T0049031

A DREAM to SHARE

SHERILYN KAY

WestBow
PRESS
A DIVISION OF THOMAS NELSON

Copyright © 2011 Sherilyn Kay

All rights reserved. No part of this book may be used or reproduced by any means, graphic, electronic, or mechanical, including photocopying, recording, taping or by any information storage retrieval system without the written permission of the publisher except in the case of brief quotations embodied in critical articles and reviews.

Scripture taken from the Holy Bible King James Version Public Domain

Scripture taken from the Holy Bible NEW INTERNATIONAL VERSION Copyright 1973, 1978, 1983, 2011 Biblica, Inc. All rights reserved worldwide. Used by permission.

WestBow Press books may be ordered through booksellers or by contacting:

WestBow Press
A Division of Thomas Nelson
1663 Liberty Drive
Bloomington, IN 47403
www.westbowpress.com
1-(866) 928-1240

Because of the dynamic nature of the Internet, any web addresses or links contained in this book may have changed since publication and may no longer be valid. The views expressed in this work are solely those of the author and do not necessarily reflect the views of the publisher, and the publisher hereby disclaims any responsibility for them.

Any people depicted in stock imagery provided by Thinkstock are models, and such images are being used for illustrative purposes only.

Certain stock imagery © Thinkstock.

ISBN: 978-1-4497-2829-8 (sc)
ISBN: 978-1-4497-2830-4 (hc)
ISBN: 978-1-4497-2828-1 (e)

Library of Congress Control Number: 2011917914

Printed in the United States of America

WestBow Press rev. date: 10/28/2011

1

Spring of 1973

A pale blue sky arched above bare-limbed oaks and traditional brick buildings on the Central Missouri University campus as Connie Oakland sauntered along, surrounded by chattering sorority sisters.

She glanced at the note which she had found in her campus mailbox and fumed. "Scholastic probation. House confinement. Social annihilation if my grades don't improve by midterm," she muttered.

She had drifted aimlessly in academia for almost two years; now, motivated to achieve, she made an excuse to the bevy of laughing girls and left them to pursue their activities.

In the alien environment of the library, she opened her algebra book. She traced the problems with a rosy polished fingernail, her lips moving as she sought to comprehend the concepts. The equations remained uncooperatively flat on the page.

The golden February afternoon sun slanting across the oak table lured her to freer spaces where her light heart could roam. She hurried outside, intending to improve her grades—tomorrow....

She paused beside a marble pillar on the wide top step with her eyes closed. After a particularly cold and dark winter, she inhaled the promise of spring and the wings of her spirit unfurled.

Impact dislodged the book from her arms and splayed it at her feet. Her eyes jolted open and she flung out her hand to steady herself. "Oh! Excuse me."

"Excuse me," said a very attractive young man simultaneously. "I was so preoccupied about the withdrawal of American troops from Vietnam I didn't see—you ..." His expression glowed with interest, and an infinitely charming smile revealed even, white teeth.

"That's quite all right," she said calmly, her pulses rioting.

"I shouldn't go lunging up steps crashing into people. I'm sorry I caused you to drop your book." He knelt to retrieve it and handed it to her.

She noticed he stood at least a foot taller than herself with dark hair feathered back over his ears. She drew herself up to her full five feet and maintained her cool self-possession while the blood warmed in her veins.

"Hello, I'm Connie Oakland."

"I'm Douglas McKenzie."

Unwilling to excuse herself she lowered her eyes in demure confusion.

"Would you like to get a Coke?" Douglas asked.

"That would be very nice," she said, sweeping her lashes up.

Douglas lifted the book from her fingers and added it to his. "I see you're taking algebra. Are you a math major?"

She was unable to admit that math frustrated her even more than her other subjects, and she smiled, her head tilted for effect. "I'm a liberal arts major," she said, giving an acceptable title to her basic course of study.

"Oh, I see," Douglas said, and she feared he did.

Douglas guided her into the student union and seated her in a corner booth away from the surging mainstream. As he ordered Cokes from an aproned waiter, she lifted her gaze from his navy V-neck sweater and blue checked shirt. She admired the line of his shoulders, the firmness of his jaw and chin, his slender nose, the gentle curve of his cheek, and dark, level brows that bent down slightly at the edge.

Douglas turned back to her and inquired, "Where were you going when I crashed into you?"

"Back to the Gamma Mu Upsilon House." For she knew that after she had wandered around looking for an intangible something, she would have returned to the House.

"You're a sorority girl? Yes, of course." Douglas answered his own question. "You won't be depledged for being seen with an independent, will you?"

"Why are you an independent?"

"I joined the army straight out of high school so I could put myself through college on the GI bill, but these days it barely covers tuition and leaves little for living expenses. I can't afford to be in a fraternity. I'm completing the five year program of architectural design in five years, when six is more likely, and it is so demanding that I don't have time for frat houses, dumb stunts, and goofing around." Douglas laid his arm on the table and leaned slightly forward. "I plan to work with an architectural firm in St. Louis whose projects have always intrigued me. When I walked past the buildings the sensation was almost magical. As soon as possible I want to design buildings I would be proud for Pop to construct. What do you plan to do after you graduate?"

Content to participate in Gamma House activities, she had never considered anything beyond her newest gown and the next dance. Now to justify herself to this dedicated young man, she said, "Surely with a B. A. from CMU I will be able to do anything."

"Oh, sure. Anything ..."

She accepted the icy glass of Coke. Douglas cupped his chin in his palm, and his sapphire eyes behind long silky lashes seemed to peer into the depths of her being with disturbing intentness. Intrinsically poised, she found some amusing things to say. She covered what she did not wish to reveal with a bubbling stream of chatter about old art and new music to buoy the interest of this current conquest.

Soon Douglas drained his Coke from its crushed ice and gathered up their books.

"If you'll excuse me, I still need to study in the library."

She was baffled by her inability to detain him, and she flashed him a high voltage smile. Response lighted Douglas' expression, but he stood and gestured with his left hand for her to precede him.

Outside the student union the magnetism of attraction slowed her departure.

"Thank you for the Coke," she said with a play of lashes. "I'll see you later."

Douglas pursed his lips and nodded as he returned her book. She hesitated until pride and social grace nudged her forward.

I've been on this campus almost two years without seeing Douglas McKenzie. What makes me think I'll see him again? With a quick indrawn breath she knew, *I have to. I simply have to.*

❧

He shifted his books and watched Connie Oakland's departure. Her platinum hair that turned under at the edge like a bell and her rounded figure in a pink sweater and short plaid skirt appealed to his architectural appreciation of form and beauty. Her allure infused him with unfamiliar pleasure. Without intending to, he waited until her fluid walk carried her from sight. The dewiness of youth and the irresistibly free spirit which lilted in her voice and sparkled in her amethyst eyes had captured his heart. No woman had ever affected him this way before. Yet this one did.

This really won't do, he said to himself in astonishment. *An architect always works from a plan, and this isn't in the plan at all.*

The conflict between his level, logical mind and his overawed heart perplexed him, and he clasped his hair in his left hand. *All right,* he told himself, *the Sweetheart Dance is next Saturday. I'll ask Connie to go with me. But no sorority girl would go to the Sweetheart Dance with an independent.*

Determined to try, he would call Connie—after he finished studying in the library.

He dialed the number to the Gamma Mu Upsilon House three times before his trembling fingers got it right, and then Connie's breezy voice eventually reached him.

"This is Douglas McKenzie. Would you do me the honor of attending the Sweetheart Dance with me?" he requested formally.

"I would be delighted."

The miracle happened!

Saturday evening he was knotting his tie in his dorm room surrounded by classical music from a radio in the background. Following a brief knock, his study partner Peter Keyes, with tortoise-shell glasses and a shock of reddish hair, entered unbidden.

"Shall we get the team together and work on our senior thesis?"

"I have a date for the Sweetheart Dance."

"I thought you didn't date."

"I don't. Connie is the only girl in the world I would do this for," he said, nervousness crinkling in his stomach.

"She must be quite a girl if you prefer her specifications to schematic diagrams."

"She has a smile like sunlight and there's this heedless sort of gaiety about her, yet she possesses the unruffled passivity of an Impressionist milkmaid."

"Oh, horrors. You must have crashed at first sight. Ever fallen before?"

He shook his head helplessly. "After three years in the army and during five years of college—including summers—I had an honor code to do well in school. I was more dedicated to architectural design than dating."

"Didn't you miss it?"

"The agony and intricacies of falling in love? They all lived happily ever after? That's for people in novels. Until I met Connie."

"If you ever have another moment of sanity, I'll get the team together. Don't forget we're depending on you to complete this municipal complex project before graduation. We'll be burning a lot of midnight oil in the design studio."

The joy and the challenge of creativity vied with his attraction to Connie. Slowly he shrugged into his dark suit coat.

"Surely I'm not the only one with a date tonight."

Peter raised his eyebrows above the frames of his glasses in eloquent accusation.

"We'll get the group together soon," he promised as he picked up the pink rose corsage and followed Peter out of the room.

While he waited for Connie in the lobby of the Gamma Mu Upsilon House, the nervous churning increased. He set his teeth to suppress it and watched the formally attired couples with feigned nonchalance.

Connie descended the circular staircase wearing a pink gown, and the exquisite scent of musky floral perfume wafted toward him. He gazed down at her enchanting heart-shaped face with its wispy half bang above golden arched brows, pert nose, full lower lip, and round chin.

"Good evening," Connie greeted.

"Yes ..." Diffidently he handed her the corsage. "I'm glad you wanted to come with me."

Connie acknowledged his attraction with a smile, her lips parting over even, little teeth. She deftly pinned on the corsage, and then she laid her hand on his arm for him to escort her.

The student union ballroom, decorated with oversized red and white Valentines, throbbed with music and voices as Connie guided him onto the dance floor.

"Don't expect much and you won't be disappointed," he warned. "I don't usually date—studying keeps me busy—so I haven't had much experience with this sort of thing. If you wanted me to explain the innovative trends in Modern architecture ..."

Connie laughed gaily—a happy, carefree child in a world he had inhabited solely as an adult. His arm closed around her waist, and her nearness caused his blood to run faster.

"You do very well," Connie said, approval shining in her eyes. "Next time you may explain Modern architecture."

Next time! Gladness spun from his heart to his head.

A blond young man wearing an unbuttoned tuxedo over a crumpled shirt, his tie hanging crookedly, ambled across the floor and cut in. Watching Connie dance with this intruder surged resentment through him, and he clenched his jaw against it.

As the golden boy waltzed Connie past he overheard him chide, "Now, Constance ... you told me Grandmother Van Leigh was ill so you couldn't attend the Sweetheart Dance. Yet here you are with an independent, not in the least concerned about poor dear Grandmother."

So that frat twerp asked Connie to the Sweetheart Dance.

Flattered that Connie had accepted his invitation, he disregarded her dishonesty. Smiling to himself, he waited for the interloper to return with her.

At his side Connie said, "Douglas, this is Blakely Whitworth. Blakely, this is Douglas McKenzie."

Blakely regarded him from beneath drooping lids before inclining his head to acknowledge the introduction.

"Blakely, this is goodbye," Connie said with finality.

"For tonight anyway," Blakely conceded, kissing Connie's hand with a flourish.

Blakely's lazy brown eyes met his with a challenge, and a strange new possessiveness leaped within him. Determined to control the situation, he tucked Connie's hand into the crook of his elbow and set his feet wider apart, waiting until the frat boy wandered away.

Connie's lavender eyes held his with a sunny friendliness, and all that was lonely and untouched within him warmed in response to it. She projected inbred poise rather than the glamor of cover girl models, and he longed to delve into the inner recesses of her refined spirit.

The music changed, and he led Connie to the refreshments where they selected an array of *canapes*. He seated her at a small, round, white cloth draped table on the edge of the dance floor. He explained his senior thesis design project, encouraged by Connie's questions and expressions of interest.

Soon after midnight he returned Connie to the Gamma Mu Upsilon House and released her fingers with some hesitancy.

"Thank you for going with me tonight."

"I had a marvelous time."

He was tempted to kiss her, but he curbed his unexpected impulses and walked across campus.

At a deserted pavilion, dimly illuminated by the full moon and light fixtures along the walkway, he sat on a granite terrace and looked into the vaulted dome of space. All the stars and galaxies seemed to be in their normal courses, yet he sensed that the plan for his life had tilted off its axis. Holding Connie warm and responsive in his arms had inspired him to create something unique—a blueprint of the longing in his soul. Despite the American economy that February of 1973, his optimism exceeded the horizon. He returned to his room, removed his coat and tie, turned on the classical station, seized a pencil in his left hand, and began to draw.

❧

Dancing with Douglas had bubbled exhilaration in her veins like champagne, and she floated up the stairs of the Gamma House in an aura of bliss.

In the room she shared with two other girls, she whirled around, hugging her happiness to her. "I'm in love, I'm in love, I'm in love."

"But you're practically engaged to Blakely," Donna said, shaking out her long blond hair.

"He's Mother's idea. But Douglas—"

"He's an independent for goodness sake," dark-haired Cheryl objected as she unzipped her red satin gown. "Your mother would never approve."

"I know I shouldn't even think of him. Mother would say it's not propa," she said, desperately, rebelliously loving him in spite of everything.

"What do you see in him?" Cheryl asked.

Despite his inexperience, Douglas McKenzie had the charm and manners to function in any social situation. Her spontaneous admiration for him surpassed her usual enthusiasm for every new acquaintance, while the genuineness of his consideration and the tender respect she had felt within his arms made her blood sing.

Unable to express intangibles, she elaborated on externals. "He's tall and extremely attractive with the most gorgeous blue eyes and a devastating smile."

"That would do it," Cheryl agreed from the doorway of the closet.

She cherished that image of Douglas, yet she knew he also possessed rare intelligence and self-discipline, a man separate from the indistinguishable mass of college boys.

"Douglas is the only man for me," she confided. "I shall love him till life no longer exists on this planet."

"Does that mean you'll keep him a week?" Donna inquired.

For the past six weeks she and Douglas had studied together in the university library nearly every evening. Following the Sweetheart Dance Douglas had called and she had requested help with algebra. She hadn't cared a fig for equations, but watching him do math in his head was unutterably fascinating. His perseverance and patient explanations had rescued her from scholastic probation. Douglas' insights and observations on science, politics, and the economy had challenged her to think while she had interspersed information about entertainment, the arts, and culture. Their conversations had acquainted her with his passion for designing and his fascination with classical music from a former music appreciation class and its association with architecture. She admired his industry and strength of purpose that his adoptive parents the McKenzies had instilled within him, yet his dedication to academic excellence baffled her.

Bored, she closed her book, propped her elbow on it, and cupped her chin in her palm to gaze at Douglas. With his head bent over his book, he rigidly underlined parts of the text and numbered them. She was delighted to be in his presence, yet she yearned to coax him from his diligence to the pursuit of pleasure. Even another ride in his rattly, old, blue Volvo would be better than being confined to the library.

She reached out to touch Douglas' lean fingers with their neat, U-shaped nails. "Let's go somewhere."

"I can't. This report is due Friday."

"A walk then."

"Sorry, Con."

"Let's get a pizza."

"You go ahead."

Frustration simmered within her. "Surely that report isn't that important."

Douglas laid his palm against her cheek. "Yes, it is."

Aggrieved she rose, Douglas' touch still vibrating along her nerves.

"Call me when you're not quite so busy."

Douglas inclined his head and returned his attention to his text book.

Accustomed to receiving what she desired, she gazed at him in bewilderment. Then she flounced out of the library. Anger seared into her soul and lodged there with a strange, dull ache.

He has a blueprint where his heart should be! Why do I have to be so interested in someone who only studies or talks about designing? The fraternity men don't spend all their time studying. You could date one, you know.

In Denver for spring break that April of 1973, she humored her parents and consented to date Blakely Whitworth, who had returned to his home nearby.

Saturday morning Blakely whirled his Porsche through the pine and cedar scented Bear Creek Canyon and the sun sparkled on spun sugar clouds. Yet Blakely and familiar surroundings and distance had not diminished her interest in Douglas McKenzie, and the uncomfortable situation of dating second choice settled darkly on her heart. During the week she and Blakely had attended ballets and concerts, had brunches, lunches, and dinners wherever she chose. Through it all she had endured being with one person when she wanted solely to be with another. She longed to recapture that breathless exhilaration which only being with Douglas produced, for what she felt in his presence exceeded her enjoyment in the usual round of social functions.

As she contrasted his industry and strength of purpose with her floating aimless ease, she contemplated how exciting it would be to share her life with someone who had such determination and planned a place for himself in the world. Having found an acceptance apart from being Armand Oakland's daughter or the propa product of a society mother that she had unknowingly sought all her life, she desired to anchor her soul in Douglas'.

Unaccustomed to desiring something she couldn't possess, she assessed her finely honed skills: her questioning glance; her practiced stimulating smile; her male ego-flattering attention that had brought other men to happy submission at her will. Nevertheless, she sensed that Douglas had a will stronger than her own. No doubt the independence and self-discipline which had intrigued her were what resisted her tactics. She was resolved to exert more effort than she had previously expended on anything, and she smiled. She snuggled more deeply into the bucket seat of the Porsche, anticipating the outcome.

In her room at the Gamma House late Tuesday afternoon, she became certain Douglas would not call to apologize. She sat cross-legged on her bed with her elbows on her knees, her chin on the back of her hands. She brooded about returning unpursued to any man, but the magnetism of Douglas' charm drew her heart to his. She changed into a new, pastel plaid safari suit and reapplied traces of makeup.

Why are you doing this? her pride demanded.

Because life isn't worth living without him, her heart answered.

Confident that Douglas would be in the library, she hurried across campus. She found him wearing his blue checked shirt, sitting at a table, engrossed in his reading. She approached silently, simply filling her mind with the image of him.

"Hullo," she ventured with a tone that didn't betray her inner turmoil. "I would like to study with you."

Douglas glanced over his book, and the lift of his dark brows reminded her she carried neither books nor paper.

He truly is determined to succeed, and even I am unable to change that.

Awed, she lifted a gaze that questioned and appealed until Douglas' expression wavered.

Thrusting a textbook into her hands, Douglas said, "Here. Quiz me on these."

Every nerve relaxed and she dropped into the chair opposite him with a disarming smile. The tension in Douglas' manner stopped her gaiety, and she read him the first question.

Douglas answered them all, and then he said, "Let's go somewhere and talk." He gathered up his books and steered her out of the library with his hand on her elbow.

When she and Douglas were seated on a granite terrace in the deserted pavilion, he spoke. "While I was on spring break I was studying for finals as well as doing some designing of my own. I barely had time to sleep but I still missed you. More than I ever thought possible." Douglas' throat worked before the next words came. "I had my life all planned. I had a goal—to graduate with honors and begin my career as an architect. Then I met you." His unguarded look of adoration quickened her breath. "You're a sweet, vivacious little girl who interests me very much, and I want to date you. However, I'll be extremely busy this next month. I know sorority girls don't just sit around waiting to date independent architectural students."

"I don't want to date anyone else."

"What about that Blakely Whitworth character?"

"I just spent a week with Blakely, and—"

"The whole week?"

Douglas' strained, white face haunted the inner chambers of her soul, and she laid her palm against his cheek in gentle reassurance.

"Every tedious waking moment. I could scarcely survive without you. I missed you, Douglas," she said without pride or pretense. "Blakely is not the man I want."

Douglas drew her into his arms, and his lips moved slightly on hers with a gentle pressure. She surrendered to the consuming joy of his exquisitely sweet kiss.

He edged away to murmur words of wonder. "You know I'm in love with you, don't you?"

"In love? With me?"

"It was rather like an avalanche. Tell me if you can that you didn't feel it too."

Mutely she nodded.

"There's something very special between us, Connie," Douglas said. "Love at first sight, the best kind. An instant attraction that strikes a spark, kindles a flame that will burn forever. But I know so little about you, and I want to know everything."

Her happiness froze. She dared not tell Douglas everything until she was certain his love was genuine. "My father is in real estate," she offered. "My mother keeps busy with her friends. My sister Penny is studying fashion design, and we live southwest of Denver."

Douglas touched his fingers to her lips. "Tell me slowly so it will take a lifetime."

She was relieved that she hadn't had to live her whole life without Douglas' love, and she nestled against him, content in his embrace.

"You're the only girl I've ever loved," Douglas confided with his cheek against her hair. "But falling in love was not in the plan. It happened, though, and there's no denying it. Yet I must not allow anything to interfere with my goal."

Gradually emerging from the miracle of Douglas' love, she mused when his plans, his goals, would involve her.

2
Graduation

*H*e had always prided himself on being logical and dedicated to a plan, and his brain had battled his emotions as he tried to argue himself out of this altogether new and overpowering situation of loving Connie. But helplessly, happily, he had capitulated to forces beyond his comprehension.

During the months he had studied with Connie, she had exhibited a rare ability to listen without fidgeting, expressing little sounds of concern and appreciation in all the right places. As he had explained specifications, space requirements, climate, and materials inherent in his senior thesis, her quiet poise had encouraged him, and her admiring gaze made the complexities seem manageable. The strenuous schedule of repeated conferences with his professor on the positives and negatives of his design project and looking at optional concepts while adhering to the idea of his main design—completing 25 weeks of work in about half that time—as well as studying for final exams and finishing his own designing had continued to press him. Yet he had helped Connie conquer mathematical concepts. Occasionally he treated them to ice cream at Serendipity's, but Connie's kisses surpassed the sweetness of any hot fudge sundae....

Now his frenzied strivings were ended, leaving his brain strangely empty. Nevertheless, he had obtained his goal: he had completed the program in five years—with honors. Brahms' celebratory *Academic Festival Overture* rang in his mind.

His gaze rested on the blueprint of his personal vision—a house, two stories high, beautiful in its exterior simplicity, startling in its interior asymmetry. *It's a dream house. A dream to share with Connie.*

He hurried to the pay phone at the end of the corridor. He received the number for Armand Oakland from Information and placed a person-to-person call. While he listened to the distant ringing, apprehension quivered in his stomach. A cultured male voice answered, "Oaklands' residence." Following his query, he was given another number. He deposited a handful of coins and waited until he reached a secretary at Oakland Enterprises. "This is Douglas McKenzie. May I speak to Mr. Oakland, please?"

Soon a voice with an air of authority said, "Hello, Douglas. Constance has written to us about you."

Flattered, he responded, "I'm glad she has, sir. I would like your permission to ask her to marry me."

The shocked silence tightened his nerves, and he gripped the phone, prepared to present his entire plan.

"I had hoped Constance would wait to graduate. I have been putting something aside for her which I would like for her to receive."

"Yes, sir. I had planned on her graduating. That will give me time to establish my career and save up enough money to build my house before we're married."

"You seem to have everything quite well planned."

"Yes, sir. An architect always works from a plan."

"I see. Constance has quite an affinity for you, but you are not the only young man to fascinate her or to be fascinated with her."

While Connie had seemed thoroughly fascinated with him, perhaps the Oaklands were partial to that Blakely Whitworth character.

"During the past few months Connie has convinced me that her attraction, enthusiasm, and commitment are exclusively mine."

"Although Constance may be quite fond of you, her mother and I would like to have an opportunity to become acquainted and meet your family."

He was determined to succeed in this ultimate endeavor, and he replied, "Sir, I realize you only know what Connie has told you about me. Understandably you are hesitant to grant your permission for her to marry a virtual stranger, but there will be opportunities for all of us to meet each other. I love your daughter as I have never loved any other person, and I vow to you that I will cherish her every day of my life."

After a brief silence, Mr. Oakland spoke with a deeper resonance in his voice. "Very well then. You have my permission to ask Constance to marry you. However, she has the impatience of youth and expects to receive anything she desires. I'm not certain she will agree to wait."

"She must. That's the only way the plan will work. And since you also want her to graduate, she has no choice, has she?"

"Right." A ripple of laughter carried along the line. "Good luck, Douglas. I'll leave convincing Constance to you."

"Yes, sir. Thank you."

In a haze of lyrical feeling, he jogged back to his room, the victorious theme of Beethoven's *Fifth Symphony* filling his soul.

That afternoon in a brightly lighted jewelry store glittering with gems in glass cases, he selected a ring. Diamonds set in a ribbon of platinum looped around a radiant center stone with iridescent facets that sparked rainbows. The intricate beauty and the reality of what the ring symbolized halted his breath. He made the down payment from his meager funds, and then he drove back to campus.

He left the ring in his dresser and went to meet Connie following her final exam.

Connie emerged from the math and science building wearing a short yellow sundress, her flowing gait of confidence and ease unable to conceal a zest for life which would eternally enchant him. The awe of loving such a unique young woman suffused him, and he pressed through the throng to reach her.

Connie gazed up at him with an expression full of vivacity as she handed him her books. "I passed! And I owe it all to you!"

He caught Connie's hand in his, sharing her accomplishment.

Perhaps I have taught her study skills which will enable her to succeed without me the next two years. The thought dimmed the sunny afternoon to a cloudy vagueness.

"Come," he said.

He seated Connie and himself on a terrace in the deserted pavilion and laid aside her books. "I want to be alone with you before my folks arrive."

"Graduation was only a date on a calendar, months away. Now it's tomorrow! It's been marvelous being together so much I almost forgot. It's been our Golden Hour in Time.... Now it's over! You aren't simply graduating—you're leaving!"

"That's the way it usually happens," he consoled, aware that his long-sought graduation deprived him of Connie's presence.

"But nothing will ever be the same."

Tears clustered Connie's sooty lashes into stars, and her full lower lip trembled.

Regretting they would never again experience this academic camaraderie, he whispered, "Please, don't cry."

How will I be able to follow my plan when Connie's tears threaten to erode it? Are the sacrifices—the enforced separations and certain loneliness—worth it to achieve my dream? They have to be, he insisted. *It's the only way the plan will work.*

Nevertheless, this final sacrifice that inflicted a heavy disappointment on Connie demanded more of him than all the others.

He held Connie to him, wanting to hold her so close graduation couldn't separate them. His mouth molded to hers and her lips moved beneath it. Her fingers crept up to fondle his hair, and then her hand trailed along the line of his neck to his chest. His body tingled and excitement brought a sick crunch to his midriff. He stilled her fingers with his and eased away on a ragged breath. Connie's expression smoldered with allure, but the goal—so long pursued, so nearly attained—loomed before him. He forced himself back.

"Please, you mustn't try to snare me in a web of passion. If you love me, let me do as I've planned—without any guilt or regrets."

"You have everything all planned, don't you?" Connie's chin came up and her violet eyes spit sparks. "You set a goal and go for it. No detours, no personal considerations. You have a blueprint where your heart should be!"

"That's not true," he disagreed, for the pain of his decisions pierced his heart. "Every day for more years than you know I've had to decide if the plan is worth the sacrifices."

"It must be," Connie flared. "Nothing will keep you from it—not even me!"

"No, not even you."

"Your stubbornness is ruining our happiness."

"Do you expect me to give up everything I've worked for all these years just because I fell in love with you?"

Her head high, her back rigid, Connie turned away. Then her gaze flickered to his. As he regarded her, not only the blithe spirit who had attracted him but also a surprisingly willful child, he questioned her ability to accept his new plan.

He cupped Connie's face in his hands and dipped his lashes over one eye. "Tomorrow after graduation I'll explain my new goal, my dream to you."

≈

Friday morning she crossed her arms on the window sill of her room in the Gamma House and stared out over campus as she contemplated living without Douglas. With him life had become a more real, earnest matter than it had been before and there had been a zest to each new day. During the glorious hours she had shared with him, she had not allowed herself to think it would end. Now all that remained were a few precious moments after graduation.

How could he do it? How could he simply walk away from our love?

Baffled, she pondered the situation. Tears didn't sway him. Temper fizzled against his cool patience. Tempting, although particularly enjoyable, generated no fires fierce enough to melt the metal of his resolve. From their first encounter, Douglas McKenzie had been the most challenging man she had ever known.

Grudging admiration mingled with frustration, yet she refused to be disregarded. She had given him a drawing set in a leather case with his name engraved in gold as a graduation gift the evening before so he would always remember her. She would see him again—if she had to track him through St. Louis with a bloodhound! Still, life would never shimmer with the glow it recently had.

Even the Gamma House graduation party with its food, friends, frivolity, and festive decorations the previous weekend hadn't lessened her unhappiness.

She applied extra blush to her ashen cheeks and selected waterproof mascara because, in spite of what her mother had taught her was propa, she knew she was going to cry in public and she didn't want to look like a raccoon. A new, white sheath, lacy white stockings, white pumps, and a slender gold neck band had seemed suitable for Douglas' graduation. However, with the cessation of life as she had lived it the past few months, she wondered if she shouldn't be wearing black....

Withdrawn and self-contained, she crossed campus to the massive stone auditorium, barely noticing the brick buildings and dark green foliage shimmering in the sultry heat.

"Hello, Cutie," a pleasant male voice said above her.

Terry, Douglas' very tall, 20-year-old brother, grinned down at her. Her heart was too leaden for light flirtation and she turned away.

"Good morning, Connie," Mrs. McKenzie greeted, her plump face surrounded by tight dark curls burnished with pride. "We are so proud of Douglas!"

Maintaining a guise of serenity, she noted the navy polka-dotted dress Mrs. McKenzie had worn to dinner the evening before. Mr. McKenzie was of medium height with a strand of dark hair combed over his encroaching baldness. He wore a suit of indeterminate style, and a camera hung from a strap around his neck. She surmised that Douglas had inherited his attractiveness from his biological parents. Mr. McKenzie laid his hand on her arm and escorted her into the auditorium.

After the long, tedious speeches, Douglas Alan McKenzie crossed the platform *magna cum laude* to receive recognition for his accomplishment in architectural design. A rush of pride and loss collided in her soul.

He's so intelligent, why doesn't he think of a way for us to be together instead of torn apart?

The building vibrated from the pipe organ's playing the traditional, majestic recessional. It was a poignant reminder that Douglas' graduation, the bridge to his shining future, had consigned her to a dark chasm.

As she waited outside in the crowd with the McKenzies, she blinked away a recurring mist. Douglas rounded the corner in his cap and gown, and her spirit revived at the sight of him. With an exuberant smile, he enfolded Mrs. McKenzie in an embrace that momentarily raised her off her feet. Mr. McKenzie clasped Douglas to him, and they stood rocking in silent celebration, patting each other's backs with both hands before Terry joined them. Releasing Mr. McKenzie and Terry, Douglas turned and caught her up in his arms, his forehead touching hers beneath his mortar board. His masculine strength and woodsy scent infused her with brief consolation.

"When Pop is through taking pictures meet me in the pavilion," Douglas said. "I'll be there as soon as I can."

Douglas stood her down beside him with his right hand holding her left, and she applied a smile to achieve the proper photographic effect.

She passed through the pedestrians and entered the pavilion, Douglas' promise of one more time together shielding her mind.

She watched Douglas trot down the grassy hill toward her wearing his blue checked shirt and tan slacks and carrying a tube of blueprints. She gazed at his tall, straight body, the set of his shoulders, the firm line of his jaw and chin, and his dark hair ruffled by the breeze. Struggling against sadness, she stored up meager memories.

I'll die without him.

Douglas clasped her hand in a bond of affection.

"Just say goodbye and end the agony," she cried.

Douglas' bleak eyes met hers, and he gave her a single, long, silent look that turned her heart over.

This isn't easy for him either.

"We'll say goodbye soon enough, Con, but there's something I want to show you."

Douglas spread his handkerchief on the granite terrace and seated her on it before he unrolled the blueprints.

Love Douglas, love his designs, she knew.

"Four bedrooms, three baths, two stories. It's beautiful," she marveled, tracing windows and doors with an oval polished fingernail. "It's a dream house."

With one knee on the terrace, Douglas set an open tiny white box in the center of the blueprints and asked, "Will you marry me and share my dream?"

Disbelief spun through her, stopping her breath. She stared at the round center stone circled by channel set diamonds.

Marry— Not to lose him—To live in that house with him— Together, forever—

"When?" she finally managed.

"In two years. After you graduate."

"A girl can get married and still graduate."

"I know, but I don't want to do it that way. You'll have a chance to mature, and I'll be able to establish my career and build my house before we're married."

"When will I see you again?"

"Next fall I'll probably drive over here and visit you occasionally."

"Occasionally? <u>Occasionally</u>? For two <u>years</u>?"

"I know it's a long time, but it's the only way the plan will work."

Confronted by Douglas' unyielding adherence to a plan, she gazed at the ring as she considered her answer. She inclined her head in demure surrender.

Douglas slipped the ring on her finger and pressed it to his lips, his sapphire eyes caressing her face. He encircled her with his arms and she clung to him in a haze of happiness while his vows of devotion fell with his kisses upon her willing lips.

Eventually Douglas said, "It's time to take you to the airport."

The inevitability of parting eclipsed the joy of their betrothal and threatened to undermine her self-control. Holding herself together, she walked with Douglas to the student union where his family waited.

"Well, do we congratulate you?" Terry asked as they crossed the visitors' parking lot.

"Yes, you may congratulate me."

"Our congratulations to you too, Connie," Mrs. McKenzie said.

"Thank you," she replied, mentally correcting it to felicitations and readily displaying her engagement ring.

"Welcome to our family," Mr. McKenzie added.

Douglas seated her between Terry and himself in the backseat of Mr. McKenzie's brown Plymouth station wagon. They stopped at the Gamma Mu Upsilon House where Douglas and Terry packed her luggage into the back of the station wagon, and then they rode to the airport. Douglas' set, white lips betrayed his inner turmoil, and she reached up to lay her fingers on his cheek. With a wan smile, he turned and kissed them.

In the congested terminal, the call for her flight drew her reluctantly toward the gate. She clung to Douglas' hand, unable to express all she felt in the final moments of companionship. "I love you, Douglas."

"I love you too, Con."

She resisted being torn apart for a very long time, and she buried her face against Douglas' chest. His arms closed around her with a fierce pressure and his hand cradled her head. Slowly he released her, and she hurried across the landing field to the plane.

Seated on board, she stared out the tiny rectangular porthole and gazed down at Douglas by the wire gate until the plane taxied forward and he disappeared from view. The desolation of separation filled her chest, and she shuddered with a long involuntary sob. Leaning back against the seat for the flight to Denver, she focused on her sparkling ring and pondered how she would survive until she saw Douglas Alan McKenzie again.

3
Summer

Wearing a short white robe over a turquoise swimsuit, she lay in a floral cushioned chaise lounge on the sandstone terrace that surrounded the blue tiled pool behind her home. A marble balustrade separated it from the expansive lawn that sloped up to a wooded hillside, yet the serenity of the Rocky Mountain beauty failed to assuage her loneliness.

Amazingly, her relationship with Douglas McKenzie hadn't been terminated by his graduation. His unforeseen proposal had provided a ray of hope for the future that would guide her through the void of separation. However, since she had said goodbye to Douglas two weeks before, the sharp pangs of loss had not faded into dull endurance. Deprived of her source of life without him, she wilted and drooped as a blossom without sunshine. Closing her eyes, she daydreamed of her beloved: his attractive features; his charming wit; the animation in his expression when he spoke of designing; the sharing of their thoughts and ideas; his noble spirit with implications of passion beneath it.

She regretted being unable to celebrate her engagement with the festal occasion she and her parents had always anticipated, yet being engaged to Douglas allayed her disappointment. But how could she tolerate living on campus with just memories to sustain her, only seeing him occasionally for two years?

Her older sister Penny dashed past in a brief red swimsuit and flung some mail in her lap. Douglas' precise angular writing on the envelope accelerated her pulse and she ripped it open.

My dear sweet Connie, the letter began. Filled only with vague references to his work, it ended with, All my love, Douglas.

She longed for one passionate sentence she could cherish in her loneliness. Nevertheless, the piece of paper that still bore traces of his woodsy scent formed a tangible link to him, and she clasped it to her chest. Eventually she laid it down and glanced through the usual social invitations, and then she entered the cool depths of her home.

Seated at the French provincial vanity in her pink wallpapered room with its rose satin draperies, she applied makeup and dressed for dinner, an idea lingering beneath the surface of her mind.

She descended the wide, curving, red-carpeted staircase beneath the chandelier into the black-and-white tiled foyer. Hearing her parents' voices, she entered the ivory-carpeted, gold wallpapered living room with its full-length mullioned windows, and high beamed cathedral ceiling. Her mother, petite and blond, and her father, heavy and graying, sat on the gold brocade sofa, sipping drinks Fenton had served.

"Constance deah," her mother greeted.

"Good evening, Constance," her father said, rising at her approach.

"Mother ... Father ... I do not want to live in the Gamma Mu Epsilon House next year."

Her mother's china blue eyes widened.

"I want to have an apartment where Douglas could—"

"Absolutely not," her father said, his gray brows bristling. "You and Douglas are not to live together until after you're married."

"We wouldn't be living together. It would just be a place where Douglas could come when he visits every weekend."

"Constance deah, we have our social position to consida, and a guhl of your culcha and breeden belongs in a sorowity house."

"I can still see my friends and attend the monthly meetings. But with an apartment ..."

A thoughtful light brightened her father's expression. "Perhaps a dormitory—"

"A dorm?"

"Ahmand!" Her mother's protest coincided with her own.

"Certainly, Camilla. I lived in a dorm when I attended CMU."

"Ahmand, it's not propa for a guhl of Constance's refinement and background to live in a common dohmitory."

"It's not proper for a girl of Constance's refinement and background to live in an apartment either."

Vexed by her father's unexpected option, she lowered her head and allowed her lip to droop with skilled pathos.

"We'll call the college tomorrow and get your room assignment. You may give the difference to Douglas for that house of his."

Disbelief whirled through her, but she remained certain her father would relent and grant her heart's desire, as he always did.

⁂

Seated at a drawing board in the workroom at Hunt and Associates with half a dozen other architects, he regarded the specifications for a project and laid his slide rule aside with an utterance of disgust. The building lacked an innovative approach, yet his suggestions had been disregarded. He had endured an entire month of uninspiring designs, and he speculated when Mr. Hunt would allow him to create unique projects. The desire to be on the leading edge of progressive architecture burned within him as a flame; the smothering atmosphere of the unimaginative dampened it to an ember. He longed for Connie's adoring gaze and expressions of appreciation that would encourage him in the midst of inconsequential drafting.

He ignored the current inane project and stared out the multi-paned window into the hazy St. Louis sky. Connie's heart-shaped face, framed by her platinum hair turning under at the edge like a bell, and her amethyst eyes filled his mind.

Connie's letters written in her circular handwriting on pink checked stationery informed him of her activities and assured him of her love, but they couldn't fill the emptiness. Two years without her companionship gaped as an eternity. He caught his hair in his hand. *Oh, Connie, you have no idea how hard it is to live without you.* In spite of the heat and humidity, it was going to be a cold, lonely summer.

Following work one evening early in July, he met Pop in a coffee shop with orange vinyl booths and clientele seated at the counter. He sat across from Pop at a gray Formica topped table beside a large window facing the street, and they ordered iced tea.

The waitress in a brown uniform with white apron and cuffs returned and hurried away.

"You miss Connie, don't you?" Pop asked.

His thin, tough coating of masculine pride prevented an answer, and he sipped his tea.

"To be separated from the woman you love is rough," Pop remarked.

But as a man unhappy in his work, he was truly miserable. He turned his glass with his left hand, reluctant to express his disappointment in Hunt and Associates to this man who had adopted him, supported him, partially paid his college expenses, and encouraged him to work toward a goal. The dissatisfaction of an unchallenging job conflicted with his loyalty to the plan to design buildings he would be proud for Pop to construct. He exhaled audibly.

Aware of Pop's scrutiny, he explained, "Architecture is like a language. Buildings communicate the values of the society that designs them. The best designed buildings rank as works of art. They're more than square footage for an inexcusable number of people to inhabit. They should provide more than shelter, protection, and privacy. They should be efficient, aesthetic environments where people can work, shop, learn, and live!" He wiped rivulets from the side of the glass and flipped the moisture from his fingertips. "But those qualities must be in the design as are available floor space, electrical outlets, and safety codes. There are more imaginative matters to consider than cost per square foot. I can't design buildings that are merely human beehives. I don't see how anyone could sanction such tasteless and redundant buildings."

Belatedly he realized Pop had made a comfortable living by constructing those tasteless and redundant buildings. Heat flushed his cheeks.

"Things not going well at Hunt and Associates?" Pop asked.

"Not as I had hoped. I used to stand on street corners and stare at H and A buildings, absorbing their dignity and elegance into my soul. Planning, functional and technical expertise, and knowledge of construction are still highly valued, but style isn't much of an issue. Mr. Hunt expects me to simply draft projects which would be better designed by a kindergartner with blocks!"

Pop leaned forward and laid a gnarled, work-begrimed hand on his arm.

"It's good to have a goal, but things changed while you were working toward it."

The basic structure of his life tottered, and he braced his hands against the edge of the table.

"It happens." Pop swirled his glass of iced tea. "Nothing in life remains the same."

"I had meticulously planned my career path, and I had an intense desire to work hard to achieve a very satisfying and rewarding career in architecture. Finally I was doing what I had planned to do. Yet being mired in mediocrity wasn't in the plan. All my life I wanted to freeze fluid music into an inhabitable form, but they aren't freezing fluid music into anything at Hunt and Associates."

"Why don't you talk to Mr. Hunt?"

"I tried. He's not interested in my ideas."

"It's fairly common for a young designer to work for someone who is a little set in his ways."

With startling clarity he realized that Mr. Hunt was too old to be as innovative, but he was too young to retire.

"You may have years of inconsequential drafting before you can experience the creative challenge you crave."

A chill curled down his spine. "No. No ..."

"You're young and impatient. Perhaps if you wait.... It takes time to adjust. Major metropolitan areas weren't constructed between dawn and dark."

He inclined his head as he acknowledged the patience to persist in attaining his goal that Pop recommended. But waiting any longer to be on the progressive edge of architectural design grated against his soul.

"I don't want to give up what I've worked for all these years, but they are not utilizing my skills. I have too much ability and potential to tolerate a career of doing what I've done this past month." Rampant discontent plagued his inner being. "Neither my conscience nor my creativity will allow the unimaginative disguised as innovative in apartments and office buildings."

"This is what you have always wanted to do, son, and I'm sorry it isn't working out." Pop reached across to clasp his arm. "You mustn't stick to a plan out of a misdirected sense of loyalty or you'll always be unhappy."

He pondered the dilemma of adhering to his plan or doing that at which he was best until he left the coffee shop with Pop.

Over the next few days he barely ate, scarcely slept, hardly concentrated, and extensively walked around the area of Hunt and Associates as well as through his neighborhood. There had to be a way, some way, anyway he could be on the progressive edge of architectural design. What way? He didn't want to change the plan. He hadn't done so for Connie, but certainty rose within him like a wave: he couldn't achieve his destiny at Hunt and Associates. By slow degrees he realized it was futile to cling to the plan because he would always be unhappy in his work. Reluctantly he razed what he had striven all his life to obtain. His goal demolished, he mentally sorted through debris and choking clouds of dust. He sought what he could salvage, for he had struggled too hard, sacrificed too much to relinquish his goal.

As he lay in the backyard hammock with his hands behind his head and his legs crossed at the ankles, his agile brain juggled risks, benefits, and contingencies. Gradually one idea settled on the solid foundation of satisfaction in his career. He redesigned his future and began to reconstruct a new plan, a new goal as the exuberant strains of Mendelssohn's *Italian Symphony* pulsed in his head.

4

#32 Cedar Ridge Trail

*H*e had requested that Mr. Hunt refer him to a more progressive architectural firm, and Evan Scott of Dixon, Scott and Hall had extended an offer in Denver, Colorado.

While he analyzed going to Denver, he debated whether it was a practical career decision from his logical mind or a desperate act of his rebellious heart to see Connie.

Explaining to Mom and Pop one evening that he had accepted a position with a different firm had been only slightly less difficult than making the decision. Mom had pretended that some dust bothered her eyes; Pop had seemed to have something caught in his throat; Terry had suggested they turn his bedroom into a den. Affectionately and efficiently they had helped him pack the most necessary items into his Volvo.

In the August dawn, he drove from Salina, Kansas, where he had spent the night sleeping in his car. Gradually the excitement of seeing Connie, the heat, and motion brought a wave of sickness. He halted beside the highway, succumbing to it.

That afternoon he stopped at a service station to shave, brush his teeth, and change into tan slacks and blue checked shirt. Using Connie's return address and a street map to guide him, he drove southwest out of Denver. The air cooled and cleared, and in the wooded foothills the fragrance of cedar and pine enveloped him. With the hymn-like fourth movement of Dvorak's *Ninth Symphony* rolling in the back of his head, he turned onto Cedar Ridge Trail. From the well-paved road, he noticed two white brick pillars with a black wrought iron gate standing open between them: beyond loomed a two-story, white brick French country house. Its impressive lines and angles, chimneys, leaded windows, and glass domed conservatory aroused his architectural interest. Amidst formal plantings and precisely trimmed lawns, it resembled a pearl in an emerald setting. Using the excuse of requesting directions from people who lived in such a residence, he drove up the long circular drive and stopped beside a fountain where a marble cherub poured a stream of water from a basin. He approached the house and tapped the brass handle of the knocker on the heavy wooden door. It opened to reveal a professionally attired man with a withered apple face.

"I'm looking for Number 32 Cedar Ridge Trail. The Oaklands' residence ..."

The butler gestured him into a black-and-white tiled foyer with a curving, red-carpeted staircase beneath a grand chandelier.

"I'll tell Mrs. Oakland you are here. Your name, please?"

A tingling began at the back of his head, and his numbed brain fought for balance. *Oaklands live here?*

"Douglas," he managed. "Douglas McKenzie."

The butler directed him to a settee beside the stairs and then bowed away.

The foyer surrounded him with an aura of affluence, and the unexpectedness of it submerged his relief at having found Connie's house. His anticipation of seeing her congealed into misgiving, while the reconstructed framework of his dream wobbled beneath him.

I asked Connie to marry me and live in my dream house—but she already lives in a dream house. When she said her father was in real estate, I thought she meant selling it, not owning it.

Unable to clear the chaos from his mind, he waited for the butler to return.

"Douglas!"

He rose an instant before Connie flung her arms around him. He crushed her to him, her soft weight assuaging the months' old ache to hold her. He laid his lips on hers in a greeting more ageless than Time.

"I missed you so much!" they exclaimed together.

Wearing a short white robe over a turquoise swimsuit, Connie led him through the house to a sandstone terrace that surrounded a swimming pool. He stared past the marble balustrade to the extensive perfect lawn that sloped up to a wooded hillside.

He pushed his left hand through his hair. "This is quite a place you have here. I seem to have missed the changing of the guard." His humor failed to diffuse his ire at Connie for her deception. "Why didn't you tell me you were rich?"

"I knew you would be prejudiced against people who weren't as poor as you."

He caught Connie's shoulders. "What was I, the novelty of poverty? What did you expect from me?"

"Excitement. Challenge." Connie lifted her shoulders beneath his hands. "Then I thought I found love and security too. I had seen stars in your eyes and I didn't want them replaced by dollar signs. I wanted to be certain you wouldn't be influenced by Father's assets. Blakely is far more interested in Father's net worth than he is in me."

"I gave you a ring and asked you to marry me. Why didn't you tell me then?"

"What should I have said? 'Yes, I'll marry you, but I'm Armand Oakland's daughter, so if you don't want to wait to be married until you're able to afford your house, Father will build it for you.'"

"Why did you lead me to believe we could share a dream and a future?"

"Because I love you."

"But when I see this house—"

"Houses have nothing to do with it."

"Houses have everything to do with it. You're society and I'm a junior architect. We have no mutual interests, no mutual friends, no mutual opinions politically or socially. We have nothing in common."

"We have our love. Love at first sight, the best kind. A sudden meeting which strikes a spark, kindles a flame that will burn forever."

No doubt the white light of love blazing in his brain when he first met Constance Oakland had blinded him to her prosperity. Now, with the veil she had woven of half-truths and strategic silences parted, he could see clearly.

"It's quite impossible," he concluded, the implication piercing the center of his being.

Connie caught his hands in hers. "We're planning to be married. Nothing has changed."

"Seeing you like this changes everything."

Connie's secrecy threatened his peace of mind; the disparity of their lifestyles threatened the foundation of his plan. Seeking solitude to reevaluate that plan, he turned to go. Connie leaned against the door jamb of the lattice porch, her curving form preventing his departure. Undeniable attraction lured him to her.

"What about that dream? Weren't you working in St. Louis? What are you doing here?"

His brain groped back to his preempted explanation, and a glimmer of satisfaction returned. "I've accepted a job with a different architectural firm."

"In Denver? I have just endured the most boring summer of my entire life, and now you're here? I have existed solely to have every weekend with you in Missouri, and you'll be here while I'm there!" Connie crossed her arms and pointed two directions with her forefingers. "What's the purpose in that?" she cried with an out flung hand.

"It's a big advantage to my career," he flared. "That should mean something to you."

Connie stalked across the terrace and sat on a chaise lounge with her nose as upraised as its construction would allow. "Why didn't you write to me?"

He realized Connie had no inkling of what turmoil had been involved in changing his plan. "It was too complicated to explain in a letter." He sat beside her and ran his fingertips up and down her arm in a tender gesture to placate her. "I know it's an unexpected change I handed you."

"But when will I ever see you?" Connie asked with an engaging little pout.

"We'll have the next two weeks."

Connie smiled and reached out to touch his cheek. "Of course it's going to be fantastic having you here. And in the fall you could fly to Missouri so we could have weekends together in my apartment."

Implication lurched through him, but practicality downed it. "I won't be able to afford weekend trips."

"You could use Father's jet."

He was unaccustomed to the instant solution wealth provided, and he started to protest.

Connie laid her fingers on his lips, and then glided them down his chin. She rubbed his chest with her palms, creating a pleasant warmth in his veins.

"Nothing will keep us apart, will it, Douglas?"

He met her confident gaze as he lifted her hand in his and turned it up, laying a kiss in her palm.

A door closed in the distance, and the butler approached.

"Will Mr. McKenzie be staying for dinner?"

"Yes, Fenton. Take Mr. McKenzie's things to one of the guest rooms."

"No, thank you. I can't stay."

"We'll discuss it later," Connie told him with a fixed smile. She waved her fingers, and the butler withdrew.

Weariness ached in his back, and valor warned him against further disagreements. Yet feeling out of place where he had inadvertently wandered, he repeated, "I won't be staying."

Connie rose and removed her lacy white robe as she glanced down at him. "Would you like to swim?"

Very aware of the tactics Connie wielded with such effectiveness, he managed a bland expression. "I've been traveling two days, so I'm very tired. You go ahead and I'll watch."

Connie dove into the pool with a quick, lithe motion and emerged in the center, laughing and blowing kisses to him. He smiled in response to her pleasure at having him nearby and stretched out on the chaise with his arms crossed on his chest, his legs crossed at the ankles. Connie swam with effortless grace, and the sunlight rippling on the surface of the water seemed to reflect a dazzling wealth of gold coins....

"Mr. McKenzie? Dinner is suhved."

His eyes snapped open and he roused with the guilty knowledge that he had been sleeping. He followed the butler across the terrace, the clarion call of Tchaikovsky's *Capriccio Italien* in his brain dispersing the cobwebs.

He arrived in the foyer as Connie descended the red-carpeted staircase with the manner of one born to wealth and position, her short white sundress accenting the honey-toned tan of her legs and shoulders.

He laid his hand on her arm. "I'm sorry I fell asleep, but I started driving very early so I could be with you."

"I'm so glad you did."

Connie came into his arms, and he lowered his lips to hers with a hunger that had nothing to do with his stomach.

Remembering his manners, he murmured, "The soup will be getting cold."

"We're having *vichyssoise*."

He released Connie, and she guided him across the foyer with her hand on his arm.

In the ivory-carpeted dining room, he noticed the choice imported wooden tiles, the handsome moldings, and high ceiling as he approached the formally set table beneath a crystal chandelier.

"Mother, I would like you to meet my fiance, Douglas McKenzie. Douglas, my mother, Camilla Oakland."

Mrs. Oakland was a slightly built woman of elegance and gracious dignity with finely etched features and golden hair arranged in professional layers; she reminded him of a smooth, lustrous vase.

"We are so pleased to have you join us for dinna," Mrs. Oakland said in a soft Southeastern accent. "Constance has spoken quite highly of you." Her cool blue glance flitted over him as if searching for justification.

She didn't tell me anything about you, he recalled.

Beside Mrs. Oakland a man of his own height, but heavier, seemed to strut when he stood still. Gray hair waved tightly back from a distinguished face with a triangular nose and straight lips.

"Douglas, my father, Armand Oakland."

The man seemed pleasant enough in a casual shirt and slacks, yet power and influence emanated from him. Mr. Oakland regarded him with an expression of appraisal as they clasped hands.

"Douglas, it is so good to meet you. Please, sit down."

He seated Connie and himself on red damask upholstered chairs where he could hold her left hand in his right under the table.

"Constance tells us you will be working in Denver," Mr. Oakland said.

"Yes, sir. With Dixon, Scott and Hall."

Connie choked on an indrawn breath, and Mr. Oakland's amiable expression hardened.

"Mista Scott," Mrs. Oakland mused.

"Is he a friend of yours?" he inquired with a chill of premonition.

"Friendly adversary you might say," Connie muttered. "Mr. Scott desires Father's business but Father keeps it within his company."

"Have you met him?" Mr. Oakland asked.

"No, sir. Why?"

"Hired you sight unseen, did he?"

"Yes, sir. We had an interview over the telephone."

"Five year program in five years? Six is more like it. With honors, I believe? Top five percent?"

"I worked at it, sir."

"Of course you did, and you certainly must have impressed Scott."

"Why shouldn't he be impressed? Douglas is intelligent, creative, ambitious—and humble," Connie said with humor in her manner.

"What is Scott paying you?"

Self-consciously he said, "If he can't pay me what I'm worth, he's at least paying me what is standard."

Mr. Oakland leaned forward, scrutinizing him. "I could use a young man like yourself in my organization. I'll double whatever Scott is offering you."

Distress twisted his heart, for every cent he earned brought him closer to his dream with Connie, but independence and loyalty prohibited acceptance. He confronted Mr. Oakland's steady pewter eyes beneath hairy brows, and resistance solidified within him. "No thank you, sir. I've been hired by Mr. Scott and I must fulfill my obligation to that firm."

"He's also stubborn," Connie added, a white line around her lips.

"Mr. Dixon died about a year ago, but that Scrooge Scott never had his name scraped off the door," Mr. Oakland informed him.

"Perhaps his clients benefit from his frugality."

"Mike Hall is a know-it-all of the worst sort. Since he passed his examination for registration he knows all there is about architecture. Ha, ha," Mr. Oakland said without humor.

"Tell us about your family," Mrs. Oakland invited. "Who are they? Where do they come from?"

Being mindful of Oaklands' social status, he deleted references to being adopted.

"Pop is a contractor. Mom is a housewife. My younger brother Terry—" Sensing Mrs. Oakland's disinterest, he subsided.

"Tell them about your house," Connie suggested.

Enthusiasm flared then dwindled into honesty. "It isn't much of a house really."

At least not compared to this one, he added mentally.

"Constance is quite enthused about it," Mr. Oakland said.

"Is she?"

"It's the only thing to be enthused about. This has been a hideously boring summer. Not only were we a thousand miles apart, but Father had to work so we couldn't take the yacht to the Bahamas."

Iced tea hung in the back of his throat and he swallowed abruptly. "Yacht? Bahamas?"

"No Douglas. No Berry Cays. See what I mean? Bor-ing. At least Penny was able to go to Paris."

"Who's Penny? Paris?" he asked with increasing confusion.

"Constance deah, you have a couple of weeks to play around before you retuhn to the univehsity."

"With moving into an apartment and starting a job, I doubt that Douglas will have much time to play around," Mr. Oakland said before he could voice the thought himself.

Mr. Oakland's peremptory manner, Mrs. Oakland's social supremacy, and Connie's mercurial moods prevented him from enjoying the gourmet fare served to him by Fenton, the man with the withered apple face.

❧

The early September light mountain air beneath the cerulean sky retained a touch of summer heat that elicited the aroma from cedar, pine, and juniper trees as she walked beside Douglas in the woods behind her home with their fingers entwined.

Douglas had rejected her parents' invitation and not stayed in a guest room. He had spent his first few days in a motel until he moved into a furnished apartment near downtown Denver. Despite his work schedule and her pre-college shopping, they had telephoned and dated, swum and sunned, biked and hiked, talked and laughed, and two weeks had drifted by in a haze of happiness.

"We have had so much fun. It hardly seems possible I'm going back to CMU without you today."

Becoming conscious of Douglas' unusual quietness, she leaned against a juniper tree with her knee bent and her foot braced against it. "What's the matter?"

Douglas laid his forearm on the tree, touching her hair with his fingertips. "We won't be able to see each other until Christmas, and I'm missing you already."

"I wish you had stayed in St. Louis," she retorted. "I almost had Father talked into letting me have an apartment where we could have had weekends together."

"I'm certain your father wasn't going to change his decision."

Deprivation weighted her spirit, yet even Blakely Whitworth knew which sort of a girl a man married and which he didn't. She tipped her head back to gaze at Douglas, observing his pale, constrained face.

"We could have at least <u>seen</u> each other. Having you in the same room, hearing your voice when you discuss politics, proposals, and population densities would have alleviated the loneliness."

Douglas gazed down at her with turbulence in his eyes, and she realized he had his difficult moments too.

"Utility rates are higher than usual, beef, milk, and bread prices are climbing, so it will cost more for me to live than I expected, but I should be able to save about five hundred dollars a month toward my house."

She was too vexed to respond to obvious optimism, and she turned away, replying over her shoulder. "You're being awfully practical about this."

Douglas brought her around to face him, his knees bent, his eyes level with hers. "It's the only way I'm able to tolerate having my heart a thousand miles away."

The unsteadiness of Douglas' voice stirred her soul, and it revolted against the separation. She locked her arms around Douglas' waist and pressed her head to his chest, hearing the hard beat of his heart. "How will I live without you?" she cried.

"We'll have wonderful memories of these past two weeks, and somehow we will survive until we're together again at Christmastime."

Douglas lifted her head and his lips sought hers. The kiss sealed in all the joys of summer and must sustain her through the fall semester. Douglas released her with noticeable regret and turned her back to the path, the airport, and another separation.

5
Returns

*O*n the cab ride from the airport to the campus in Center Springs, Missouri, memories of riding there with Douglas after his graduation haunted her and loneliness obscured the present.

She entered an austere institutional room and set her luggage down at her feet. Even with two beds, two dressers, two desks, two windows covered by avocado-colored draperies, and a sink set in a small white counter beneath a mirror, it seemed as vacant as her heart without Douglas on campus. Miserably tearful and ready to weep, she intended solely to exist until she could return to Douglas. How her father had prevailed over her mother and herself so that she was living in a dorm rather than the sorority house yet baffled her. Gritting her teeth, she wished she had never mentioned an apartment. To expend her pique, she made up one of the beds and covered it with a brightly flowered bedspread.

She had arranged her clothes in the closet and was placing her cosmetics on the counter by the sink when the salmon-colored metal door clicked open. Startled she looked up at a tall young woman with long black hair around a bronze rectangular face and bangs cut straight across her forehead. Wearing a red checked Western shirt, blue jeans, and boots, the young woman stepped forward, and the door swished shut with a distinctive metallic click.

"Hi. I'm Linda Sevenstars."

She stared before innate courtesy prompted a reply. "I'm Connie Oakland."

Linda's obsidian eyes beneath heavy brows skimmed over her. Full lips revealed uneven teeth in a surprisingly pleasant smile that crinkled Linda's cheeks. She returned it with unexpected pleasure.

"I guess we're roommates," Linda said.

She perched on her bed with her hands clasped around one knee as she watched Linda hoist the suitcase onto the other bed and efficiently unpack. She half expected Linda to pull out moccasins and a beaded dress. Linda shoved the suitcase under the bed and made it with practiced ease, covering it with a brown plaid blanket. Linda sat on the bed, leaned back on her elbows, and shook out her hair.

"I'm a pre-veterinarian major. And you?"

"I'm a liberal arts major." She wasn't sure how else to describe her basic course of study.

"But for how long?" Linda inquired, nodding at her engagement ring.

"Two years," she sighed. "On Douglas' graduation day last spring he asked me to marry him." She held her fingers so the light refracted from the diamonds. "He is starting his career as an architect and plans to build the house he designed before I graduate."

"It sounds like he has your life well-planned," Linda acknowledged. "I plan to be a vet and help my people. For the past two years I went to a community college that wasn't far from where I lived, so this is my first time in a dorm."

She refrained from mentioning her own newness to the dorm. She was certain Linda was far too removed from the sorority culture to understand the vast difference.

"I came to CMU for its pre-vet course, but I just found out a lot of my credits didn't transfer. I must work very hard the next two years to make them up, and I need a scholarship for vet school."

"Your parents—?"

Linda shook her head. "They both work so we do okay, but I have an older and a younger brother and an older and younger sister. They can't put us all through school. I have a job on campus that helps with my tuition costs."

She failed to grasp the concept.

Linda's honest, unaffected, open spirit infused the room with energy and touched something deep within her. Unintentionally she found herself drawn to this young woman who was the opposite of herself.

Soon after classes started, she participated in the Gamma Mu Upsilon sorority rush and pledge teas, enjoying the familiar activities with her friends. They had responded with the appropriate oohs and aahs and lighthearted envy to her superb engagement ring. In the parlor of the Victorian style house, she was surrounded by her sorority sisters with their flickering candles at a ceremony to celebrate her engagement, and her love for Douglas burned like a candle in her heart.

During lunch with Donna and Cheryl, they patted her hands, consoling her about living in a common dormitory, and they inquired about her new roommate. As soon as she mentioned Linda Sevenstars, Donna said, "I guess that's what comes of being from the wild, wild west of Denver, Colorado."

"She wants to live with the Indians!" Cheryl added.

She was stunned and outraged by her former roommates' attitude and barely maintained her civility. Having been rebuffed, she took refuge in her dignity and soon politely excused herself.

Gradually she noticed Linda's passion for scholastic success and an intense quest for destiny. As she contemplated Linda and Douglas' examples, her own basic course of study seemed too simplistic. Inspired by Linda and desiring to be an ideal wife for Douglas, she changed her major to home economics at the last hour.

She recalled what she had learned from Douglas in the library, and she applied what he had taught her. With direction and purpose, she diligently read and underlined and completed assignments, using more ambition than she ever had before. Even though she and Douglas remained too far away to touch, her efforts to do what she knew would please him and their frequent letters to each other connected her more closely to him.

In one of his letters, Douglas wrote that Mr. Scott hadn't removed Mr. Dixon's name from the door out of respect for him as the founding member of the firm and in deference to his wife and daughter. He described Mr. Scott as so thin and wan he questioned the condition of the man's health. With Mr. Scott's light reddish hair that curled down into sideburns and his nearly invisible eyebrows and eyelashes, he reminded him of a Charles Dickens' character. She giggled because the few times she had met Mr. Scott that had been her impression. Douglas observed that although Mr. Scott appeared frail, he rigorously invented new forms of architecture to reflect the spirit of life today and he was an effective businessman. His long white bony fingers drafted a design with rare artistry. Mike Hall was very bright and knew a lot about architecture. He answered when asked, but there wasn't much non-architectural conversation between them.

Linda was well enough organized to attend classes, study, work, help her with science, and walk with her around campus. She treated Linda to pizza and hot fudge sundaes at Serendipity's from the ample allowance her father provided, and Linda shared the homemade cookies her mother often sent.

Talking together, studying together, learning together, laughing together, Linda's presence mitigated Douglas' absence. In addition to the time she spent with Linda, she attended activities at the Gamma House.

In mid-October OAPEC imposed an oil embargo on the United States, and by December the oil crisis required urgent conservation action. In the chilly, partially lighted dorm, Gamma House, and the homemaking house, the holiday spirit had dimmed. Learning to do for herself what someone else had done for her while conserving energy challenged her.

The aroma of cinnamon bread pervaded the homemaking house kitchen, and she inhaled the scent, recalling Mrs. White's cooking. Christmas vacation began two weeks from Saturday; after months of yearning for Douglas, she would soon return to him. Then being wildly, intensely happy would warm her even though she knew she would be cold and lonely again.

When she entered the dorm room, Linda was kneeling at a desk, removing a small wooden structure from shredded newspapers.

"See what I have, Con."

"A *creche*," she murmured, laying her coat on the bed and kneeling beside Linda. "Where did you get it?"

"Mom just sent it. It was given to me by the mission church for my 10th birthday—which was also Christmas—and I've used it every year since. I hope you don't mind my setting it up."

"Not at all."

As she watched Linda place a little manger in the midst of plump ceramic cattle, small sheep, and intricately carved figures, her mind drifted back to her father's reading of the Christmas story for as many years as she could remember.

"Where's the Christ Child?"

Linda's bronze fingers hovered over the manger then moved away, leaving a tiny Baby in white swaddling clothes on the straw.

"You know, Con, a lot of people accept the Baby Jesus of Christmas but reject Him as the crucified Christ and risen Savior. God gave us His

Son as a Baby, but He grew up and died on the cross for our sins so He could bring us to God."

"We're all God's children anyway," she said.

"God created us, but we've all done things that separate us from Him and will keep us out of Heaven."

Troubled by her roommate's comments, she countered, "My idea of Heaven is pizza and hot fudge sundaes."

She helped Linda to her feet, hustled them into their coats and out the door to Serendipity's with her arm around her roommate.

Through the flurry of holiday activities at the Gamma House, last minute assignments, and studying for finals, she noticed Linda's *creche* standing in a beam of light during the morning and as a silhouette during the night. Linda's statements about the Christ Child puzzled her, but she was a good Christian girl from a good and proper Christian family.

❧

Saturday morning he dressed to meet Mr. and Mrs. Oakland for the drive to Stapleton International Airport. He slipped the medallion with its red caduceus from around his neck where he wore it when he slept and tucked it into his wallet where he carried it during the day. Perhaps sometime he would tell Connie about his rare blood type and drug allergies, but he refused to hang his albatross around her spirit during Christmas vacation. He glanced at the clock beside his bed, knowing that in an hour she would return. As his heart soared, his stomach fluttered. He suppressed the queasiness and shrugged into his dark suit coat. Emerging into the hazy December day, he drew in an icy, steadying breath.

A dark red Mercedes purred up beside him, and he let himself into the back seat with its classic luxury of maroon leather. He greeted Mr. Oakland, who wore a gray cashmere overcoat and Mrs. Oakland who wore a sable fur.

While he waited beside Oaklands at a gate in the airport, a wave of incoming travelers flowed past bearing Connie toward him. He raised her off her feet, her body in her white fur jacket perfusing him with pleasure as their lips met in welcome.

He set Connie down, and she greeted her parents. "It's so good to be home!"

Mrs. Oakland kissed the vicinity of Connie's ear. Mr. Oakland wrapped his arm around his daughter and drew her to his side.

"When is Penny arriving?"

"Her flight is due in very soon," Mr. Oakland answered.

He followed Mr. and Mrs. Oakland through the crowded concourse to another gate, his fingers linked in Connie's. With all the inconveniences in flight cutbacks, he mused how they had scheduled these two so conveniently.

Amidst disembarking passengers, a statuesque young woman in a silver fur coat and matching hat on her short dark hair met his eyes with a little click of appraisal. He noticed her gray eyes behind mascaraed lashes, delicate nose, and bow shaped lips. He smiled in automatic response, but his heart belonged to Connie. The young woman paused beside Mr. and Mrs. Oakland, greeting them each with a quick kiss. She embraced Connie in a mass of fur while her unabashed gaze ranged the length of him. His cheeks burned but he endured her regard.

"Penny, this is my fiance, Douglas McKenzie. Douglas, my sister, Penelope Oakland."

"Hello, Hero. I didn't recognize you. From what Connie has told us, I thought you wore a long red cape and had a big red "S" on your shirt." Penny's green-shadowed eyes flitted over his suit. "You must find a phone booth. You look positively destitute. You'll give Father's company a bad name."

"I don't work for your father. I work for Mr. Scott."

"Ah, yes. Mr. Scrooge and Bob Crachit." Penny arched her fingers against his chest. "How quaint."

Anger tingled his tongue, and he questioned her rapid shift from approval to disdain. "You must be the Wicked Witch of the West."

Penny's eyes narrowed, and she stalked out of the alcove. Mrs. Oakland scarcely repressed a shudder, and Mr. Oakland seemed to have difficulty clearing his throat as they followed her.

"Never mind Penny. She loves being loathsome," Connie said.

Laden Red Caps stowed an incredible amount of luggage in the trunk of the Mercedes, and then Mr. Oakland smoothly accelerated into heavy traffic flowing from Stapleton.

"Why isn't Potts driving Mother's Continental?" Penny demanded.

"I prefer to drive myself," Mr. Oakland said.

Connie lifted her mouth to his own, and he drew her into his arms. The sweet fire of her kiss melted the cold, hard ache of loneliness which had built up in his chest all these months.

"A public conveyance is not an appropriate place for such an unseemly display of affection," Penny hissed next to his ear.

Penny vexed him to speechlessness and he retreated into himself.

During the Christmas season, Connie whirled him through parties—the one at her home as lavish and crowded as all the others—and a flurry of socializing. The uniformed Potts chauffeured them around in the Continental, seemingly unaffected by the gasoline shortage while he had to wait in line for his allotment every payday.

On a less brightly lighted, economically uncertain Christmas Eve in 1973, he drove up to Oaklands', where red and green shafts of light illuminated the front of the house and the glow from the windows spilled gold onto the frosty lawn.

He existed in a world of shortages and rising prices, and as he approached the front door with its large wreath of lacquered fruits embedded in evergreens, he sensed the powerful undertow of Oaklands' wealth. Resisting it, he hesitated on the step. Commitment to Connie and the sharp wind cutting through his suit coat urged him forward. His teeth chattering, he tapped the brass knocker.

Fenton swung the door open, admitting him into the warmth and light, scents, and tangible excitement. The red leaves of a poinsettia tree brightened the foyer, and a garland of evergreens entwined with lights trailed up the banisters. He glanced down at the small package he carried, regretting the paltriness of his offering, but relentless inflation left little for gifts.

"I'll put that under the tree for you, sir," Fenton offered.

Connie descended the stairs wearing a long floral-sprigged gown enhanced by a gold chain necklace. She paused on the bottom step and laid her hands on his forearms, her luminous lavender gaze overflowing with love and glad welcome.

"Merry Christmas, Douglas."

"Merry Christmas, Con," he murmured with a downward sweep of his lashes that deepened her color.

He escorted Connie into the dining room, and Mr. Oakland joined them wearing a suit with a white shirt and black tie. Mrs. Oakland entered in a green velvet gown with a diamond and emerald brooch at the shoulder, generations of sophistication in her manner. Penny followed in a vibrant red satin enhanced by a single strand ruby and diamond necklace, deigning not to look upon him.

Glimmering white tapers in silver candelabra and red velvet runners beneath evergreen boughs on the table accented the vast array of holiday fare. The variety of colors and alignment of the *canapés* appealed to his aesthetic sense, but practicality balked at the expense. Connie selected a shrimp puff from a tray, and he had the impression that Life had been served to her from silver platters while he had forged his own destiny. Aware of the Oaklands watching him, he caught Connie's inquisitive glance and wondered if he looked as displaced as he felt.

I could never live like this, a stranger in paradise, he knew as Borodin's melodic *Polovtsian Dances* sang in his brain. *It's quite beyond me.*

After dinner Connie edged him away from her family's conversation into the living room where a fire in the fireplace flickered shadows on the beamed cathedral ceiling. In the far corner a mammoth white flocked Christmas tree, decorated with red glass ornaments, red velvet bows, and garlands of red tinsel, loomed amidst a mountain of unopened gifts.

Mrs. Oakland and Penny seated themselves on the gold brocade sofa, and he sat next to Connie on the matching love seat. Mr. Oakland removed a Bible from the mantle and sat in the chair beside the fireplace.

"Father reads the Christmas story every year," Connie whispered.

He fingered the gold chain on the back of Connie's neck, and she trembled at his touch so that he scarcely heard the biblical account of Christmas, which he could have recited from childhood.

Abruptly Penny thrust a rectangular package into his lap. "Open it," she ordered rather than the more customary, Merry Christmas.

"You shouldn't have ..."

"Penelope seemed to think you could use it," Mr. Oakland said.

With a wary glance at Penny, he pulled away the red foil and opened the box. A gray wool overcoat lay before him. He peered up at Mr. Oakland through a haze of humiliation and rebellion. "I can't accept this."

"Nonsense, you're practically one of the family," Mr. Oakland said.

Resistance rose within him, but courtesy subdued it. "Thank you."

"I have a present for you too," Connie murmured.

"I was afraid you did."

Connie removed two packages from beneath the tree, and he opened the gold-foil wrapped one which revealed a gold pen and pencil set with his name engraved.

"It's very nice," he said, trying to smile.

Connie turned to the gift in her lap that he had brought, and which she, with the unerring accuracy of a child, had retrieved, unintentionally depriving him of the small honor of presenting it to her. She ripped aside the gaudy reindeer paper and pulled out a ceramic music box with a brightly colored little boy and girl perched on a stump.

"It's darling!" Connie exclaimed, cradling it in her palms as it tinkled *Close to You*. "It's much the nicest present I've received."

"I'm glad you like it," he said, knowing it was the only present she had as yet received, but he longed to give her something more impressive.

If you must impress Constance Oakland with expensive gifts, you better stop right now, he warned himself. *All you'll ever be able to give her is yourself and your dream.*

Eventually Oaklands' living room resembled an exclusive gift shop with mounds of clothing, jewelry, and personal appliances. As Fenton served eggnog from a silver tray, Penny surveyed the scene with a lift of her aristocratic brows.

"Well, that's the loot for this year."

With impossible speed Connie's vacation reeled past. Penny had returned to Paris, and all too soon he was taking Connie to the airport. On the way they stopped at a 1960's style coffee shop where he sat across from Connie and ordered hot chocolate. He clasped her hands beneath his chin, their elbows on the table.

"In spite of not being with my folks and the nation's problems with a fuel shortage that is turning the world colder and darker, this has been the warmest, brightest, happiest Christmas I have ever had because of the love we share."

"But if you had kept—"

He laid his finger on Connie's lips, silencing her repeated objections to his returning the overcoat.

In their scant remaining moments, he savored Connie's nearness until the rough reality of parting dragged through his heart. "When I originally made the plan to share my dream with you, I hadn't calculated that being separated would be so difficult. But when our dream is reality, all the pain of parting will be worthwhile. In the meantime my career and your studying homemaking will help us survive the next three months until you return."

6

Consultation

*T*he March wind hurled itself off the Front Range and gusted against the brick building of Dixon, Scott and Hall, where he sat sketching at his drawing board with light from the two-story tall north windows. Being part of the solution to climbing building costs with designs that produced the maximum esthetic benefit for the minimum cost had resolved his former rampant discontent and revived his creative soul.

"Douglas, Rev. Jefferson would like to speak with an architect," Miss King informed him. "Mr. Scott and Mike Hall are meeting with the commissioners."

Gradually he focused on Miss King in a green shirtwaist dress, her brunette hair curling around her shoulders. He followed her to the conference room where a plump young man with a pleasant face surrounded by curly light brown hair waited at the highly polished table.

"Rev. Jefferson, Douglas McKenzie will consult with you," Miss King said and withdrew.

The clergyman, wearing a tan-and-gray plaid suit, rose at his approach. The pastor's brown eyes behind wire-framed lenses were on a level with his own, and the man's quick smile and firm handshake conveyed a warmth of manner and a gracious pastoral spirit.

After they were seated at the table, he inquired, "How may I assist you?"

"We would like an educational addition at Central Bible Church."

As Rev. Jefferson explained the needs to him, he took notes, blending innovative ideas into the basic requirements.

"Mr. Scott, as the principle architect, will overview the project at the beginning, but I would like to see the church in order to design something which will complement the existing facility."

Rev. Jefferson's cheeks vibrated with a low chuckle. "The existing facility has been there for 75 years, and I wish you could redesign the whole thing, but we're stretching our budget and our faith with the educational addition."

Adding a modern educational complex to a 75-year-old church while still maintaining its historical integrity challenged his creativity and his spirit soared.

"I would like to see the church tomorrow morning if that's convenient."

"I'll be there any time after 8:30."

The next morning he parked beside the white frame building with narrow, arched, stained glass windows and louvered bell tower beneath a spire. He paused to visualize an addition which would enhance its style and charm. With a sense of satisfaction, he entered a small anteroom that smelled of waxed wood, old books, and dust. Rev. Jefferson emerged from a doorway in front of him, his white shirt sleeves rolled past his elbows. The clergyman led him through double doors into the sanctuary where wooden pews were illuminated by colored shafts of light drifting in through the windows. In a room behind the sanctuary, which had been added on as an afterthought about 25 years ago, partitions divided the floor space.

Rev. Jefferson paused and said, "With over a hundred people in Sunday school, you can see why we need more teaching space, a kitchen, and restrooms."

The clergyman opened the back door for him to view the site for construction. He listened to Rev. Jefferson's explanations and offered suggestions until the man looked up at him with amazement in his expression.

"You're able to visualize my dream even more clearly than I am."

A sense of accomplishment for communicating his unique vision pervaded him, and he inclined his head.

Rev. Jefferson's gaze lingered on the middle distance as he asked, "How much will it cost?"

"It's next to impossible to state the cost this quickly."

The clergyman turned and led him back into the small office lined with bookshelves and gestured for him to be seated in a chair facing the desk.

Rev. Jefferson leaned back in the desk chair. "That building is a step out of our too deeply rooted traditionalism into the future where we will be more effective in our ministry to the community. See, I have this dream ..."

Sentience touched his heart and he said, "Architects are in the business of building dreams."

"But at what price the dream?"

"The highest you're willing to pay."

Rev. Jefferson leaned slightly forward with genuine interest in his expression. "What are your dreams?"

"I've designed a house I plan to build before my fiancee and I are married next year."

"It sounds as if you have your life well planned."

"An architect always works from a plan."

"How does God fit into your plan?"

He blinked, groping for an answer to a question he had never considered.

"Our lives are like a construction project designed by the Master Planner. No one will truly realize his dreams until he has discovered the plan God has for him. Whatever dreams you pursue, only those built on the solid foundation of a personal faith in Jesus Christ will last."

He politely tolerated the speech and then rose. "I'll work with you on this because I know how important it is to have a dream become reality, but I'm not a religious person. There are too many problems religion can't solve."

Rev. Jefferson stood up. "That's true. Religion isn't the solution to life's problems, Jesus is. All a man needs will be found in Him."

"I'll design something suitable for your needs. I'll draw up a proposal and have it ready for you in a few days."

He returned to Dixon, Scott and Hall and directed his attention to the project from the day before, but his mind strayed into a void. Insistence retrieved it, yet creativity refused to flow.

Annoyed, he chided himself. *Come on. You have your life planned, and religion isn't in that plan. Religion is an emotional crutch for people who are unable to direct their own lives. You're the captain of your destiny, the master of your fate, and you don't need religion any more now than you did when you left the church. Less, actually, because now you have Connie's love.*

Yet something indefinable refused to settle within him. He wandered around the small room, rapping his knuckles on the drawing board.

That evening in his apartment, he put a Chopin record on the turntable and seated himself at his drawing board to write to Connie. The inability to concentrate pulsed irritation through him, and he clasped his hair in his right hand as he willed himself to compose sentences with Chopin's turbulent *Revolutions Etude* accompanying his inner turmoil.

At Dixon, Scott and Hall the next morning, he stared at the incomplete sketch on his drawing board until it blurred, his mind strangely incapable of functioning.

After a week of the unimaginative and an unusually surly disposition, he sprawled on the black vinyl couch in his apartment.

Unable to contain his edginess, he rose and paced, noticing the unfinished letter to Connie. Compunction and futility collided. He paused at the window and pressed his forehead against the cool glass to stare into the light-pierced darkness below. Not one of a million people could touch his heart, sustain his existence, or fill the hollowness that ached inside him. He closed his eyes against intolerable lonesomeness.

When I originally made the plan to share my dream with Connie I hadn't calculated being separated from her for such long periods of time. When we finally share our dream, all the pain of separation will be worthwhile, he had told Connie. Often he needed to remind himself. *A year ago we were together almost constantly. Now I scarcely see her. Loneliness is the hardest thing in the world to live with and it's starting to bother me.* Honesty surfaced and he struck the window casing with his palm as he turned away. *I've missed Connie before. This is something else.*

Since he had achieved his goal of working with a progressive architectural firm, enthusiasm and optimism had filled his days. So why did this deep dissatisfaction plague him now? He let his mind wander until it traced the trail of its discontent to his conversation with Rev. Jefferson.

I was doing all right until he said attaining my dream comes from faith in God. I planned my dream and I'm achieving it. There's no reason to bring God into it.

He unrolled the blueprints for his house onto his drawing board. Unaccountably, looking at them failed to lighten the heaviness in his spirit.

He put on the olive drab jacket he wore when it was cold and left his apartment to walk toward downtown Denver. He passed department stores, tall office buildings, banks, multistory apartments, and storefront restaurants, marveling at the structural systems which blended lines and angles into functional beauty. Appreciation tingled through him to his fingertips, as it had for as long as he could remember, and his hands clenched, clutching his destiny. The passion to create burned in his veins, but the flames cooled and ashes swirled through his soul. Mentally he searched beneath the structure of his goals until within the chambers of his being he encountered a hollowness he had forgotten existed. *A man must have his dream*, he insisted. But there was something more somewhere, something inexplicably he lacked. Confronted by this dark hole in himself, he determined to discover what could rid him of the gnawing emptiness that lingered beyond the reach of Connie's love or his creative endeavor.

Utterly alone and needing to talk to someone, he thought of Pop or Mr. Oakland, Mr. Scott or Mike Hall, but discarded each of them. Certain that the one who had caused his distress should be the one to alleviate it, he turned back toward his apartment.

He sensed Rev. Jefferson was a man to whom he could open his heart, and he found the number and dialed.

"Good evening, this is Pastor Jefferson."

"This is Douglas McKenzie, the architect you talked to about your educational building."

"Yes," the pastor said, recognition in his tone.

"Could you meet me at your church? I need to talk to you."

"Certainly."

When he was seated across from the clergyman, he began tentatively. "The design is taking longer than I expected."

"That's no problem." Rev. Jefferson met his eyes, probing his soul. "You're not here to talk about architecture, are you?"

The clergyman's perception eased the conversation.

"Not really. Last week you said something about the Master Planner having a design for my life."

"Yes."

"I already have my life planned, but there's an emptiness neither designing nor my love for Connie can fill."

"That's because there exists in man a God-shaped hole, and in His love for us He has a plan for filling it. 'Jesus saith, ... "I am the way, the truth and the life: no man cometh unto the Father, but by me.' When you confess to God that you cannot run your own life, that you need Him and His salvation, He will give you eternal life."

The concept conflicted with his independence so that it jolted the depths of his nature. Automatically he dissented. "I don't think religion—"

"Not religion," Rev. Jefferson countered. "Belief in Jesus. His death on the cross for your sinfulness and His resurrection are the only means of achieving a personal relationship with God and discovering His plan for your life."

The concept of God, the Master Planner of the universe, entering his life floated beyond his comprehension while the hollowness continued to gnaw at him. He recalled what he had heard as a child in Sunday school about Jesus that hadn't seemed to apply to his life, but Rev. Jefferson's explanation sounded relevant. A struggle raged within him, shortening his breath and darkening the light around him until he dropped his forehead in his palm.

"It's up to you. You may ask Jesus into your heart and receive forgiveness and a life filled with direction and purpose, or you may incur the terrible consequences of separation from God forever. What do you want to do?"

A Force which he couldn't deny propelled him toward belief, and he accepted his need of God. "Yes," he murmured to the One he had rejected in his youth. An unexplainable fullness replaced the emptiness in his spirit.

"Great!" Rev. Jefferson exclaimed, his eyes alight behind his glasses.

The clergyman opened a booklet on the desk and showed him several scriptures. "God's Word, the divine blueprint, provides the design for your life."

As he focused on the page, one question intruded.

"What if God's plan for my life is different from my own?"

Rev. Jefferson handed him the booklet. "Then you'll have to decide whose plan you're going to follow: yours or God's."

And what am I going to tell Connie?

7
Spring Break

*H*er day either spiraled up or circled down, depending on whether a letter from Douglas lay in her campus mail box. The woodsy-scented pieces of paper with his precise angular handwriting spanned the distance between them and brought life and breath into her leaden soul.

She maintained her obligations to the Gamma House and endeavored to achieve academic success, yet longing for Douglas hovered over her restless nights and seeped into the endless days. She often isolated herself in memories—his tall straight body, his attractive features, the clarity of his sapphire eyes, and his long silky lashes.

Today she had daydreamed too long and burned her casserole to a dark crust. In her humiliation she stood at one of the sinks in the homemaking house, scrubbing away the residue. With her lips set, she plunged the glass dish into clear water and whisked it around, thinking through what she needed to do before her flight tomorrow.

Her heart outraced the clock until the plane taxied to a stop at Stapleton International Airport late Saturday afternoon.

The sight of Douglas urged her forward, but his overgrown hair and outdated gray suit sounded a discord in her mind. He caught her up in his arms, and she clung to him with one knee bent as she savored his strength and masculine fragrance. His lips on hers dissolved the lonely past and began the joyous present.

Douglas drove her to meet her parents in his rattly, old, blue Volvo with classical music playing in the background. They rode through several neighborhoods where Douglas described the various architectural styles, his knowledge and enthusiasm fascinating her. Her conversations of Gamma House activities and events and scholastic challenges intermingled with his incidents from the office to energy and building woes. He explained that the oil crisis had provoked a change in legislation for the Trans-Alaska Pipeline System with the hope that it would be a solution to the sharp rise in oil prices despite difficulties for its construction. She smiled and murmured, much more interested in the sound of his voice and his agile mind than the topic. She gazed up at him in silent communication of her delight at being in his presence.

In The Grotto the profusion of tropical plants muted the lighting, and water cascaded over a rock wall to splash in a lighted pool where brightly colored fish darted. As she and Douglas followed a tuxedoed waiter to the elegant dining area, serenity pervaded her. Her father rose with dignified affection in his manner.

"Welcome home, my dear."

She pressed her lips to his broad, smooth cheek, and he circled her with his left arm as he shook Douglas' hand.

"It is good to have you home, Constance deah," her mother greeted. "We are pleased to have you join us too, Douglas. We see so little of you."

During dinner her mother's narration of social events and Penny's experiences in Paris fell around her like gentle rain.

❧

Connie gazed up at him in silent communication of her delight at being in his presence, and he gently squeezed her left hand in his right beneath the white linen tablecloth to acknowledge his happiness. Wearing a yellow jumpsuit over a white long sleeved blouse, Connie possessed a unique blend of sophistication and youthful exuberance, and affection throbbed in his soul.

The gourmet feast of smoked salmon, rice pilaf, and an array of desserts contrasted with his meager daily fare, and the disparity of their lifestyles still threatened his peace of mind. Yet he was certain his love for Connie—that compelling force which had redirected his future—could transcend it.

On the drive from the restaurant to Oaklands' house, Connie chatted of her classes and dorm life with Linda in more detail than could be contained in letters, while he tried to think of a way to tell her about Jesus.

He stopped at the edge of the fragrant pine and cedar woods behind her home and drew Connie into his arms. He covered her mouth with his, and her eager response touched his heart with flame. He longed always to have the pleasure of her presence, and he knew it would be very difficult to wait another year to marry her. He contemplated consenting to Mr. Oakland's repeated offers of a position at twice the salary so he could save more rapidly for his house. Despite the force of Connie's allure, he knew he must wait until after she graduated. Furthermore, his integrity insisted he succeed on his own ability. He must resist Oaklands' influence, which Connie so subtly wielded. He spurned the enticement of their wealth to retain his independence, for he would not become a parasite.

Sunday morning, wearing a pink suit with a short banded jacket and flared skirt, she rode to church beside Douglas, noticing again that his shaggy hair and that suit lessened his attractiveness.

"Paul Jefferson is the pastor who asked me to design the addition for the church we're going to," Douglas said. "It means as much to him as my house means to me, so we understand how the other feels. He also explained that I'll only achieve my dream if I build it on the solid foundation of faith in God and His Word."

Startled by Douglas' statement, she said, "You have a dream—a dream we're sharing. I just want you to build your house now so we could be married rather than spending the next year a thousand miles apart."

Soon Douglas stopped beside a quaint, little church without a particle of style to it. Carrying a Bible in one hand, his other hand on her back, he guided her into a small tiled anteroom where he introduced her to Rev. and Mrs. Jefferson. Neither one of them had a particle of style either. Rev. Jefferson was tall and rotund in a tan corduroy suit. With light brown curly hair and brown eyes behind wire-framed lenses, he was not at all what she expected a clergyman to be like.

"I'm pleased to meet you," Rev. Jefferson said with an amiable manner.

"And I'm Margie. We're so glad you could come."

Wavy, shoulder length, coppery hair framed an unexceptional face, and she noticed the woman's nondescript beige sweater and brown skirt with an artful smile.

While she listened to the congregational singing, she recalled Linda's miniature Christ Child in the manger. Yet she sensed the hymns and Rev.

Jefferson's enthusiastic Palm Sunday sermon contained more than accolades to a sleeping Baby. She left questioning the importance of knowing Jesus and why it mattered.

Thursday evening the sun sank behind the Front Range, outlining the dark mass with a golden halo. She paced the terrace behind her home, her new, pink platform sandals clicking. The turquoise sky faded to indigo, and her pink qiana shirtwaist blurred in the encroaching darkness. She peered at her watch, her inability to distinguish the time increasing her impatience. She and Douglas had dated during the week, but now his lateness wasted precious moments.

When Douglas emerged from the lattice covered porch, she turned away and raised her chin, chastening him for his tardiness.

"I'm sorry to have kept you waiting," Douglas said behind her.

"You did say six o'clock."

Vexed by Douglas' lack of response, she turned to him. "Why are you late?"

"Business." With his hand on her arm, Douglas led her around the house to his car.

"I never see you," she said with a practiced droop in her voice.

"You're the one on vacation, I'm not."

The dome light illuminated the rigidity of Douglas' jaw, which reminded her of his compulsion to succeed.

Why did I think he would be less dedicated to starting his career than he was to preparing for it?

As Douglas drove, she ran her fingers through the hair covering his suit coat collar, its length too long to be stylish. "You need a haircut," she observed.

Douglas' shoulders twitched. "I can't afford it."

"Surely Mr. Scott pays you quite well."

"I make about fifteen hundred dollars a month. The IRS, et cetera, takes about a third, and I save five hundred. Food prices have jumped twenty percent in the last year. With the continuing rise in fuel prices, I barely manage to buy gasoline, eat, pay rent, and utilities at this year's ten percent inflation rate."

"Don't be too frugal," she said, Douglas' unkempt appearance disenchanting her.

"Con-nie, don't you understand? I'm saving it for my house."

"We could help you with your house."

"You could probably buy it twice, but when I designed it and proposed to you I didn't know that."

Encountering the impenetrable wall of Douglas' obstinacy, she fumed. *He's as implacable as ever! But nothing will interfere with our attaining our dream.*

Douglas stopped in front of a neon lighted diner, the yellow lights flashing on and off across his face. "Is this okay?"

Okay for what? she mused.

Douglas escorted her into the building where the dingy tiled floor, rattle of dishes, scent of hot oil, and the rough clientele at the counter halted her in mid-stride. She stifled a gasp of dismay and accompanied Douglas to a red vinyl booth.

Seated across from her, Douglas asked, "What would you like?"

"To go someplace reasonable for dinner," she hissed.

Douglas' dark brows lifted. "What's unreasonable about this one? The food and service are good and the prices are reasonable," he said with the slightest emphasis.

She snatched the paper napkin from beneath her flatware and laid it in her lap, anger tightening her lips.

It shouldn't matter, part of her insisted. *You're together. After all those meals in the cafeteria when you missed him so much, you should be deliriously happy.*

But Douglas' styleless hair, college days' suit, and palpable tension diminished the usual breathless joy of being in his presence.

Nibbling her chef's salad, she raised her gaze to Douglas who seemed oblivious to her inner turmoil as he bit into his hamburger.

"This isn't a luxurious dining place like I'm accustomed to," she said with a demure smile.

"When we're married we won't be living the way you're accustomed to. We'll be living on a budget—something I'm sure you've never had to do."

The chasm between their lifestyles jeopardized her happiness, and she sought to bridge the gap with charm. Adjusting her manner to ego-flattering attention, she held Douglas' gaze with an intentionally melting expression. His face softened into a smile that revealed his even, white teeth and erased all traces of ill temper.

"As long as I'm married to you, we'll be rich in love and nothing else will matter," she declared.

The blue flames in Douglas' eyes kindled warmth within her.

"I better take you home or I'll forget myself and go someplace where I can kiss you."

"That's quite all right with me."

Douglas shook his head and his smile faded. "I don't trust myself. You're very attractive and we've been apart far too long."

At least we agree on that.

Douglas drove her home, but her light chatter failed to draw him into conversation, and in the circle drive he turned to open his car door.

Desperate to detain him, she caught his arm. "Douglas, please—"

Douglas turned and enfolded her against him, his lips clinging to hers before they trailed across her cheek, around her ear, and lingered on her throat. She trembled in his embrace and clasped his hair in her fingers as she slanted her lips across his, reveling in the fire which sparked between them.

Douglas drew a quivering breath and eased away. "You know you have a devastating effect on me, but please don't take advantage of it."

She leaned against him, serene and confident in the power she wielded over the man who adored her.

"I could hold you like this forever," Douglas murmured with his chin against her hair. "But I must take you in before my resistance crumbles with a crash and I forget all my plans—and principles."

Douglas walked her to the door where he cupped the back of her head in his palm and laid his lips on her forehead in a quick, good night kiss.

The next morning she and her mother rode in the back seat of the Continental as Potts drove them downtown on a mutual endeavor. Her mother was impeccably dressed in a light blue suit with wide lapels on the three button jacket, and she wore a lavender dress and matching coat with a shawl collar. They entered the office of Dixon, Scott and Hall and waited in the brown shag-carpeted lobby where orange open weave draperies covered the windowed wall while Miss King notified Mr. Scott of their arrival.

"Mista Scott," her mother greeted the thin, pale, rather gangling gentleman. "You rememba my daughta, Constance? Constance, Mista Scott. We have come for Douglas. I undastand he was to be free today."

"He hasn't asked for time off or indicated to me he planned to be away."

Her mother patted Mr. Scott's dark green suit coat sleeve. "The deah boy doesn't know it yet. Ahmand seemed to think he could shuly have Good Friday off. We'll wait heah," her mother said and sat in a rust colored leather tub chair with gracious ease.

She seated herself in another tub chair beside her mother.

Douglas entered, his eyes giving her a surprised greeting. A brown-haired man of average height and attractiveness followed a step behind him.

Douglas paused to perform the introductions. "Connie, this is Mike Hall. Mike, my fiancee, Constance Oakland."

Mike clasped her hand in his and gazed at her with the you-are-so-lovely, where-have-you-been-all-my-life? look she usually evoked and generally enjoyed.

Douglas removed her hand from Mike's and held it in both of his. "What is the purpose of this pleasant diversion?"

"Mother and I have come to take you shopping."

Something indefinable flitted across Douglas' face, but she maintained a gentle pressure on his arm and led him from the building.

Potts opened the door of the Continental for her mother, and they seated themselves.

"What soht of clothes would you prefeh?" her mother asked. "I'm afraid we haven't time for them to be propaly tailohed, but we should be able to select somethen suitable."

"Clothes? I don't want you to buy my clothes."

"Ahmand said you wuh a detehmined young man."

"What is this—a conspiracy?"

She gazed at Douglas with a smile designed to bedazzle any man. "You could accept a few outfits."

Douglas' defiant eyes shifted from her to her mother's cool stare but fell away from the strength of it. "One outfit," he conceded, his voice sounding strained.

"Yes, dear, one from each of us."

Douglas crossed his arms on his chest, his breathing measured.

A silence much louder than sound vibrated between them and continued into the carpeted dressing room of the fashionable men's shop. Douglas stood before the mirror wearing a white turtleneck sweater, white slacks, and a navy blazer. Her heart beat high with admiration. Smiling, she met her mother's eyes.

"Clothes certainly make the man. Now, if we could only get his hair cut."

Her mother smiled with a barely perceptible nod before turning her attention to the salesman who waited at Douglas' elbow. "He'll weah that one, and we'll take the silva one he tried earlieh as well. Come, Constance deah, we shall select shirts and ties then go with Douglas to puhchase his shoes."

"I'd like to speak to Connie—alone," Douglas said, his tone brittle.

Her mother gathered up her gloves and handbag and preceded the salesman out of the dressing area.

"This has to stop. I am not the kind of man who accepts handouts. I want to live the way I'm used to living—buy my own clothes."

"But on what's left from your salary, you couldn't possibly." She traced the golden emblem stitched on his blazer pocket with an oval fingernail. "When you get used to dressing the way men are supposed to dress you'll enjoy it."

"Really?" Douglas said, his eyes a cold, hard blue.

Uncertainty chilled her, but she laid her hand on his arm with a little pat. "Now you have something appropriate to wear to take me to the Good Friday service."

She slipped out of the dressing room, pausing with her hand on the door knob as she questioned the wisdom of persuading Douglas to accept what he didn't want.

In the elite Mr. Maxwell's aromatic glass and ebony salon, where she had her hair trimmed when she came home on vacations, she waited beside her mother for Douglas. She was certain her mother had worked magic to secure an immediate appointment.

Finally Douglas emerged, still wearing the white slacks and navy blazer, his hair trimmed and styled. Attraction swelled in her heart.

"It's so rewarden to see Douglas propaly groomed," her mother murmured.

She approached Douglas and slid her fingers through the hair over his ear. "You look wonderful."

"Thanks," he said curtly.

With his hand on her elbow, Douglas guided her out of the salon and into the Continental where her mother and Potts waited. They returned to the office of Dixon, Scott and Hall, and then Potts drove her mother home.

Douglas seated her in his car and sat beside her.

"Where are we going for lunch?" she asked.

Douglas hunched his shoulders and started the motor.

"Since I had my hair cut, I can't afford to take you out."

She glanced at him to detect a jest, but his grim expression denied humor.

"I thought Mother—"

"Her buying my clothes is one thing, getting my hair cut is quite another!"

Mr. Maxwell's services floated through her head. "You couldn't possibly have afforded it."

"If I don't eat this week I'll come out about even."

"We didn't intend for you to do <u>that</u>."

"I <u>told</u> you I couldn't afford a haircut."

Douglas drove to the Gothic style church she and her parents occasionally attended. As he sat beside her on a blue upholstered pew in the dim sanctuary, she remembered his sizzling kisses the evening before. She almost preferred him in his old suit and overlong hair to this cold, stylishly dressed man.

Rev. Murphy, short and graying but distinguished in his long clerical robe, began the service. Escaping the monotonous drone that sounded pious, her mind pursued its own path. *Rev. Murphy eulogizes a Great Teacher Who was murdered. Rev. Jefferson claims Jesus is God's Son and could live within me. Linda has told me I need Someone in my life besides Douglas.*

Unable to form a conclusion, she discarded the problem; she was more interested in coaxing Douglas back to affectionate humor.

Outside in the crisp, bright April air, Douglas opened the car door for her. "Would you like to get a Coke?"

"Can you afford it?"

Anger glinted in Douglas' eyes.

Regretting the jibe, she proffered him a conciliatory smile. "Yes, that would be very nice."

In a nearby coffee shop, Douglas seated her in an orange booth, and silence persisted between them until after they were served.

"Could we go to my church Sunday?" Douglas asked.

"But it's Easter. Mother and Father always go to church on Easter. You must come with us."

"During the service this afternoon, did you hear Rev. Murphy explain what was accomplished when Jesus died on the cross?"

Certain she hadn't listened that closely to Rev. Murphy she remained silent.

"Jesus took the punishment for all the things we do wrong and gives us everlasting life so we can go to Heaven to live with Him there."

"What difference does it make?" She laughed a little as she spoke, poking the ice with her straw in an unusual display of nervousness. "We're all going to Heaven anyway."

Douglas' eyes, dark and serious, held hers. "We have to believe that Jesus is the only One Who can give us a right relationship to God before we can get into Heaven. In the meantime we can discover His plan for our lives."

"But you already have a plan for your life."

"I did have my life all planned, but I had left God out, and leaving God out is the worst possible thing to do. Pastor Jefferson has explained how Jesus could help me—"

"Help you? You who relies solely upon yourself?"

A dark wave of color suffused Douglas' cheeks. His gaze slid away from hers, and a vast distance seemed to separate them. Seeking to reach him across it, she laid her fingers on his and smiled with practiced charm. His expression remained guarded, and her inability to enchant him stilled her heart.

Saturday morning when she entered the sunny breakfast room, her father was already seated at the round maple table.

"Good morning, Constance," her father greeted, rising. "You've been home a week, but I've not seen much of you."

"Between your schedule and mine ..." She leaned against his shoulder and smiled up at him.

Her father seated her and then returned to his chair. "I must say that young man of yours is—quite a young man."

She blinked at so profound a statement. "Yes, he is. Quite ..."

"One could also say he's a little bit stubborn."

One could also say he's very stubborn, she added mentally.

"That house for one thing. It's going to be more expensive than he planned. I know he wants to have it completed for you before you're married, but this energy crisis has drastically affected the building industry. Buying power is eroded by high prices, and interest rates are at an all time high and still rising." Her father extended his hand toward her. "Constance, I would like to help Douglas, but Thursday evening when I suggested it, his pride prevented him from accepting anything from me."

Insight into Douglas' ill-temper filtered into her mind.

Her father cleared his throat behind his thumb and forefinger. "I opened a savings account in your name. When Douglas encounters financial difficulties—as he inevitably will—you shall be able to assist him." Her father removed a booklet from beside his plate and slipped it under her hand.

Curiosity prompted her to peek. She stared at the amount, amazement halting her breath.

"Twenty five thousand dollars?"

"A man must retain his pride, my dear, so don't mention this little transaction to Douglas. Just watch and wait and let the interest accrue then help him discreetly as the need arises."

"Yes, of course. There's no way he will ever find out."

8

Easter

$\mathcal{T}$he dazzling sun in the robin egg blue sky on Easter hadn't dispersed the April chill, and patches of snow remained on the northern edges.

Wearing a white eyelet dress, she rode beside Douglas in his Volvo. "I'm glad you decided to attend church with Mother and Father and me."

"But did you hear what Easter means?"

Wearing new clothes and white shoes seemed not to be the answer Douglas expected. Sensing that it was more significant than ushering in spring, she inquired, "What does it mean?"

"Easter is the reminder of Jesus' dying and—"

"That's a particularly morbid view."

"The death and resurrection of Jesus are linked. Jesus died for our sins and was buried and raised by the power of God on the third day. Easter is the joyous occasion to celebrate His victory over sin and death. It's the most incredible event in all of history! Jesus is alive!"

"Um hmm," she murmured, assenting to the tradition of Easter she had heard from her earliest years. "I'm so happy you are joining Mother and Father for dinner as their guest today."

"I had no choice. Your father wouldn't take no for an answer."

Trying to placate Douglas with a compliment, she said, "I love you in that silvery suit. The yellow shirt and striped tie—"

"So that's it," Douglas said, his voice harsh and angry. "The way I dress determines how you feel about me. Well, I would much rather have worn my own clothes to my own church!"

Masking her dismay, she leaned her head against Douglas' shoulder and ran her fingertips along his lapel. "You look exceptionally handsome in that suit," she amended.

Ahead of them, her father swept his red Mercedes to the crest of a hill and parked in front of a glass domed, marble columned building. Douglas followed.

Douglas escorted her into the elegant dining room where Grecian statues in marble chitons stood among broad-leaved plants. Sunlight glinted through the dome and sparked rainbows from delicate crystal. Heavy silver service lay on white linen napkins.

Douglas seated her at a table separate from her parents.

"Isn't this a perfectly marvelous place? Mother and Father come here on special occasions, and Easter—"

Douglas' face resembled those of the statues behind him.

"You don't like anything we do, do you?"

"It's very nice. It's late Fifth Century Greek. Greek architecture is graceful and harmonious. The thin, slender columns have a classic aesthetic beauty." Douglas' gaze rose to the ceiling. "The glass domed roof is a masterpiece of engineering."

"Must you appraise everything as an architect?"

"I _am_ an architect. I may not recognize myself as a man, but I am still one _very_ _good_ architect."

Douglas' bright blue eyes had a sharp fierceness she had never seen before.

A palpable silence hung between them, and she tried to coax Douglas back to attentiveness during the dinner of savory lamb. With lowering brows he remained uncommunicative and impervious to her charm. The festive meal had gone absurdly flat, and when they left the restaurant irritation isolated her from him.

As Douglas drove west, their few remaining hours passing in brooding silence caught at her heart.

"Being separated from you is unbearable, and I live for the moments we're together. Please, let's not waste them."

She stroked Douglas' jaw and lips with the back of her fingers until they softened, and he drew her against his side, driving with his left hand. They rode through several neighborhoods where he described the various architectural housing styles, his knowledge and enthusiasm fascinating her.

In the juniper and cedar woods behind her home, Douglas stopped his car and cradled her in his arms. She lay back against his chest, satisfied that he could be as civil and affectionate as always. His gaze caressed her face and her lacy white stockinged legs protruding from her short skirt.

"This is the way we should spend our engagement, with you in my arms."

She spoke from her sense of contentment. "It's too bad we can't bottle this and uncork it in our loneliness."

"Perhaps that's what memories are—an antidote for loneliness."

She abhorred more months of only memories. She had agreed to wait two years to marry Douglas, but she never fathomed their separations would be so abysmal. The future, which had been a tunnel with only a dim light in the distance, now emerged before her. She opposed waiting further for what she desired, especially when it could be purchased immediately.

"Let's get married now and end all these separations."

"We can't, Con. I haven't saved enough money and—"

"It doesn't have to be that way. We could be living in your house in six weeks."

"I can't afford to build my house yet, and you must graduate."

"I don't care about graduating. All I want is to be married soon."

"But, Con—"

She sat up and covered Douglas' lips with hers, silencing his protests. She furrowed his hair as his mouth moved on hers, the sweetness of his kiss quickening her pulse. She touched her lips to Douglas' eyelids until they flickered beneath her feathery kisses. With a quick indrawn breath he buried his face in her neck, his hand stroking her ribs and hip with delightful pressure. She slid her mouth over to nibble Douglas' ear while she rubbed his shoulders beneath his suit coat and eased him out of it. His lips trailed to her throat, flooding her with pleasant sensations. Her mouth forged to his with unmistakable urgency, and she freed him from his tie and unfastened his buttons.

"Con, please— Please, don't— Don't tempt me. It could be disastrous."

"It could be fabulous," she replied, kissing his bottom lip.

"No," Douglas said on a wavering breath and caught her hands in his. "Not now. Not like this. Not until we're married and living in my house."

"It could be soon."

Impatient to possess the dream, she turned and knelt beside Douglas, drawing his head toward her. Her purse slid to the floor from where she had laid it next to her on the seat. She ignored it, but Douglas eased away and reached down to retrieve what had spilled out. He replaced the lipstick, comb, compact, and wallet, and then he stopped and straightened, flipping open a savings account book.

Alarm froze her blood. "May I have that please?"

"Twenty five thousand dollars!" Douglas stared at her. "I thought my passbook had fallen on the floor, but—" His steel blue eyes impaled her. "Why do you have twenty five thousand dollars in passbook savings?"

Panic squeezed calm logic from her mind. "Father gave it to me."

"Why would your father give you twenty five thousand dollars?"

"Please—" She reached for the passbook and sat back on her heels.

"He gave it to you for my house, right? But I have told you and told you and TOLD YOU I don't want your help! I planned to build my house myself and I will."

"But you can't possibly—"

"What were you going to do? Sneak it into my account when I wasn't looking?"

Stung by Douglas' perception, she opened her lips to protest.

"This is why you were so sure we didn't have to wait—why you came on to me so strong." Disbelief and betrayal darkened Douglas' expression. "How far would you have gone to lure me from my plan?"

"Why can't you accept a little help instead of flaunting that accursed plan?"

"A little help? I have scrimped and scratched and saved for seven months, and now you show up with a balance of over seven times what I have. How do you think that makes me feel?"

"It should make you feel grateful, but apparently it doesn't."

"You bet it doesn't! It's a cruel scheme to undermine my independence."

"No ... we were only trying to help."

"I would rather die than accept your help! Neither you nor your parents will ever—by any means—force anything more on me!"

"Don't be so stubborn! Your ingratitude is exceeded only by your naivete."

"I'll build my house my way with no interference. Do you understand?"

She was spurred to furious response and hoped to shock Douglas into obtaining the dream quickly. She snatched the ring from her finger and thrust it into his hand. "If you're going to be so stubborn, proud, and independent—!"

"I'm stubborn, proud, and independent. You're childish, selfish, and deceitful. Hardly traits on which to base a marriage!"

Douglas dropped the ring in his shirt pocket.

Wait! she wanted to cry out. *This is all a horrible mistake! I do want to marry you.* But Douglas' savage expression halted her admission.

Douglas slammed the Volvo into gear and spun onto the roadway.

The extent of her miscalculation whirled through her.

"I'm sorry. I won't give you the money."

"You bet you won't!"

Her composure wavered, and she clasped her hands in her lap to keep a grip on herself until she could disintegrate in private.

In front of her home, Douglas jolted his car to a stop and reached across her to jerk open the door. The inference was unmistakable, and she stepped out. He banged the door, and the Volvo roared down the drive.

Woozy from shock, she groped her way upstairs and flung herself onto her bed. She moaned, uttering undignified noises in her despair, muffling them in the pink quilted bedspread she clutched in her fists. Bereft of Douglas' love, she pulled a pillow over her head, waiting for the feeble flame of life to flicker out.

❧

He parked and walked around to his apartment, the frigid breeze invading his shirt where Connie had unbuttoned it.

Inside he leaned against the door and withdrew the ring from his pocket, wondering what he should do with it. He flipped it between his thumb and fingers until a scalding mist obscured his vision.

He sought escape at his drawing board, but the blueprints for his house were there. He dropped his forehead onto them. The dream was gone—razed before it became reality—and there was nothing to replace it.

He turned to bitter introspection. *It's been a ridiculous situation from the beginning. A poor architect engaged to a sorority girl. I should have known I was an unsuitable suitor for Armand Oakland's society daughter. Ever since I moved to Denver, she and her parents have been trying to buy me. Now it's the propa clothes and a high-priced haircut. Twenty five thousand dollars was the final installment. Perhaps her father's generosity was merely misguided, a misjudgment of my independent nature, but she—* Accusations sizzled in his brain. *She has manipulated me with her subtle allure and temper tactics right from the beginning.*

He recalled the times Connie had sought to entice him from his plan, but this time she had brought the full battery of her charm to bear. The anguish in his soul forced a strangled sound between his teeth.

Why did it have to end <u>this</u> way? Why did she try to deceive me?

Almost in answer memories from the Sweetheart Dance returned with startling clarity. Blakely Whitworth had chided Connie for telling him Grandmother Van Leigh was ill so she couldn't attend the dance, but he had been so flattered that she would break a date with a frat boy to go with him that he hadn't questioned her methods.

She deceived Blakely then. She deceived me now.

Connie's deception and the withdrawal of her love rent something inside him asunder with an annihilating sheet of pain. It gaped and quivered as an open wound, the like of which he hadn't experienced since he was very young and his father had gone to Korea and was missing in action and his mother had died soon after. Subject once more to such desolation, he felt shattered into a thousand pieces. Distraught, he ripped the blueprints into shreds and hurled them away, tattered remnants of a dream that would never see reality. Then he sat doing nothing, knowing he would never do anything again.

Ever.

9
Broken Things

S he awakened the next morning damp and rumpled, still wearing her white eyelet dress and lacy stockings. Unbidden Douglas' harsh words and stone-faced fury loomed in her memory, replacing her first thoughts of him that normally tingled delight through her. The awful realization that her ploy had tumbled in on her and she must endure all her days without him disrupted her pulse. She fled to her pink tiled bathroom and immersed herself in a tub of bubbles, waiting for the heat to soak away a hurt which nothing could diminish. Her tears mingled with the water until no more remained.

She considered calling Potts to have him drive her to the airport so her parents wouldn't know that Douglas hadn't taken her, but they needed to learn of her broken engagement.

She applied extra makeup to conceal her pallor and dressed in a new, long sleeved blue floral dress with a wide collar.

She entered the breakfast room, and Fenton seated her at the round maple table across from her mother, who sipped tea from a delicate china cup.

"Good mornen, Constance deah. Your fatha and I wuh out with anotha couple yestaday and missed your retuhn."

"Where is Father?"

"He was called away on business. I'm not suhe when he will retuhn."

Initial relief expand within her, yet she knew she must explain the debacle to him.

"Do you have anything scheduled this morning, or could you go with me to the airport?"

"I ratha thought Douglas had ahranged to take you."

The sound of his name caused her to tremble, and she could not trust herself to speak.

Her mother's eyes searched her face. "Constance deah, you look absolutely haggahd."

The wound was too deep, too fresh for words, and she summoned the semblance of a smile.

"Is anything the matta?"

"There has been a change in plans," she stated, using a socially acceptable phrase to describe the devastation of her life.

She phoned Potts, and with impeccable timing he arrived to load her suitcases into the Continental, and then he seated her mother and herself for the trip to the airport.

As she waited for her flight, she was unable to avoid the inevitable and she said, "Douglas has broken our engagement."

Her mother's genteel features shadowed. "How humiliaten. What will our friends think? Thank goodness there hadn't been a fohmal announcement and only a few people knew."

Bereavement had so wounded her heart she scarcely noticed her mother's usual insensitivity. Anguish surpassed her dignity and she boarded the plane with a small, helpless cry.

When she entered her dorm room, the brightly colored music box with its evocative *Close to You* caught her attention, and the loss of Douglas' closeness overwhelmed her again. Images of the past dissolved, leaving only reminiscence of what had been and the hopeless realization of what would never be again. She buried her face in her pillow until, wretched and weak, she finally sniffed and blotted and blew.

She emerged from the pall which engulfed her and forced herself to unpack, becoming aware of Linda's absence.

Eventually the door knob clicked, and she glanced up to see the back of Linda's left shoulder push the door open. Linda turned and entered, carrying a suitcase in her right hand. The sight of her friend's left arm in a sling and a cast produced a hollowness in her knees that anyone's injury caused.

"Linda! What happened?" She rose to take her friend's suitcase and eased her onto the bed in spite of the mists swirling behind her eyes.

"My kindest, gentlest horse shied and threw me."

"How awful!"

Linda leaned back against the wall and regarded her. "How was your vacation?"

Her throat ached with the effort of suppressed tears and no words came.

"Connie, what happened?"

She caught herself in a figurative grip and regained enough control to explain. "Father offered Douglas money to build his house because it will cost more than he planned, but he wouldn't accept it. He's the I'll-do-it-myself-or-not-at-all type. *I Did It My Way* should be his theme song. Anyway.... Father put some money in a savings account for me, and when Douglas encountered financial difficulties I could deposit a few hundred dollars into his account. If my purse hadn't fallen on the floor, he wouldn't have known where the money came from."

"Connie, that's not even honest."

Linda's echo of Douglas' attitude irritated her.

"Besides I don't think it would have worked," Linda added. "He seems like a bright guy. He could figure it out."

"I thought if it was in his account he would use it. Why didn't he want to do that?" Anger blazed a path through her brain. "Because he's absolutely intractable, that's why!"

"But what you did wasn't right either. You know that, don't you?"

Regretting the destructive outcome, she tilted her chin.

"I wanted Douglas to build his house now so we could be together rather than always being torn apart. Instead of slipping the money to him gradually and discreetly, maybe I thought if he saw it— Only not that way— Oh, I don't know.... I got it all muddled!"

"What you did broke your engagement and ruined your happiness. Sin does that. But if you confess your sin to God, He will forgive—"

"God has nothing to do with it. Douglas overreacted, that's all."

"But if you would—"

"Stop it, Linda," she warned and paced. "It's something I'll have to work out."

"No one can work out their own sin, Con. That's why God gave us Jesus to take away our sin."

"It can't be a sin to give someone money."

"Giving money to someone isn't, but deceitfulness is. 'The heart is deceitful above all things and desperately wicked.'"

"I don't think wicked—"

"It's the wickedness you're born with that Jesus died to save you from."

"I never thought of myself as <u>that</u> bad."

"You're not as bad as you could be," Linda agreed. "But without Jesus you're as bad <u>off</u> as you can be—sinful and sad and separated from God. But, 'the blood of Jesus Christ, God's Son, cleanses us from all sin.' If you believe He gave that blood for the wrong things you've done then you will be freed from the penalty and power of sin."

She refused to believe what she had done merited bloodshed, and she turned away from Linda. Yet Truth gnawed at her conscience and she averted the face of her soul. Still she sensed an exposure to God's unrestricted view. Driven deeper into herself she encountered unexpected darkness. She didn't know how the Holy Spirit moved convicting her of sin or how He revealed Christ to her, but an awareness came that her own efforts were powerless to rid herself of her guilt; only the power of Jesus' blood and His resurrection could do it. Faith had been created in her heart, and she received the offer of salvation.

"If what everyone has told me about Jesus is true, I will accept Him into my life."

The cleansing of forgiveness poured through her, bringing peace, and Jesus had made all the darkness depart. She sensed the significance in what had transpired and met Linda's searching gaze.

Joy burnished Linda's coppery features. "When Jesus comes into your life—in the Person of the Holy Spirit—He gives you eternal life that assures you of going to Heaven. You will also find that He is with you in every situation and His love will comfort you as nothing else will."

Weariness dimmed Linda's radiance, and concern for her friend prompted her to prop the cast on her own pillow. Touching the cold, hard thing did queer things to her stomach, and as soon as Linda's eyes closed she hurried from the room with a sense of having escaped.

In the hall she leaned against the salmon-colored metal door, realizing that in spite of adversity, Linda had led her to Jesus. Her spirit soared in silent awe. Her stomach rumbled a reminder that she hadn't eaten in over twenty-four hours, and she hurried to the cafeteria.

Grieving and directionless, she wandered into the Gamma House, where she received comfort and sympathy.

Later she reentered her dorm room where Linda was struggling out of a plaid blouse. She laid her hand on Linda's shoulder to quiet her.

"Let me do that."

She gently freed Linda from the restrictive blouse and slipped a flowered gown over her head.

"I refuse to wear my cast under my clothes and look deformed," Linda fumed.

Fondness for her friend prompted her to patiently ease the wide sleeve over the cast in spite of her aversion to contact with it.

"Mom dressed and undressed me all last week, but I thought I could manage alone."

"You're going to need a lot of help," she observed. "Broken arms present more practical problems than broken hearts. They say it's your heart that gets broken, but it's your stomach where you feel it, and it's the worst feeling in the world."

"Broken arms is bad, but broken hearts is worst," Linda sympathized.

"And broken English is terrible," she said with an airy laugh.

"I'm sure you hurt as badly as I do, so we'll help each other," Linda said. "Having Jesus in our lives will help too."

Nevertheless, every day she awakened to the tragedy of her lost future. She had called her father to inform him that the plan to aid Douglas discretely had gone drastically awry; Douglas had broken their engagement and she wouldn't need the $25,000.

Remorse dampened her existence, and she endured each day as it came. She aided Linda with showers, shampoos, dressing, eating, and typing assignments, staying as near as possible, and she collapsed in bed each night with a weariness too profound for words.

She noticed that Linda persevered, enduring discomfort and inconvenience with a gentle and quiet spirit of peace and a strength beyond stoicism.

One evening early in May as she strolled across campus with Linda, the fluorescent crimson sun turned the window panes to sheets of flame and paved the roadway with molten brass.

"I'm almost glad I broke my arm," Linda remarked in the twilight serenity. "At least with everything you've been doing for me, you haven't had time to mope."

The unhappiness which dwelt within her reared up. "You have no idea what it's been like," she cried. "Helping you has kept me from having to scream, but not <u>one minute</u> has passed that I haven't missed Douglas and wanted him back! From the first moment I saw him, I wanted him more than life itself, and I still do! I had found an unconditional love apart from being Armand Oakland's daughter or a propa society guhl. Douglas' love and direction altered my destiny—then one day I woke up and he was gone. The source of my life was torn away, and there's this dreadful hole. I've been bleeding to death inside, but I won't just decently die."

Linda turned to look at her. "I'm sorry. I really didn't know. If you love him that much, why don't you write and apologize?"

"He's the one who broke our engagement and destroyed our future."

"Weren't you responsible for that?"

Truth pierced her, and her voice refused to function.

"You confessed your sin to God and He forgave you. Now you need to ask Douglas to forgive you too."

"What about all the hurt he caused me?"

"You need to forgive him too."

Linda's suggestion suspended her thoughts, and she paused on the drive until her mind revolved into action. Gripping Linda's arm, she hurried back to the room.

At her desk she drew her pink checked stationery to her with trembling fingers. Half-drowning in the confluence of love and sorrow, she wrote to Douglas and apologized for the fallacy of assisting him with her father's money. She explained that she had confessed her dishonesty to Jesus and accepted Him into her life. She concluded by expressing regret that she had betrayed a precious love and lost it.

Exhaling a long quivering breath, she carried the envelope to the campus mailbox, where it disappeared with a *whoosh*.

10
The Letter

He entered his apartment building and the unexpectedness of the pink checked envelope in his mailbox stopped his stride. By making a special effort he had almost succeeded in putting Connie from his mind, and he would not allow loneliness and surprise to jeopardize that. Coldness seared his heart, and he dragged his eyes away and continued on upstairs. After supper he listened to a record of Schoenberg's *Piano Concerto Opus 42,* which matched his inner dissonance while he read an architectural journal.

The next morning when he was in his office at Dixon, Scott and Hall, Miss King announced his scheduled appointment with Rev. Jefferson.

"The building committee and the church board are impressed with your inventive addition to the existing building. However, they would like it to be less expensive while still maintaining its versatility." The pastor handed the design to him.

"That's typical. The client always wants to change it. We'll pull out the best of each idea."

Seated at the conference table, he sketched possible alterations to accommodate the needed various functions, his right hand on his forehead to keep his ideas flowing smoothly.

Pastor Jefferson leaned over his shoulder, attentive to the process.

"You do that so well. It still amazes me that you are able to visualize my dream even better than I."

"It's my job to visualize dreams," he said with satisfaction.

"What about your dream?"

Blood which had rushed and rioted with love for Connie pooled around the iceberg where his heart used to be. "My dream will never see reality."

"Oh? Why not?"

The question which had tormented him for weeks remained unanswered, but the pastor's concerned gaze compelled him.

"It's all Connie's fault. I should have been warned against rich girls who have had their way since boarding school. They're well-trained in the art of breaking hearts."

"Okay," Pastor Jefferson encouraged. "What happened?"

His helpless rage rising, he pushed his hands through his hair and strode around the room.

"She concealed her wealth, but it was there like a tiger waiting to spring and tear our dream apart. I had saved every penny possible for seven months, and then she wanted me to get my hair cut! She and her mother bought me new suits because she loves me in that kind of clothes. When I wouldn't accept her father's financial assistance, he gave her a savings account so she could help me—without my knowledge or approval."

"And you didn't want her help," the pastor stated.

"No way! No man with any fortitude would live on a woman's money. I designed my house and I planned to build it. I don't need some scheming, rich sorority girl to undermine me with her money."

"Is this girl a Christian?"

Dismay tightened beneath his ribs. "Connie thinks any upper class American is a Christian. I tried to explain it to her, but she didn't understand."

Pastor Jefferson's brows appeared above his wire-framed lenses. "With your diverse financial, social, and spiritual backgrounds perhaps this is best."

The month's-long dissatisfaction with their dissimilar lifestyles congealed into inevitability. He had deluded himself into believing Connie and he could share a future, but the sheer force of his will could not generate a basis for marriage. Still, his soul rebelled.

"Only you still love her," Pastor Jefferson said.

The truth increased his anguish, and he peered at the pastor through a haze of misery and disillusionment. "But she deceived me and destroyed everything!"

"You trusted your immortal soul to God, now trust Him with your dream."

He recalled the fragmented blueprints and dissented. "I've taken care of it."

"Anything which is purely ambition is bound to fail because human plans are warped by selfishness and pride," the pastor cautioned. "Only as you trust your life and future to God will you truly succeed. 'Except the LORD build the house, they labour in vain that build it:' Seek God's will and obey it." Pastor Jefferson clasped his shoulder.

Annoyed, he opened the door. "I'll redraw the design so these revisions will suit your needs."

"I'm sure they will. You're a very intelligent architect. I trust you'll soon use that intelligence to design your life according to God's plan."

Following Pastor Jefferson's departure, he returned to his drawing board, but the pastor's comments buzzed around him like bees. He brushed them away and concentrated on another project.

Late that night, pink checked envelopes drifted through his uneasy sleep, and he awoke with a strange sensation in his chest. He elevated himself against the head of the bed while the conflict in his soul battered his determination. Gradually his heart rejected the caution urged by his brain. He crept downstairs in his pajamas to retrieve the letter.

◈

She seemed to have lived longer in the 21 days since she wrote to Douglas than in her 21 years.

She returned to her room from the campus post office, irritation shredding her disposition. She flung her books on the bed and flounced down beside them.

"Still no answer, huh, Con?" Linda asked, her arm in its cast on the desk useful as a paperweight.

"No, there's still no answer. Even though the price of postage is now ten cents, he could surely afford to mail a letter. Unless he doesn't want to accept my apology." Unable to tolerate the possibility, she pressed her fingertips to her temples.

"I'm sorry, Con. I wish I could do something to help."

"The only thing that would help is to have Douglas back in my life, but I'm sure he doesn't want that. And I feel so hollow, so utterly hollow, without him."

Linda moved to sit beside her and laid an arm around her shoulders, sharing the hurt.

"Remember, you have the Spirit of Jesus living within you. He wants to fill your life with a perfect, never failing love, and His presence will be a great source of comfort."

Yet she found doubt rather than comfort.

"You're a great source of comfort, Lindy," she said, circling Linda's waist with her arm. "What would I ever do without you?"

Linda hunched her shoulders and lowered her head. "You may never find out. I went to the Housing Director and requested you as my roommate for the summer session."

"I requested you too!" she said with pleasant wonder. "I shall have something to look forward to during a horridly dull summer."

Distracted by Douglas' continued silence, she lacked concentration and floundered through finals.

She sat on a mauve upholstered chair in the distinctive Victorian parlor of the Gamma House, sipping fizzy apricot punch from a clear glass cup. Despite the decorations and merry atmosphere of the graduation party, she remained more disconsolate than she had been last year. Then she believed she would lose Douglas McKenzie forever. This year she had known his love and betrayed it, an even greater loss.

Saturday when she entered Stapleton International Airport and noticed her mother waiting for her, the faint, desperate hope that Douglas would also meet her withered as if brushed by a frigid breeze.

As she rode beside her mother in the Continental, the finality of Douglas not answering her letter and the certainty that she must endure every day of her life for as long as she lived without him crushed her spirit. Discreetly she blinked a mistiness from her eyes but she could not stop the intrusion of a choked sob into her breathing.

She vaguely heard her mother's comments about Penny's finishing her course of fashion design in Paris and returning home and the schedule for the family's annual cruise following her own summer session.

"Constance deah?"

She roused when her mother spoke directly to her.

"Are you all right?"

She held herself together with an effort, and only her inbred self-control kept her from collapsing into tears. She waved her hand in mute response, unable to explain her continued grief over her broken engagement.

However, she began to comprehend that no matter how well she disguised Douglas in fashionable suits and a Mr. Maxwell hairstyle, he would retain the fierce ambition and independence of one born poor while she would remain accustomed to a life of luxury and ease. No doubt her lifestyle did seem too rich for him.

It's not as if I'm a chocolate mousse, she fumed. *He asked me to share his dream. And I lost it—* She covered her groan with a little cough.

Craving Douglas' love despite his obstinacy, she desperately sought an idea, a word, an action, a prayer which would restore it, for she had no life, no fire, no purpose without him.

Resolution descended on her mind and she leaned back, her lips quivering on the edge of a smile.

❧

Saturday afternoon as he washed an accumulation of dishes, the unease of having forgotten something nudged his brain. Mentally he sorted through his responsibilities. Drying his hands, he leaned his forearm against the wall and stared at the date circled on the calendar months in advance—the day Connie was to return from college.

Connie— The thought of her charged blood through his frozen veins.

"You still love her," Pastor Jefferson had said.

He didn't deny he loved her. Connie was the life of his life. Her vivacity and sweet gentility attracted him beyond measure. He ached for her adoring gaze, her expressions of affection, the sound of her airy laughter, and her body within his arms. But from the center of his being he couldn't trust her. For weeks his heart had rushed toward accepting her apology and reestablishing a future; his soul quailed at the havoc her betrayal had inflicted.

Now that she was home her proximity seemed to demand action, but he still oscillated between hurt and hope.

He left his apartment and walked around his neighborhood sensing the grand sweeping passion of Rachmaninoff's *Piano Concerto #2* as the duel between his ardent heart and rational mind continued to rage across the battlefield of his soul.

God, what should I do? he finally inquired. *I must know if she is the girl for me.*

A soundless voice in the depths of his being resounded, and the delusion that he could exist without Connie vanished. His tattered will capitulated to his love for her. In the humility of surrender, peace unfurled its banner and logic emerged to lead him forward. He must see her, look into her amethyst eyes, and discover for himself if her apology had been genuine or if she had manipulated him again. Yet her letter sounded sincere. She said she had confessed her dishonesty and accepted Jesus into her life. With a stirring of excitement in his spirit he knew that God had forgiven her and he should too.

Back in his apartment as he contemplated becoming reengaged, nervous excitement welled up. He hurried into the bathroom where he hung over the bowl as he had the night before he proposed to Connie. With a sort of gone-in-the-middle sensation, he showered and brushed his teeth. He dressed in his blue checked shirt and tan slacks and slipped the ring into his pocket.

As he hurried through the living room, knocking on the front door disrupted him, and curiously he jerked it open. Connie stood before him in a brick red dress, her eyes dark in her colorless face.

The unexpectedness of her arrival disconcerted him. "I was just getting ready to go— I wanted to see— I didn't expect—"

"I'm sorry to interrupt," Connie said, her calm exterior vying with her look of determination. "I must talk to you. Potts brought me back into town after we took Mother home from meeting me at the airport."

He gestured Connie in and closed the door. "Sit down," he invited.

Connie sat on the black vinyl sofa, and he seated himself, half turning to face her.

Eventually Connie said, "I sent you a letter." Stilted silence hung between them, and then she continued. "After what you and Rev. Jefferson said about Jesus, Linda told me that being deceitful was sinful and only Jesus' blood could take it away. I asked Jesus into my life. It's so freeing to know I have a clean heart and I'm right with God."

"That was fantastic news." He pressed Connie to him and raised his eyes in thanksgiving.

He released her and said, "I owe you an explanation for why I didn't answer. From the moment I saw you I loved you, but when you deceived me you destroyed that love. The shock and hurt were almost more than I could endure." His voice faltered, and he waited for it to steady. "I couldn't risk that happening again."

Connie laid her cold fingers on his. "I'm sorry."

"I had to see for myself if you meant what you said before I could believe it."

He tilted Connie's chin with his fingertips, and the sincerity in her amethyst eyes dissolved the last residue of doubt.

"I meant it more than I ever meant anything in my life. I would give up everything in exchange for your love."

Connie's pledge infused his soul.

"That's not necessary. All you need to give is honesty and loyalty."

"Nothing has ever been more willingly given."

"Then we still have a dream to share?" he asked.

"However you plan to pursue it. I won't interfere again."

As he absorbed reality, Beethoven's triumphant *Ode to Joy* rang in his mind.

He took the ring from his pocket and slid it onto Connie's finger. He encircled her in his arms, inclining his head to possess her lips. The fire that had always sparked between them flared again, but commitment forged a more durable bond.

"Douglas," Connie murmured, "we won't let anything jeopardize our dream again, will we?"

He lowered his lashes over one eye in a gesture of assurance. "What could possibly interfere with destiny?"

11
December of 1974

*S*moke curled from the cheese sandwich in the skillet, and vexation
pulsed through him. *How could something be so light on one side and
so burnt black on the other?*

He was loathe to throw away his last two pieces of bread and slice of
cheese, and he bit into the charred crumbs. Wiping the inedible cinders
from his mouth, he heated a can of soup and spread a thin layer of peanut
butter on crackers.

Too desperately engaged in acquiring his dream to trifle with less than
life's necessities, he accepted pinched circumstances as purely transitory, an
investment in his future. Every penny he earned went into savings before
its coppery sheen could brighten his life. He had less after taxes than last
year, but he had saved over $7000.

Six months had passed since Connie returned to CMU for the summer
session that would enable her to graduate in the spring with a major in
home economics. At the end of her course she had flown to Nassau to join
her parents for their cruise to the Outer Islands. He hadn't sailed with them
because he hadn't earned vacation time. With the rising unemployment
rate, a curiously modest time for architects with home building down
thirty-three percent from 1973, and his tenacious pursuit of the dream,
he had been thankful for his job. He had missed spending the summer
with Connie, but he had used the time to redraw the blueprints he had
shredded in his despair.

Connie's letters had kept him informed of her activities, and she included insights on what she had been reading in her Bible. She also expressed an appreciation of him, his ideas and interests, but in his loneliness he longed for more than could be contained in an envelope.

He had answered her letters and also written to his folks regularly, explaining the Oaklands, apprising them of his career, and informing them he was attending a church where the pastor was his friend. He had eaten dinner with Paul, Margie, and their toddler son Davi every Wednesday before the church service, and the weeks had sped past.

The economy had been skidding down over the past 12 months, but since October the United States was plunging deeper into a recession that seemed to be the longest and could be the most severe since World War II. It had picked up enough momentum to drag the economy lower; for a while yet the recession was continuing, and the American way of life was ebbing. A Christmas season hadn't begun with so many tidings of discomfort and lack of joy about the economy for many years. Reasons for cheer were sparse. This Yuletide would be a time of less elaborate meals, less frequent parties, fewer and cheaper presents except, he suspected, for the Oaklands.

❧

Inside the frigid airliner that December morning, she huddled into her white fur jacket and braced herself against the turbulence. *This has to be the worst flight since the one at Kitty Hawk*, she fretted. *But when it's over, I'll see Douglas.*

The imminence of seeing his quick, tantalizing smile and hearing his pleasant voice set her heart skittering.

During the two weeks she and Douglas had been together in June, they had nurtured the fragile blossoms of faith, love, and trust which had emerged from their broken engagement. They had talked and laughed, telephoned and dated, swum and biked, and those memories had sustained her during this most interminable of separations.

The plane bounced to a stop, and she hurried into the holiday congestion, seeing only her beloved. She flung herself into Douglas' arms, and the warmth of his welcoming kiss dispelled the chill of separation and winter travel.

Douglas drove his Volvo through heavy traffic with a classical music station softly playing, and they chatted in a fragmentary, laughing conversation which eclipsed the past and oriented her in the present.

Douglas stopped on the edge of an expanse which rose into the snow-covered foothills, and the white, silent world closed around them. He laid his arm across her shoulders and pointed out the windshield.

"How would you like to live here?"

Puzzled, she peered up at him.

"This is where I plan to build my house. I bought the property for you as a Christmas present. It's the first tangible element of our dream."

"It's happening," she marveled. "After an eternity of waiting, it's finally happening!"

"When shall we be married?" Douglas asked, his eyes alight with eagerness.

"Tomorrow!"

Douglas' face dimmed. "You have to graduate first."

"Why?"

"I have my reasons."

"But you never say what they are!" The urge to rage at Douglas to discard his stubborn reasons blazed through her. Nevertheless, she had promised to allow him to pursue the dream as he had planned, and she subsided.

"How about the first Sunday in June?" Douglas suggested.

Considering the extensive preparations that would be necessary for her wedding, she said, "That would be too difficult so close to graduation. Mother will need at least a month for last minute details."

Without moving Douglas gave the impression of stopping. "Yes, of course."

"The last Friday in June would be best."

"Our wedding will have to be on a Sunday afternoon."

"Sunday is no day for a formal wedding."

"Sunday afternoon would be much better for my folks' travel plans around Pop's work schedule. They could come for the rehearsal on Saturday evening and leave right after the reception. Besides, if the wedding is in the afternoon, we'll have time to catch a flight and start our honeymoon before it gets too late."

Douglas' smoldering gaze sparked anticipation within her.

"The last Sunday in June," she agreed.

In Oakland's dining room the next evening, he waited near Connie, who was radiant in a frilly white Victorian blouse and long red velvet skirt behind the white linen covered table with numerous buffet dishes. He wore a blue velvet double-breasted suit Connie had insisted upon giving him prematurely for Christmas. He abhorred having her buy his clothes, but he admitted that nothing he owned fitted this occasion.

White ribbons with "Constance and Douglas" written in gold script festooned one wall, formally announcing their engagement. A string quartet played softly as women in colorful gowns and men in dark suits flowed in and out of groups to sample the gourmet fare. Black-clad caterers bearing silver trays of champagne circulated among the guests. He was introduced to 50 of Oaklands' closest friends, including that Blakely Whitworth character. Blakely regarded him from beneath drooping lids as before then smiled in acquiescence and shook his hand.

He managed polite conversation, but he was too intensely in earnest for society. Connie was so perfectly trained by a society mother, so finished in every expression and movement with a gentility and offhand ease that perpetually intrigued him. He longed solely to withdraw from the babble and concentrate on her.

Mr. and Mrs. Oakland and Penny led Connie and himself through the throng, and halfway up the red-carpeted staircase Mr. Oakland paused to propose a toast.

"Constance and Douglas have chosen to spend their lives together, and I wish them every happiness and success."

"May all their dreams come true," Mrs. Oakland said.

"Yes," Penny added, raising her drink. "Constance has found her knight in shining armor, and they will live happily ever after."

He glanced from all the people looking up at them to Connie. The wonder of their love flooded through him, and her eyes reflected his delight in their future.

❧

She reclined on the pink velvet chaise in her room and spread her fingers to allow the rosy polish to dry, feeling truant from her arduous class schedule. Knocking on her door roused her, and she glanced up to find Mayla in the doorway.

"Your mother wishes to speak with you."

She followed the maid to the sitting room where her mother and Penny waited at a round, gold cloth covered table in front of the bay window.

"Do sit down, Constance deah. We should begin plannen your wedden."

"My wedding—" She met Penny's excited eyes as she seated herself in a blue velvet tub chair. "Shouldn't we wait until Douglas can be here?"

"Why? Everyone knows the groom is the least important person in the wedding," Penny said. "Just tell him what time to show up and where to stand. We don't need him cluttering up the place."

Before she could retaliate, her mother said, "We shall make our plans, deah, and Douglas shall be expected to adheah to what is customary."

Briefly she questioned Douglas' reaction to what was customary, but her mother opened a white satin wedding planning book and poised a gold pen over the first page.

"Have you and Douglas set your wedden date?"

"We've decided on Sunday afternoon, June 29th."

"Sunday—? Sunday aftanoon isn't propa for a fohmal wedden."

The joy of marrying Douglas eclipsed any former hope of when the formal event should occur, but she knew her mother would never understand the McKenzies' schedule or Douglas' insistence upon it. Expecting the success she had achieved since infancy, she developed the brooding expression of an impending tempest. Her mother's lips thinned, but she made a notation on the page.

"Sunday, June 29th, at foh o'clock," her mother said, her tone brittle. "We'll make ahrangements with Rev. Muhphy for the chuhch and the ohganist, but shuly there won't be anotha wedden scheduled for Sunday aftanoon. Tell Douglas he and his motha must staht compilen their guest list and give it to me as soon as possible. Now, what do you wish your colors to be?"

Visualizing the beautiful chancel of the church her parents occasionally attended, she mentally sorted through various hues, selecting blue and yellow.

"How many attendants do you wish to have?"

"Six, including Penny as my maid of honor and Linda as first bridesmaid."

"Linda?" Penny queried.

"Linda Sevenstars, my roommate."

"An Indian?" Her mother's voice shook. "Constance deah, we couldn't possibly— She wouldn't fit in at all with the soht of affaih we are plannen. Pahaps some of your otha friends ..."

Loyalty to Linda strengthened her resolve and she said, "Linda's my dearest friend, Mother. She led me to believe in Jesus. It wouldn't be right not to include her."

She applied the sunshine of her smile until her mother nodded, scarcely concealing a shudder.

"I suppose as long as you provide the gown ..."

"We'll shop for our gowns after Christmas," Penny said with rare tact.

"We must include Cousin Peggy, and I'll also invite Susan Devonshire, Victoria Ormandorff, and Barbara Whitworth. She doesn't object to my not marrying her brother. Kimberly Leighton would be an adorable flower girl."

"Douglas will need six attendants as well," her mother continued. "Have him make his selections as soon as possible. Their fohmal weah must be ohded months in advance of a June wedden to give the propa identical look to the pahty. Now for the reception...."

"Let's have a buffet. I don't want to sit around eating a wedding breakfast after an evening ceremony when Douglas and I should be off on our honeymoon."

With a startled glance, her mother said, "We shall consult with the cateras about buffet menus and ahrange with the maitre d' for the bridal table."

Wedding decorations ... floral arrangements ... participants ... photographs ... music ... the location for the reception ... transportation ... cakes ... menus ... beverages.... Myriad details.... Questions.... Answers....

As her mother continued with extensive plans, she envisioned Douglas in black and gray striped trousers, cutaway coat, white wing collar shirt, and gray ascot with a sprig of stephanotis from her bridal bouquet as his boutonniere. Expectancy surged through her, and she pressed her palms to her cheeks.

"There's nothing more beautiful than the pageantry of a formal wedding," Penny sighed, her hands crossed on her chest. Slanting a narrow look at her, Penny asked, "Under the circumstances don't you think you could find someone more presentable to marry?"

Instant wrath flared toward Penny, who retreated behind a sardonic smile.

Sunday evening before Christmas, she sat with Douglas on a wooden pew in the sanctuary of Central Bible Church. The serenity of candlelight, the woodsy scent of pine boughs, and the organ music filled her with reverent peace. She questioned the social whirl of her parents' party and Mrs. Dixon's and the Farrs' and the Fischers' and the Whitworths' along with other holiday activities which usually enthralled her. Although slightly subdued, they completely ignored God's purpose for Christmas; here Christmas' meaning revitalized her spirit.

During the full-voiced congregational singing of "... born that man no more may die ..." Then "... sorrowing, sighing, bleeding, dying, sealed in the stone cold tomb," she paused to ponder the importance of Jesus' birth and the unimaginable price paid for her free gift of salvation. The significance of the sacrifice impeded her voice.

"Are you all right?" Douglas asked, bending at the knees, his eyes on a level with hers.

"All these years I've sung these songs ... I never knew— I never thought—" Unable to express her awe and appreciation, she shook her head. "Jesus did that for me." With a flash of insight she clasped Douglas' hand in hers. "Mother and Father don't know—"

"We'll have to tell them," Douglas said.

She wasn't sure she could explain to her parents that Jesus was born as a baby so they could be born again and have everlasting life. Nevertheless, yearning ached in her throat during the remainder of the service.

On Christmas Eve Douglas looked exceptionally handsome in his blue velvet double-breasted suit. He sat beside her on the gold brocade love seat in the living room, their fingers entwined against the long skirt of her Christmas plaid taffeta gown.

Her father read the Christmas story aloud from the Bible, and the necessity of sharing that Jesus could be her parents' Savior churned within her.

Before she could phrase her thoughts into speech, her father laid the Bible on the mantle and then presented a diamond bracelet to her mother and a diamond and ruby bracelet to Penny. The flurry of gift giving ended her opportunity to speak.

When opened gifts and discarded wrappings had partially obscured the living room, her father set the remaining box in front of Douglas and herself.

"I wish to give my gift to the both of you."

Unease emanated from Douglas but excitement prickled through her. She pulled away the silver wrapping with an exuberance which shredded it and opened the box to find it filled with crumpled newspapers. She flung them aside, and Douglas leaned forward to retrieve the dislodged candy, fruits, and nuts. At the bottom she discovered a flat box and opened it, revealing the deed to the property Douglas had shown her.

An icy tide of dismay coursed through her.

Father, how could you? she protested mentally.

Douglas pushed his hand through his hair and rose in one angry motion.

Tension replaced the festive atmosphere, and her mother rang for Fenton. He appeared carrying a tray of eggnog, but Douglas declined with a flick of his fingers. In her distress, she also waved Fenton away.

Her father accepted a glass and rose and bade Douglas follow him with a nod. Hoping to prevent conflict, she hurried after them. Loyalty to Douglas vied with love for her father, who had undeniably interfered again. She entered her father's study and paused beside Douglas. His blue eyes blazed as he tossed the deed onto the desk.

"I bought that land for Connie as a symbol of the progress toward our dream. You have no right to deny me the privilege of giving it to her!"

"I should have known you wouldn't be thankful that I paid this off and gave it to you as a gift. I had hoped that you would have the good sense and common courtesy to accept it. I accepted your gift."

"There's a lot of difference between a desk set and a piece of property!"

"What?"

"Price!"

"Piffle. It's the thought that counts."

"And I don't want you thinking I need your help! It's my dream and I'll achieve it the way I planned!"

"You have a plan and that's admirable, but are you pursuing it for your own ego, or do you want it badly enough to restrain your pride? What advantage is there to having a plan if it's impossible to achieve?"

"What advantage is there to having a plan if everyone circumvents it?"

Her father rose and leaned forward, his hands flat on the top of the desk. "You decide how much your plan means to you, but it's Constance's happiness that is of concern to me."

"That's what concerns me too. That's why I bought the property for her."

Douglas' jaw set in an uncompromising line, and he stood rigidly in a still, cold fury. Hostile silence persisted between him and her father until valor prompted her to intervene.

"It was a kind and generous gift, Father—"

"But I don't want your handouts disguised as gifts!"

"Still," she continued, giving Douglas a warning stare, "you shouldn't have done it. That was a sacrifice which meant a lot to Douglas in the giving." Her father seated himself, his face blank as she continued. "Douglas must decide if he will accept it as a gift. If not, then you must allow him to pay you for it."

Her father leaned back in his chair and sipped his eggnog with a long look at her that gradually shifted to Douglas.

"You might want to keep this in a safe place until you decide what to do," she suggested.

She held the deed out to Douglas, and he hesitated before he took it. Still a trifle white, a trifle grim, he tucked it into the breast pocket of his jacket. With a breath of relief, she laid her hand on his elbow and drew him out of her father's study.

In the hallway Douglas leaned his forearm against the oak wall and peered down at her, turbulence in his eyes.

Answering his unspoken question, she said, "It's your decision whether you accept it. I risked our love before when Father tried to help, and I'll never do it again."

Douglas' tension eased a bit, and her arms closed around him in a silent vow.

❧

Late in the afternoon on the first Saturday in January, he met Mrs. Oakland, Penny, and Connie in a plant-filled tea room following the ladies' shopping trip for wedding gowns. He seated Connie at a linen covered table while Penny and Mrs. Oakland were seated across the room.

He ordered two hot chocolates with whipped cream before he asked, "How did you do?"

"I wish I could explain—show you my gown!" Connie outlined her head and shoulders with her hands, and images visible in her mind roused his curiosity. "And Penny's and Linda's and the other bridesmaids' gowns! Everything is going to be so beautiful—" Connie clasped her hands beneath her chin, incandescent in her happiness. "Now that I've chosen six attendants, you must also select six as soon as possible because their formal wear must be ordered months in advance. We will inform your mother as to what is expected of her to comply with our wedding plans.

Oh, Douglas," Connie bubbled, unable to restrain a little bounce of joy. "Do you know what this means?"

Captivated by Connie's exuberance, but rather overwhelmed by it, he shook his head. Connie's lips parted over her round, even, little teeth with excitement that stirred his heart.

"After waiting forever, we're going to be married this year!"

12
Adjustments

*H*e approached his Volvo, the dry, brown, late winter grass crunching beneath his shoes. As he turned the key in the ignition, silence replaced the familiar *chug* of the engine. Getting out of the car, he peered beneath the hood at the baffling assortment.

That's all I needed—to have my car die.

Resenting its ill-timed demise, he stalked to work, the March wind biting through his suit coat.

From the corridor at Dixon, Scott and Hall, he noticed Mr. Oakland seated at the table in the glass walled conference room, and surprise expelled what breath he had left.

"Douglas," Mr. Oakland greeted. "Is something the matter?"

He paused in the doorway. "My Volvo wouldn't start."

"I'll send Potts around to check it."

"There's no need to do that, sir."

Mr. Oakland chuckled and folded his hands at his waist. "You can't be walking to work. You also need an overcoat."

"I have a flight jacket I wear when it gets too cold, and the exercise will do me good."

Mr. Scott approached from the lobby and Mr. Oakland said, "Sit down, Scott. I have rather a lot to do today. Douglas, join us."

He eased into a chair as Mr. Scott's green-eyed gaze flitted from him to Mr. Oakland. While Mr. Oakland proposed an office park complex—and

Mr. Scott objected to the technical problems inherent in the design—his own fascination increased.

"Well, Douglas," Mr. Oakland queried. "What do you think?"

He knew that Mr. Scott, as the principle architect, wanted to be the designer, but Mr. Oakland had brought the work to him. Professional courtesy slowed his response, and he glanced across the table at Mr. Scott, who rubbed his long, white fingers across his chin.

"Do I receive benefit of your innovative, young architect's counsel, Scott, or do I take my business home?"

At Mr. Scott's nod he replied, his agile mind having meshed with the problem. "Sir, you don't simply want offices set in a parkway. You want the wide open spaces, the mile high atmosphere, and the Rocky Mountain sunshine to be an integral part of the design."

"Of course, that's it!" Mr. Oakland exclaimed. "I knew you were good!"

"Exceptionally so, but you've worked with enough architects to know that," Mr. Scott said.

From the doorway Miss King said, "It's the City Commissioner's office calling, sir."

Mr. Scott excused himself and followed her.

"Explain how your idea works," Mr. Oakland said, leaning forward.

Designing had always been the inner fire at which he warmed himself; now, challenged by such a progressive concept, the force which sustained his existence kindled and flamed. Yet he sat with his chin between his thumb and forefinger, the dilemma of creating something unique for Mr. Oakland clashing against his resolution to establish his own architectural identity without any assistance.

"Are you hiring the architectural firm of Dixon, Scott and Hall to design this for you, sir?" he asked as a clarification.

Mr. Oakland waved his hand. "Evan Scott can't see past his nose. You, on the other hand, seem to have grasped the potential of it. I need your architectural ingenuity to meet the current building challenges."

Anticipation pulsed through him, and eagerly he described the use of light and air.

"By Jove, I think you've got it! Sketch those ideas of yours, Douglas," Mr. Oakland said, tapping the reflective table top with a manicured fingernail.

The next morning he walked to work against the wind, analyzing the financial implications of repairing his car.

In his office, the complexities of Mr. Oakland's business park claimed him, and externals faded away until the telephone rang. With his attention on his drawing board, he answered automatically. "Douglas McKenzie."

"Armand Oakland here. Potts informed me that your Volvo hadn't been properly maintained. It will cost over a hundred dollars to repair it."

He realized Mr. Oakland had sent Potts around to check on it despite his objection, and he seethed.

"Sometimes preventive measures cost less in the end than negligence, but I didn't call to give you an economics lesson. While you may find walking to work entertaining, it isn't possible for you to escort Constance. Unless you would prefer to have Potts drive you."

"No way."

A low chuckle came along the line. "You must have transportation to sites as well. Since used cars are quite risky, and even with the incentives from the automakers today's automotive prices are prohibitive for you, what do you plan to do?"

Without a solution, he remained silent.

"If you're unable to afford repairs, I'll sell you my Mercedes for a hundred dollars."

Disbelief coursed through him. "One hundred dollars?"

"It is an older model, but it's in excellent condition. You'll not find this quality of machine for such a reasonable price elsewhere."

"Then why are you selling it?"

"I've been thinking of buying a 350SL. Perhaps now is the time to do so."

Opposing Mr. Oakland's attempt to sell him the Mercedes when he couldn't afford to repair the Volvo, he questioned, "Why would you sell a car for a hundred dollars that's worth thousands?"

"I knew you wouldn't take it if I gave it to you."

Mentally assenting, he inclined his head. He sought for words of absolute refusal, but the necessity for transportation and the difficulty in securing it obstructed them. Even one hundred dollars jeopardized his budget, but without alternatives he gradually accepted a price his pride could afford.

"Very well then," Mr. Oakland said with finality. "I'll have it delivered to you. Oh, and Douglas ... Potts will buy your car and repair it for himself. He'll give you one hundred dollars for it."

The dial tone buzzed in his ear.

98 | Sherilyn Kay

Weeks of academic challenges, social events, and personal activities slowly inched along.

She lay awake in the darkness of her dorm room, as she often did, savoring the vision of love and longing in Douglas' expression. How she loved him—how utterly she loved him—and every fiber of her being yearned to be with him.

Each time she walked from the dorm to the Gamma House, she realized they were separated by more than the few blocks between them. She attended the monthly meetings, but she admitted to herself that the Gamma girls were proud, pretentious, and prejudiced.

She spent less time with them and more with Linda, whose optimism and enthusiasm to pursue a God-given destiny with dedication, determination, diligence, and discipline inspired her.

Classes had finally ended for spring break, and she dressed in a periwinkle blue cable knit sweater and matching skirt. Brushing her hair under at the edge along her jaw, she met Linda's gaze in the mirror above their sink.

"It's vacation! This afternoon I shall be with Douglas!"

"I hope this one is better for both of us than it was last year," Linda said.

She met Linda's shadowed obsidian eyes, memories tumbling through her like wild surf. "I certainly hope you don't break your arm again. Since Douglas broke our engagement and I almost lost a love which was more precious than I knew, I've learned the necessity of honesty and commitment. You know he and I have been reading our Bibles, a chapter for each day of the month from Proverbs, and writing to each other about what we've learned. My initial affection has grown into a powerful force which will transcend our social and ideological differences."

Linda regarded her, shaking her head.

"I know you wondered if I was capable of a thought that wasn't trivial or selfish." She closed the latches on her suitcases. "I've always needed a purpose in life, something worthwhile to work toward. Nurturing the love Douglas deserves and balancing my lifestyle against his is my greatest challenge."

"I used to think you were made of cotton candy, but perhaps there are stands of steel in there."

"It will require the strength of steel to achieve this dream, but sharing a dream with Douglas is worth any effort."

She entered the crowded alcove at Stapleton and rushed toward Douglas with the amused awareness that his tan slacks and blue checked shirt enhanced his attractiveness. She threw her arms around him, and he twirled her around. He set her down and guided her through the terminal, his arm across her shoulders. The exhilaration of being with him quickened her stride to an unfettered skip as they went to get her luggage.

Nestled beside Douglas as he drove with a classical music station playing softy in the background, she inquired, "Why are you driving Father's Mercedes?"

"My Volvo died last week and I couldn't afford to fix it and buy groceries. Your father sold me his for one hundred dollars—the price he had Potts pay me for mine."

She slanted a look toward Douglas, questioning her father's tactics and his tolerance of them.

"The worst may be over for the building industry, and since there's an improved flow of money to the mortgage lenders and a drop in interest rates, your father has decided to develop the property he owns north of Denver. I am his architect."

Astonishment rose within her, and she met Douglas' sly look with an airy laugh.

"I designed it, but as Mr. Scott's faithful employee. I'm part of a team that works to contribute to the success of our projects. That way I'm not working for your father—he's my client."

She pressed her head against Douglas' shoulder. "How is your house progressing?"

"I'm almost glad the land was a gift because the house is going to cost much more to build than I planned."

Accepting Douglas' comment as casually as he made it, she asked, "When may I see it?"

"There isn't much to see. The frame is going up now."

"But I want to see it." She allowed her voice and lip to droop for effect.

"You won't be able to see the progress every step of the way. Since you'll be at college until shortly before the wedding, you'll be spared all the complications and technical details of building a house."

"You can't possibly expect me to wait." She expelled a quick, audible breath.

Douglas touched her lips with his forefinger. "When I showed you the blueprints, I intended to give my house to you as a gift, complete in every detail. That's when I want you to see it for the first time." Douglas met her eyes with a gleam of anticipation.

Memories of the blueprints and images of what the house would look like danced in her head, but Douglas' lofty romantic ideal to present it to her subdued her impatience. With a sense of suppressed expectancy, she gripped Douglas' hand.

Monday morning she paused beside Penny's black Audi on the drive in front of her home wearing a wide legged blue pantsuit with a large polka-dotted collar similar to Penny's gray one. The late March mountain breeze ruffled her hair with a hint of spring, and her spirit soared free from her rigorous class schedule.

"Well, get in," Penny said. "This one doesn't have an automatic door opener."

Penny's facetious reference to Douglas darted annoyance through her, but she lifted her chin and seated herself in the black leather bucket seat, deigning not to reply.

She and Penny wandered through chic boutiques and fashionable dress shops, selecting their spring wardrobes and items for her trousseau. Disbelief that she would wear them for Douglas' pleasure as his wife isolated her in a world of delightful images.

In a happy daze, she followed Penny into an exclusive men's store.

"It's too bad Douglas won't consent to being measured for the clothing he so obviously needs," Penny said as she made the first selection with a shrug.

"Douglas won't like your buying his clothes."

"Someone has to. Did you see him Saturday night?"

She visualized Douglas at dinner, the familiar tan slacks and blue checked shirt eliciting memories of their courtship, and she sighed. Penny's step on her toes jolted her back to reality.

"His appearance— The way he dresses— It's simply not acceptable."

"You'll make him angry."

Malicious satisfaction covered Penny's face. "He's going to like the way he looks, I guarantee."

Penny continued to select an array of clothing, undaunted by her own hissed admonitions. Wary of Douglas' anger and unable to prevail against her sister without wresting the garments from her grasp, she followed in a futile, silent frenzy.

After Penny locked their purchases in the Audi, she guided her into a blue-carpeted jewelry store with lighted glass cases.

"Look at what I've laid aside," Penny whispered in excitement.

A suave little man presented a strand of pearls, and her breath caught as she touched their lustrous beauty.

"The groom's gift to the bride," Penny announced. "If the groom could afford it that is. Father said—"

"Oh, no," she objected. "You and Father are <u>not</u> going to buy the groom's gift to the bride. Neither the groom <u>nor</u> the bride will allow it."

"You would like to have them, wouldn't you?"

She displayed the pearls on her fingers, longing for them. *I'd be crazy not to want those lovelies. But what is more important? A pearl necklace or Douglas' happiness? Will I accept expensive gifts from Father when Douglas isn't able to afford them, or will I be content with what he is able to provide?*

The habit of a lifetime struggled against commitment to Douglas, but resolution firmed within her; she pushed the pearls across the counter with trembling fingertips.

"No, thank you," she said, her voice uneven. "The groom's gift must be selected and paid for by the groom."

"Oh? Does the groom like Cracker Jacks?"

Anger seethed, paralyzing her tongue.

When she entered her home, she heard Douglas' voice in the living room, and she hurried to see him. Penny and the package laden Fenton continued on up the stairs. She paused in the doorway and watched as Douglas leaned toward her mother with quiet attention.

"Ah have everythen a woman could want. A loven husband, two beautiful daughtas, a luffly home, social standen, charity wuk. I have my own chuch. What need do Ah have of anotha religion?"

"It's not another religion, Mrs. Oakland. It's coming to God through His Son, Jesus. Then we have true peace and the blessed assurance of knowing we're ready for Heaven."

"Ah am pehfectly fine," her mother said, her fingers fluttering.

"No one is perfect enough to go to Heaven on their own good works. We try to be good, but our futile attempts to earn God's favor fall short. We have no ability within ourselves to please Him. We need to accept the righteousness of Jesus that God gives us by His amazing grace."

Her mother rose, hurried past her and up the stairs.

She regarded Douglas as he sat with his palms on his knees and his head bowed. She entered with her hands extended.

"Thank you for trying to explain to Mother."

Douglas twined her fingers in his and drew her down beside him. "I don't know what else to say. I've written this to his folks too, but I haven't gotten a positive response from them either." He bounced her hand on his knee, evidence of his frustration. "I would give my life if our folks could know Christ."

Something indefinable coursed through her, and her fingers tightened on Douglas'. Uncertain how to encourage him, she kissed his sleeve at the shoulder and laid her cheek there in silent recognition of a mutual disappointment.

Douglas' mood changed and he glanced around. "I was to meet your father to get the sketches I drew for his business park, but he isn't here, is he?"

She laughed low in her throat. "No, he isn't."

Douglas encircled her with his arms and his lips lingered on hers in a long, slow kiss.

"Luncheon is suved," Fenton announced from the doorway.

"Will you please stay?"

"I can't refuse. Even when you're home I scarcely see you."

With Douglas' hand on her back, she entered the dining room and sensed her mother's glacial manner.

"Well, well, well," Penny greeted. "If it isn't The Princess and The Pauper."

Douglas stiffened against her though he gave no other sign of anger, and he seated her with a smooth, easy motion. Fenton discreetly laid a place for him and luncheon began.

"What will you be doing this afternoon, Mother?" she inquired politely.

"Ah do believe Ah shall visit pooh Miz Ramsey."

"How is Mr. Ramsey?"

"Poohly, deah, poohly."

She remembered Mr. Ramsey's invalidism, and familiar agitation quivered through her.

"You won't catch me mollycoddling a sick hubby," Penny declared. "And since Connie faints during every particularly interesting play at sporting events, she would be absolutely useless in anyone's illness or injury."

Penny's candor surged hot blood to her cheeks, and she clenched her hands together in her lap.

"Are you all right?" Douglas asked.

"Constance always has been pehtubed by anyone's illness."

"I helped Linda after she broke her arm," she managed in her own defense. "But please don't let anything happen to you."

Douglas' steady, level gaze calmed her. "Nothing is going to happen to me."

Reassured, she clung to Douglas' hand and regained her composure.

After lunch Douglas spoke to her with tender protectiveness. "Rest this afternoon, Con. You look tired." He rose and turned toward her mother. "Thank you for allowing me to stay, but I must meet with another client. If you ladies ... Penny ... will excuse me...."

Douglas departed and Penny called out, "Take your white steed out of the front hall, Sir Galahad."

She ignored Penny and excused herself to go to her room.

She lay on her pink canopied bed, not so much tired as disturbed by the recent occurrences: giving up the pearls in exchange for accepting a lifestyle with Douglas; the tragedy of her mother not understanding her need for Jesus; poor Mrs. Ramsey with an ailing husband.

What would I do if anything happened to Douglas?

Ice trickled around her spine. Douglas' love and strength of purpose sustained her life. If he died, she would die. Her mind retreated from the possibility, and every taut nerve in her body relaxed.

A noise roused her from sleep, and she descended the stairs to discover the source. She heard her father's voice in his study, and she paused with her hand on the banister.

"I will have him working for me, Scott. He's an intelligent young man, a gifted architect."

"And my employee! Look here, Oakland, just because he's marrying your daughter doesn't mean you own him."

Unease skittered through her, and she crept forward, listening.

"No, but I want him on my staff."

"You always have."

"Yes, and I'm prepared to pay him well for it. No bright young man would turn down such an offer."

Yet Douglas did turn it down, she recalled.

Surely her father knew Douglas' refusal was adamant, and his efforts to lure him from Mr. Scott flooded apprehension through her.

"Certainly you know there's an energy crisis which has drastically affected the building industry."

"Of course I do, Scott. Even though it is showing some signs of improvement and the interest rates continue to decline, it remains a major concern. I also know that innovative architects are in high demand to help resolve it. Innovation is not an inexpensive commodity, and I intend to pay the price. What about you, you old Scrooge? Your scant remuneration hardly represents his true worth."

She didn't miss the intensity of Mr. Scott's reply, and she was certain that in his effort to retain Douglas, he would submit to her father's tactics.

"With his talent and my money, it will be too bad for you if we team up."

"Yes, it will," Mr. Scott replied.

"I'm certain you'll allow him to have next Monday off so he may take Constance to the airport. Shall I make my offer then or wait until Tuesday?"

"I drove out here to get the sketches he drew, not to have you dictate to me when my employees work!"

"Monday or Tuesday?"

"Oh, all right. If I can't pay him what he's worth, I can pay him what's standard."

Chairs scraped back, and she hurried upstairs, her footsteps silenced by the red carpet.

In her bathroom she reclined in a tub of scented bubbles, contemplating the implications of what she had overheard. Her father had interfered yet again, and his strategy for raising Douglas' salary appalled her. Considering what she knew, did she have an obligation to tell Douglas, or should she remain silent about her father's business affairs? If she told him, she risked his ire justifiably flaring at her father for manipulation; if she didn't tell him and he discovered it, she risked his ire flaring at her for deception. She feared jeopardizing their engagement, and honesty vied with secrecy. Loyalty to both Douglas and her father tugged at her heart. She was tempted to abandon the issue, to hope he would accept the financial worth Mr. Scott suddenly attributed to him. She would keep this secret, and if he detected her father's scheme then she would seek to mollify him.

Wearing a pink dress with a pleated skirt that fell just above her knees, she descended the staircase with her inner turmoil undetectable as Fenton admitted Douglas.

"Hello, Hero," Penny greeted, her gaze roaming over Douglas above the rim of her glass.

Douglas' lips whitened, and she hurried past Penny toward him.

"Good evening," her father greeted, shaking Douglas' hand in front of her. "I'm glad to see you after missing connections today. I had Scott meet me here and we discussed your work."

Aware of her father's double meaning, she laid her hand on the sleeve of Douglas' navy blue blazer and smiled into his face with visible effect.

During dinner Douglas' right hand sought her left one beneath the table, and her fingers curved over his, conveying the sheer, unalloyed joy of having him close by.

Comprehension reflected in his expression, and his affectionate gaze played with hers, isolating them in a private universe.

"I notice you're wearing last year's suit." Penny's sharp tone burst the iridescent aura.

Her sister left the table, and she whispered, "Please, don't be angry."

Douglas' face tensed, but before she could explain, her sister returned. Penny thrust several packages at Douglas, forcing him to push back his chair. He sorted through the contents with a sardonic smile.

"So you're the good fairy godmother after all and not the Wicked Witch of the West."

Penny paled with indignation. Her mother's aristocratic brows raised in disapproval, and her father hid his amusement behind his napkin. She took a sip of water to stifle her giggles.

"You'll have to excuse Penelope."

"That's quite all right, sir, I consider the source." Douglas leveled a cool, direct stare at Penny. "You have the subtlety of a train wreck."

Penny's nostrils flared and her eyes blazed in her livid face. "Of all the ungrateful, disrespectful—"

I warned you, she chided mentally, squeezing Douglas' hand in silent triumph.

Her father, more florid than usual, pushed his chair back.

"If you'll excuse us, Camilla, Douglas and I have business to discuss."

Douglas stood and touched his fingertip to her nose and then to her shoulder before he followed her father out of the dining room.

Her father's study door closed with its heavy click, and her heart questioned the course of the conversation with a slow, thick beat before she aimed her ire at Penny.

"Well, really...!"

❧

Saturday morning he approached Oakland's front door, feeling buoyant in the casual slacks, red sweater, and shiny blue jacket he had chosen from the assortment Penny had given him. He had stuffed his stiff Scots' pride in his empty pockets and accepted the clothing because it was the style

Connie preferred. He blessed her for not saying anything about his shirt or longer than usual hair. On his stringent budget it was impossible to maintain a hair style or purchase the type of clothing Penny selected. Even with the decrease in grocery prices and the increase in his pay check the day before—which he suspected Scrooge Scott had given him to insure his continued service in spite of Mr. Oakland's attempts to hire him away—couldn't be spent on clothing and haircuts when he needed it for the rising costs of his house. Even his and Connie's entertainment the past week had been very economical. Nevertheless, he had eked out enough to take her on a date to a special destination.

Fenton admitted him, and he followed the butler to the breakfast room where Penny stood in rainbow hued harlequin pajamas sipping coffee.

"Well, well, well, if it isn't Prince Charming." Penny lifted her cup toward him. "Sleeping Beauty hasn't graced us with her presence yet. Perhaps a magical kiss from your sweet lips would awaken her." Penny arched arrogant brows. "A few more magical kisses and you'll have her sleeping again. With you ..."

Annoyed, he turned to stare out the wide bay window and ignored Penny.

Connie's evocative scent reached him, and he turned toward her. Even in casual wide legged blue slacks and a plaid blouse beneath a burgundy jacket, Connie radiated sophistication. Yet that irrepressible inner spirit which sparkled in her amethyst eyes and animated her expression, that youthful vivacity she would never outgrow no matter how long he waited to marry her, captivated him. In the space of a heartbeat, he caught her to him and his lips sought hers.

"Well, well, well," Penny remarked, ending on a high note. "You're not going to need coffee to wake you this morning, are you, Con?"

Irritation grated within him, but before it burst into a retort he drew Connie out of the breakfast room.

"What, leaving so soon?" Penny cried in mock dismay. "Y'all be good, ya heah?"

As he drove toward Denver with Connie beside him, the spring sunlight sparkling through the windshield gilded his happiness and Penny's influence vanished.

"You look very attractive in that outfit," Connie said, circling his knee with her fingertip.

"Thank you. I appreciate the shopping Penny did."

"Oh, yeah, sure," Connie disparaged with a little laugh.

"No, really. I wondered what it would take to stabilize the economy. Penny intended to insult me with her rampant purchases, but why should I give her the satisfaction by being insulted? Besides, there's no revenge so complete as forgiveness. However, this is the last thing I will accept," he stated, wagging his finger. "Your family has already pressured me into land, a car, and clothing. From now on, I'll have only what I'm able to buy for myself."

Connie flicked him a sidewise glance.

"I'm so glad we could be together today," Connie said. "In spite of the phone calls and dates, it seems as if I've scarcely seen you this week."

Curious about a lifestyle he failed to understand, he asked, "What does a debutante do?"

Connie listed a round of society functions with her friends and wedding preparations, but his mind balked at the perpetual rushing here and there with never a moment to think and reflect.

"I missed going to the Good Friday service with you yesterday afternoon," Connie said.

The tension of maintaining his lifestyle against Oakland influence erupted. "You know I prefer the way Paul preaches. He—"

"He explains that through the death of Christ we have eternal life," Connie interposed. "But we could have taken the time during Rev. Murphy's sermon to celebrate the new life in Christ we've had this year and to meditate on the power in Jesus' resurrection and His victory over sin and death. Our eternal future is no longer hopeless."

Regretting that he had represented Dixon, Scott and Hall at a rather mundane meeting, he inclined his head.

He parked the Mercedes and walked toward the Denver Art Museum with his hand on Connie's waist. The one million shimmering gray glass tiles covering the exterior of the seven-story, twenty-four-sided castle-like facade reflected the Colorado sunshine in infinite shifting patterns.

"It is bold, innovative architecture," he marveled. "I'm amazed whenever I see it."

Its two towers didn't look like a traditional museum, and inside the elevator whisked them to the galleries. He and Connie slowly explored Renaissance, European, and American art. They discussed the works, the history and philosophy associated with them. Connie's comments displayed an unforeseen appreciation and knowledge of art. He realized the extensiveness of Constance Oakland's education and experience, she having been surrounded by culture as well as society since childhood.

Early that evening as he eased the Mercedes into traffic, he asked, "Do you know what I would like to do tonight?"

"I thought you promised Father we wouldn't."

Comprehension scudded through him, but he said, "I would like you to cook dinner for us."

"I've known I was preparing to cook for you, but to do it now— We are achieving our dream, aren't we?"

He caught Connie against his side and steered with his left hand.

In his living room, Connie laid her hands on his arms and asked, "What would you like me to prepare?"

Suddenly aware of the complications in not planning ahead, he shrugged. "I don't know. See what's in my refrigerator."

Connie opened his minuscule freezing compartment and turned to him with her lips parted. "Three TV dinners? That's no test of my culinary skills. We could have lobster or lamb chops. What shall I order from the grocers?"

He realized the next few moments would form the basis for the rest of their lives, and he sought for tact and clarity of expression. "When we are married we will be eating differently from the way you are accustomed to. The cooking must be very economical. Let's be thankful for TV dinners and not waste our time together arguing over what to eat."

"You're right. We aren't married yet."

Connie's humor buoyed his mood.

"It's going to be glorious being married to you. And although we'll eat only what I'm able to provide, I promise we won't starve."

"As long as I'm married to you, I'll have everything I need," Connie said, lifting her lips to his.

Connie's sweet kisses increased his appetite for a richer form of sustenance, and he sensed that marriage to her would provide an abundance that financial scarcity could never diminish. He gazed down at her, her eyes mirroring his realization that they had initiated an adjustment of their lifestyles.

"We're so close to our dream," he said. "The construction of my house, your cooking dinner—TV dinners."

"Yes," Connie agreed, "and three months from today is our wedding!"

13
April of 1975

*T*he sun sparkled through the mullioned windows and refracted into rainbows on the pastel blue carpet in her mother's sitting room on Monday afternoon. Dressed in wide legged slacks and a print blouse with a large pointed collar, she sat in a blue velvet tub chair at the round table. Her mother handed her the wedding planning book and she read the notations amid rising excitement.

"It's going to be marvelous. One of the most elegant weddings of the season."

Her mother nodded, a sense of accomplishment in her manner. "Yes, deah, it shall, and Miz McKenzie has been infohmed of all our plans as well. Now we must—"

"Douglas is here to see Miss Constance," Mayla announced.

Pleasure at his appearance propelled her forward, and she circled Douglas' waist with her arms as she pressed her face against his pink striped shirt.

"I have the afternoon off, so we'll have some time together before I take you to the airport," Douglas whispered.

"How nice," she said, not the least surprised.

"Douglas, come be seated. There is much involved in plannen a wedden such as Constance's, and pahaps you should be infohmed of our progress."

Douglas' gaze flitted from her mother to her, but he seated her and then himself between them.

Her mother's narration of the plans for the wedding that would unite her with Douglas created vivid images in her mind. She sought his eyes for mutual understanding but found a strange blankness there.

"We should discuss the wedden invitations now also."

"We would like our invitations to explain the importance of God's love in our lives and that He— We—" She faltered.

"We're uniting our lives in the One Who designed marriage, and we would like the guests to share in our celebration," Douglas clarified.

"What you are suggesten isn't propa. A wedden invitation is a beautiful and fohmal notification of the desiah to share a joyous occasion, not a sehmon. Simply ohda five hundred invitations wohded in the usual manna."

Douglas' lashes fluttered and his eyes flashed to hers.

"Afta you have ohdaed your invitations, you should regista your crystal, china, and silva pattehns too."

"Crystal, china, and silver?" Douglas' echoed.

"There are some luffly new pattehns available. Have a good flight, Constance deah." Her mother rose and brushed the vicinity of her ear with her lips.

Douglas drove her to the stationers her parents patronized, and she finally selected exquisite wedding stationery with nominal response from him.

In another fashionable shop, she registered white floral on white china, platinum banded stemware, and lustrous silver service. She paused to view her selections displayed on a lace and linen covered table and visualized dining with Douglas in his house. She gazed up at him with expectancy, but his shadowed expression dimmed her glimpse into their shining future.

Douglas' manner perplexed her, yet she chattered gaily as she rode beside him.

"Why didn't you tell me that wedden was going to be the most elaborate one of the season?" Douglas burst out. "You and your mother have more plans for it than Ike had for the invasion of Normandy! Good grief, Con!"

"No one ever said we were going to have a middle-sized wedding! I have a dream too, and it's having a wedding which is one of the social events of the season! It will be a great occasion, something beautiful to remember all my life. Surely you don't object." She stroked Douglas' cheek with the back of her fingers. "At least we'll be married. After two interminable years our dream will be reality."

The allure of living with Douglas prompted her to seize the dream now instead of being separated for more abysmal days and nights. She raised Douglas' hand to her lips and kissed his knuckles, letting her lips linger there as she gazed at him with mute appeal. Perception flared in his eyes, and he rocked the Mercedes to a stop in a nearby park. His arms closed around her as his mouth fused to hers.

"Please," she whispered beneath Douglas' lips. "Please ..."

"Please what?" Douglas said, answering her kisses. "Spend the night together or elope?"

"We could be together tonight, apply for our marriage license tomorrow, and be married in three days."

"This definitely is not in the plan," Douglas said with a shaky breath. "You haven't graduated. My house isn't finished."

Her urgency conflicted with Douglas' plan, and she knelt beside him to thread her fingers through his hair. Her mouth played upon his face and eyelids before returning to his lips as she spoke. "I could return to school and still graduate. You could still complete your house."

With his hands on her arms, Douglas eased back. His eyes mirrored her desire, but he said, "Being together for one night wouldn't prevent our separation."

"But we would be ultimately sharing our dream."

"It would only tarnish our golden dream. It wouldn't be the wedded, committed love God designed for our lives we read about in Proverbs. Nothing would ever be as we planned—including the wedding."

Images of her wedding and the truth of Douglas' statements constrained her passion, and she settled back into the seat beside him.

"The separations have been much harder than I planned," Douglas said. "It tears my heart out every time you leave, and it is no less so now just because it's the last. But next time you return, we will share our dream. After the wedding—however elaborate you want it—we'll celebrate our perfect union." Douglas' sapphire eyes touched her with the warmth of promise.

Douglas tilted her chin with his forefinger and laid his lips gently on hers. She cupped his face in her palms, accepting it for what it was, their final farewell.

Seated at his drawing board that evening, he read an architectural journal while Holtz's turbulent *Mars* provided the background for the battle between relief and regret that he hadn't yielded to Connie. Harassed with loneliness and abstinence, he ached for her presence. With his elbow on his drawing board, his chin in his palm, he visualized the great gray jet thundering into the clouds, tearing Connie away, and his soul strained after her. But he had controlled his body in a way that was holy and honorable and his plan remained intact: he would complete his house and they would be married. His spirit lifted and soared until the telephone rang.

"Hello, Hero. You do want to make Connie happy, don't you?"

More than anything in the world, he thought.

"What did you have in mind?" he asked, on his guard.

"What are you giving her for a wedding present?"

I had always thought of my house as a wedding present, he realized.

"Pearls are traditional. There's a gorgeous matched set Connie would love to have."

Overwhelmed by the suggestion, he blurted, "I couldn't possibly—"

"Connie could have had those pearls if it weren't for her misguided sense of devotion. You don't expect her to relinquish everything for you, do you?"

Truth pierced him, and he shook his head.

"Well? What are you giving her?"

"Me!"

"<u>You</u>?" Penny disparaged.

He crashed down the receiver, his chest rising and falling rapidly.

The next evening when the telephone jangled, dismay that Penny may be calling grated within him.

"Hello ..." he answered cautiously.

"Douglas, Armand Oakland here. About that necklace ..."

He didn't waste any time, did he? Resistance rose within him, and he braced his feet wider apart.

"It is traditional, of course."

"Yes, sir. But tradition is expensive."

"Ah, yes." Mr. Oakland paused. "I could help you."

"I'm sure you could," he said, loathe to accept anything from Mr. Oakland.

"I could loan you the money—at a small rate of interest."

A loan, not a gift. A suggestion, not a scheme.

"I'll think about it, sir."

"Come by my office and I'll give you a check." Mr. Oakland hung up as if that settled the matter.

The temptation to accept the loan and give Connie the gift she desired wrestled against his Scots' pride until pride was subdued. Again he sacrificed his integrity and capitulated to his desire to make Connie happy and fulfill the Oaklands' expectations.

At the end of the week, he was ushered into Mr. Oakland's private office by a woman who was almost as tall as he was with gray hair in a sculptured French Twist and an interested light in her hazel eyes.

The massive desk at which Mr. Oakland sat in front of a windowed wall, black leather furniture, thick russet carpet, and heavily framed graphic designs on the mahogany walls bespoke Mr. Oakland's wealth and prestige. He regarded the man with increased awe.

"Please be seated. Have you seen the pearls Penelope had laid aside?"

"No, sir."

Mr. Oakland withdrew a check from a drawer and slid it across the desk toward him. He glanced at it, the amount holding his gaze on the numerals, and he sat down rather abruptly.

As he picked it up, he asked, "When would you like to have me start repaying this?"

"Whenever it's convenient."

Convenient. The magnitude of the task tightened his chest. He slid the check into his jacket pocket.

"I'm afraid— That is— We should make a definite arrangement."

"Definitely. You may repay me when it's convenient."

Mr. Oakland leaned back in his black leather chair and crossed his hands at his waist. "Camilla and I have been thinking about a wedding present for you and Constance. Would you prefer carpet of your choosing or a honeymoon cruise?"

Determined not to accept such expensive gifts, he said, "I would rather you not give us either, sir."

"Discuss it with Constance and let me know your decision."

He rose and laid his palms on the desk, leaning forward. "That is my decision. I'll buy my own carpet and take Connie on the wedding trip of my choice."

With a soft chuckle of ill-disguised skepticism, Mr. Oakland stood and clasped his hand. "Good evening, Douglas. Thank you for coming."

Thank you for coming, his mind echoed. With the amount of money he had obtained, he felt as if he had swindled the man.

In the lobby of his apartment building, he noticed several bills protruding insistently from his mailbox. He glanced through them and mentally deducted the total from his dwindling savings. With building costs continuing to rise, he would have to apply for another loan to complete his house.

He withdrew the check and stared at it with a stirring of envy. *What would it be like to spend this much money unreservedly?*

On Saturday he purchased the pearls and placed the black velvet box in his top dresser drawer. He definitely would have to start repaying Mr. Oakland. The weight of his financial responsibilities buckled the knees of his spirit.

During the evenings and weekends he worked on his house, the activity and pride of accomplishment assuaging his loneliness. He stapled up insulation and laid flooring with the classical station playing from the radio; then the end of April he listened to news reports on the fall of Saigon.

He crouched in the utility room laying floor tile until encroaching darkness stopped him, and he stood to massage the tightness from his neck. Knocking on the front door startled him. He hurried down the hall and opened the gold double door to Paul Jefferson as the last glow of twilight reflected from the pastor's lenses.

"Hello," he said in surprise. "What are you doing out here?"

"You weren't in your apartment. I've missed having you in church."

"I've been busy. Come in while I work."

He guided Paul through the dim house to the utility room. He turned on the trouble light and knelt to spread more adhesive on the floor.

"How are you doing?" Paul asked, leaning his shoulder against the door frame.

"Despite the tragic situation in southeast Asia, there are some signs of sunshine in the spring outlook for the economy. The recession is receding and we may see an upturn. Nevertheless, this house is eating salary and savings at a tremendous rate, so I'm doing some of the inside work myself. When I designed it in February of 1973, I had no idea that an energy crisis, which is one of the greatest perils confronting the industrialized world, would cause the worst economic slump in a third of a century.

"Are you still planning to have it completed before you're married?"

"Absolutely."

"This house means a lot to you, doesn't it?"

"More than anything."

"It is unique, evidence of your innovation, but have you ever thought that it may be too important?"

Surprised he glanced up. "It's my dream."

"Be careful that your dream doesn't displace God in your life."

"The American Dream of owning one's own home is becoming the impossible dream, but I may as well build it now—expensive as it is—because prices may continue to rise."

"Yes, I know," Paul said on a long breath. "That's why the plans for the education building are filed away until the church is able to raise adequate funds."

"Perhaps if everyone in the church had lived on peanut butter and crackers for the last year, they would be able to achieve their dream too."

"You have an admirable dedication to your dream, but only as you trust it and your life to God will you truly succeed. 'Except the LORD build the house, they labour in vain that build it:'," Paul reminded, handing him a tile.

"With good health, another loan, and hard work, I'll have my house finished before the wedding—two months from now."

"Perhaps it would be a good idea for Connie to help finish your house. Not only could you select your furniture together, but it would give you something to occupy your time. Being alone with her before you're married provides a great deal of temptation."

The idea of being with Connie elevated the temperature in his veins, but his will lowered it.

"We'll be occupied all right. There are numerous social events before our wedding. I'll also be working and completing my house, so I won't have time for anything else."

"Maybe so, but be careful of compromising situations. While yielding offers certain pleasure, it violates God's holy standard and the consequences are devastating. You'll have only remorse, broken hearts, and shattered dreams. Make decisions that are sensible and rational, not hormonal."

Certain of his ability to control himself, he spoke with extreme patience. "I'll manage, all right?"

"You may need more than hard work, a strong will, and a loan to attain your dream." Paul handed him another tile. "God, the Master Planner, has a plan for your life, and it includes seeking His guidance. Nothing is as important as knowing and obeying Him. Read your Bible and pray every day. Avoid immorality. Utilize the strength God will give you to resist temptation. 'For the grace of God that brings salvation has appeared to all men. It teaches us to say "No" to ungodliness and worldly passions, and to live self-controlled, upright and godly lives in this present age,' Purity before God is more important than momentary satisfaction."

He slapped the tile onto the sticky adhesive. "Just because I've missed your sermons doesn't mean you had to come clear out here and give me one!"

14

Bridge to the Shining Future

She stood at the window in her dorm room and gazed at the dark green rolling Missouri hills, but the panoramic beauty failed to ease her dismay. Mentally she recited the meager contents of Douglas' letter which still dangled from her fingers. *Dearest Connie, It's taking every penny and every minute to finish my house, so I won't be able to attend your graduation. I know it's important, and I'm sorry to disappoint you. I look forward to seeing you at your party. Please excuse the brevity of this letter, but I am very busy. I eagerly await your return. Your own, Douglas.*

Dissatisfaction displaced the vibrant force which had driven her through the past two years of effort and separations. She turned away in a haze of unshed tears.

Desire to have Douglas present for her triumph stirred her spirit, and she moved with decision. Her eyes narrowed as she spun the dial on the telephone.

"Are you serious about not coming to my graduation?"

"I'm sorry, Con."

"How can you be so thoughtless?"

"I must stay within my time line and on budget for my house. I can't afford the time off to drive and I can't afford the additional expense of flying."

"I'll send you the money."

"Your solution to every problem is to throw money at it, but not every problem can be solved by waving a checkbook like a magic wand."

"It can if one has enough checks. If your coming to my graduation is what I want most in the world, why shouldn't I pay for it?" She paused for Douglas to accept her logic until impatience propelled her on. "Are you going to let your stupid, stubborn pride keep you from attending it, or are you going to be sensible and accept my help?"

"Con-nie—"

"You must come," she pleaded from the depths of her necessity. "It should be important to you too."

"Certainly it's important to me, but you don't understand the financial implications."

"Now look here, Douglas Alan McKenzie. That misdirected independence of yours caused you to break our engagement. Since then I have submitted to your will and protected your pride, but I refuse to let you miss my graduation. I have worked harder these past two years than I ever have so I could graduate this semester as you planned. This is what you made us wait for. You better be here. You can come on Father's jet," she said with new insight.

"I—I'll think about it."

"You think very hard," she advised with some heat. "You decide if your house means more to you than having you here for my graduation means to me!"

She hung up with a snap of finality and flounced across the room, her ire still simmering.

The door burst open, and Linda flung herself on her own bed, sobbing.

Surprise diverted her from her distress. She sat beside Linda and patted her heaving back until her friend sat up, tears cascading down her bronze face.

"What's the matter, Lindy? You haven't cried since we've been roomies."

"I just found out I'm not getting the scholarship to the Colorado State University veterinary school I applied for. What am I going to do?" Linda's voice rose to a wail.

She held her sobbing friend in an unspoken bond, sharing Linda's unhappiness as Linda had often shared hers.

Linda pushed back her tangled mass of long hair. "I'm sorry I fell to pieces. I know God has a plan for my life, but sometimes it's just so hard to understand. My whole future is uncertain right now. Still, I'm not to ask 'Why?' or 'How?' I must trust that because God **is** God and loves me, He'll do what is best," Linda concluded with a watery smile.

Unable to comprehend the struggle of her friend's faith, she remained silent, holding Linda's hand in both of hers.

Gradually an idea blossomed in her mind. "I'll give you the money."

"I couldn't ..."

Linda's refusal following Douglas' chafed her spirit. "Don't you be stubborn too! You have a problem. I have the solution. Let me help. Two years ago when I moved from the Gamma House into the dorm, Father started saving the difference and said Douglas could use it for his house. Well, we know that won't work! Please, let me give it to you."

Linda peered at her, indecision clouding her face.

"I want to do it, Lindy, truly I do. I was very unhappy when Father insisted I live in a dorm instead of an apartment, but I had no idea it would be one of the most fortunate decisions of my life because you became my roommate and best friend. You've been so wonderful to me. Your love and acceptance and example of academic excellence made the past two years not only bearable but pleasant and productive. Your sweet spirit and faith in God have inspired me. I couldn't have survived without you."

Linda rose and turned about the room with one hand on her hip and the other on her forehead as if coping with some inner conflict.

"You not only shared your life with me, but your Lord as well. You did the best thing any friend can do—you led me to Jesus. I am eternally, unutterably grateful, and I will never be able to repay that, no matter how much money I give you."

Linda sat beside her, and they put their arms around each other's waists. "You're a special friend too, Con. I admire your loyalty and generosity. I appreciate what you're doing for me."

"I'm glad you'll let me help. Father will give you a check."

As she functioned in the high-pressure atmosphere of studying for and taking final exams, the normal progression of time seemed to alternately rush forward and capriciously draw back. At unexpected intervals the thought of Douglas not attending her graduation surfaced, and her heart lurched in its need for him.

Her prayers dwindled to, "Dear God, please make Douglas come."

Late one evening as she walked with Linda to Serendipity's for their last hot fudge sundaes, the hazy, humid air surrounded her with the intermittent lights and erratic pattern of lightening bugs.

"You're upset about Douglas not coming to graduation, aren't you?" Linda inquired with her usual insight.

"After all the years of loneliness, all the work—Then for him not to come—" Disappointment lodged in her throat and restricted her voice.

"Sure you want him to be here." After a few steps Linda added, "You invited Jesus into your life, now invite Him into the situation you're in.

He could help you in your loneliness. His presence will fill the void in your life."

"All I need is Douglas."

"Don't let Douglas be more important to you than Jesus," Linda cautioned.

She sat in the gaily decorated parlor of the Gamma House with her chattering sorority sisters at this year's graduation party. Outwardly she was able to celebrate, and she should have been ecstatic about graduating, but with Douglas' coming questionable, she was only slightly less unhappy than she had been the previous two years.

On the eve of graduation, Linda pulled her laughingly along to the dorm lobby to meet the family. Half a dozen bronze faces radiated pride and expressed courtesy; then the family withdrew to their own activities. She returned to the room with its accumulation of boxes and trunks to avoid appearing overly anxious in the lobby. Unable to quell her anxiety, she rebrushed her teeth and hair and reapplied lipstick.

When my parents arrive, I'll be paged. The longing for Douglas disrupted her pulse, and she paced in her uncertainty. She tapped her fists against the full skirt of her blue polka-dotted pinafore. *And if he doesn't come—* She forced herself to accept the probability. *I'll see him tomorrow. It's only one more day— But it's the most important day of my life.*

Finally the intercom crackled open and the dorm assistant announced the arrival of her family. She sauntered down the hall, and from the doorway she viewed the lobby. Uncle Orville, a shorter, stouter version of her father; Aunt Dotty, a fluttery woman with an artificially darkened coiffure; her cousin Peggy, who looked enough like Penny to be her twin, and Grandmother Oakland, a stately woman with gray hair that waved around a face similar to her father's, stood waiting. Gratified by their presence, she entered with cool aloofness and received a flurry of affectionate congratulations.

"We drove all day to meet your parents here," Grandmother Oakland said, glancing around the crowded lobby.

"When Uncle Armand can find a place to park that jet of his and rent a car, they'll be here," Peggy stated.

Grandmother Oakland seated herself in a vacated easy chair and inquired about classes and final exams until the French doors opened and her parents and Penny entered. Douglas stood in the doorway wearing the white linen suit Penny had given him and with his hair neatly styled. She wrapped her arms around his waist, and his hand on the back of her head pressed her cheek against his wide brown tie. She savored his fragrant masculine strength, tears of relief dampening her face. Douglas' mouth sought hers, and she stood on tiptoe to relish the richness of his kiss.

"Well, well, well. What else do you want to do tonight?" Penny commented.

Douglas released her, and her mother brushed the vicinity of her ear with her lips before her father enveloped her in his arms. Following the greetings and introductions, her father withdrew a key from his pocket and handed it to Douglas.

"You and Constance bring the car around. We'll wait here. The ladies want to freshen up a bit from their travels before we go out to dinner."

"My room is at the end of the hall to the left," she said, linking her fingers in Douglas' and backing out the door.

"I'm so glad you came!" They both spoke at once then had to stop and repeat after a brief interval of laughter.

Douglas paused and inclined his head toward her. "Where is Grandmother Van Leigh?"

She blinked and gazed up at him in bewilderment.

"Grandmother Van Leigh? She and Grandfather died years ago. That's when Mother received her inheritance."

"But—" Douglas appeared to be groping mentally. "You told that Blakely Whitworth character you couldn't attend the Sweetheart Dance with him because Grandmother Van Leigh was ill."

She waved her fingers airily. "Blakely knows all about our family."

"So then he knew—?"

She circled Douglas' arm with both hands and led him forward.

She strolled beside Douglas in the balmy spring evening among aromatic trees as they had during their courtship, their words overlapping, and pleasure suffused her. Sights and sounds shifted in a kaleidoscopic pattern where the past intermingled with tonight and Douglas' presence spanned the past two interminable years.

Douglas guided her to the abandoned pavilion and seated her on a stone terrace.

"You have no idea how much I've missed you," he sighed and drew her to him.

Douglas' lips found hers, and she answered with the hunger of separation as her fingers furrowed his hair.

"Don't you dare say anything about my needing a haircut."

Reveling in the silky flow through her fingers, she shook her head and recaptured Douglas' mouth with hers. A current of electricity flowed through every kiss, every touch until she buried her face against his chest, hearing the rhythm of his heart.

"Oh, Con, it feels so good to be this close. It's going to be very difficult to resist you this next month." Douglas eased away.

She nodded in admission. "We must be very careful."

With a brief, pleasant pressure on her ribs, Douglas set her away from him and stood up. He grasped her hands in his and lifted her to her feet. He guided her toward the rented car in the parking area, his conversation excessively architectural.

Friday morning she set the black mortar board flat on her platinum hair with a feeling of culmination that suspended her breath.

"We made it, Lindy," she marveled, giddy from release.

"It's hard to believe, isn't it?"

She gazed at her friend with her heart and mind in a tumult. "I've longed to graduate since Douglas did, but now I'm sorry to be leaving. You are the dearest, truest, friend I have ever had, and I'll miss you!" She blotted away a mist, doing the least possible damage to her makeup.

"I'll miss you too, Con."

The bond of friendship constricted her soul, and she clung to Linda with her arms around her shoulders.

She and Linda marched with the graduates past emerald lawns into the massive stone auditorium, triumph vibrating through her. During the long, boring speeches, she recalled Douglas' graduation and the specter of separation that had overshadowed it.

"Constance Leigh Oakland."

She crossed the platform with swift, graceful ease to receive her diploma. Emerging from a dark chasm, she passed the last barrier between Douglas and herself and the future unfurled before her as a golden bridge.

In the crowd after the ceremony, she noticed her father shaking Linda's hand to slip her a check.

She chatted with her friends and family and the McKenzies who had driven over from St. Louis. All these people had come to see her graduate, but she saw only Douglas. He swept her up in his arms and whirled her around, his forehead touching hers in private salute. Success rang inside her like a carillon and she held her diploma in both hands behind his neck, her hat askew in the celebration of her victory.

The Oakland Enterprises jet roared forward, straining to be free of the earth, and the powerful impetus of Mozart's *Jupiter Symphony* soared in his head. As the lush carpet of wooded hills fell away below, he glanced down at Connie.

"Oh, Douglas, it was fantastic to have you share the most important day of my life! From now on we'll always be together. No longer will I have to rely on letters, which have been not only scarce but brief lately."

"I've been busy with the mix of projects at the start up of the construction season," he said, stroking Connie's wrist with his thumb. "And I'm working on my house—"Nausea rolled through him and he clamped his teeth together determined not to disgrace himself.

"Are you all right?"

He laid his hand on his stomach. "I don't think so."

His determination was powerless to quell the churning in his midriff, and he bolted; behind Occupied he abruptly discarded his lunch. Weak and shaky, he tottered down the aisle.

"Are you ill, deah?" Mrs. Oakland peered up at him.

"Not feeling well?" Mr. Oakland inquired.

Seething with humiliation, he shook his head and sagged down beside Connie.

"You look a little green, Frog Prince."

He ignored Penny and leaned back in his seat, still uncomfortably queasy, but with not much left inside him to come up.

"Do you usually get air sick?" Connie asked, her eyes violet pools in her white face.

Remembering her aversion to illness, he erased the line between her golden brows with his fingers. "Don't worry, Sweetheart, I'm just excited."

"Excited about what?"

"Your graduation, your coming home to stay after all these years."

The excitement in Connie's expression mirrored his own, and he laid his fingertips on her chin in a gesture of mutual understanding.

"I hope you don't become ill every time you're excited. You won't enjoy our honeymoon at all if you do."

"I'll be fine, and we'll have a glorious honeymoon."

"Where shall we go?" Connie queried, toying with his lapel.

"It'll be a surprise."

I'll be surprised if I can afford anything, he added to himself.

Connie's bubbling conversation of honeymoon destinations and appropriate fashions eddied around him while he retreated into introspection. He had taken his tax rebate and a day and a half off work and further compromised his integrity to come with the Oaklands. Yet Connie hadn't even asked how he had been able to attend her graduation, and he contemplated making sacrifices for one who didn't appreciate the extent of it. Connie had always pursued every whim without exchanging one thing for another, and he couldn't expect her to understand that everyone couldn't do the same. He glanced down at her, serene and confident, and he struggled with another stirring of envy.

What _would_ it be like to have _enough_ money?

He rode from the airport to his apartment in the back seat of Mr. Oakland's white Mercedes 350SL with Penny and Connie, noticing their enthusiasm for her party. When Mr. Oakland stopped, Connie's fingers on his wrist detained him.

"You do feel well enough to attend, don't you?"

The gently stated question disallowed refusal, and he managed a hopeful smile.

After a brief rest and a shower, he dressed in a blue denim suit with a red tee shirt and drove to Cedar Ridge Trail. He parked as directed in the congestion and emerged into cacophonous sound. Resisting the impulse to cover his ears, he ventured to the terrace where a mass of people writhed to the blatant music pouring from the band electronically barricaded against the house. The caterers had set tables on the lawn with silver trays of assorted meats, cheeses, crackers, breads, and fruits. Recognizing Oaklands' style of picnic, he smiled ruefully, missing burnt hot dogs and gritty potato salad.

At a touch on his arm he turned to find Connie, and she clasped his hands in hers, swinging them wide.

"I knew you would come!"

His fingers still in Connie's, she backed into the gyrating throng, pulling him along.

"Penny selected the band," Connie informed him above the din.

"How nice," he shouted, already dizzy from the deafening beat.

He led Connie to a padded chaise beside the pool and drew her down beside him. Her presence filled the great, dull, empty ache in his chest which had built up the day he had graduated and had never quite gone away. Freed from the bonds of loneliness, he tightened his arms around her as the passionate strains of Liszt's *Liebestraum* in his mind isolated him from the clamorous party.

"Together forever," Connie murmured.

With a throb of expectation, he inclined his head and lowered his mouth to hers.

"Well, well, well," Penny remarked beside him. "What else do you plan to do this summer?"

15
Surprises

Saturday afternoon as she rode beside Douglas in his Mercedes with the radio softly playing classical music, she disclosed her schedule of showers, teas, brunches, and lunches she and Penny and her mother had written that morning. She reveled in the gala pre-nuptials she had dreamed of all her life, but Douglas' guarded manner perplexed her.

Douglas stopped the car and said, "I had planned to present my house to you as a wedding gift, complete in every detail, but it isn't as finished as I hoped it would be. However, I knew you would want to see it." He pointed out the windshield. "There it is."

The house was larger and more striking than she had imagined—two stories high with gold siding on top, ivory brick beneath, and an ivory brick chimney to the right. A single-story attached garage with four windows in a horizontal row and three narrow, two-story windows on the house gave it an asymmetrical dimension. To the left, two square windows aliened vertically on each story. A window above the gold double doors, which were framed on the outer edges by amber Plexiglass, balanced the center.

She turned to Douglas in awe. "It's beautiful."

Douglas assisted her past wood chips and bits of broken bricks scattered on the scarred earth and unlocked one of the gold doors.

Inside an entryway, a black wrought iron railed stairway climbed to a balcony that started at the front of the house on the left, ran toward the back, and angled at 90 degrees to the right. Douglas directed her into a spacious two-story living room to the right of the entry. Stepping over scraps of lumber, she inhaled the scent of new wood, plaster, and sawdust with a lightheaded sense of disbelief at being in Douglas' house. She paused beside the white brick fireplace, its solidity against her hand transmitting the actualization of the dream. She passed through the living room into the dining room, beneath the balcony, with sliding glass doors that opened onto a patio. To the left was the galley style kitchen, recognizable by its skeletal cabinets. Douglas described distinctive elements and energy efficient features as she walked through the utility room, bath, and two other rooms off the hall next to the stairs. His attention to detail and aesthetics had blended into unique practical beauty, and her heart stilled with admiration.

"It's absolutely superb."

Douglas guided her up to the balcony where to the right were two bedrooms with an unfinished bath between them.

To the left, at the angle in the balcony, Douglas stood aside for her to enter a room. She first noticed a sliding glass door which opened onto a small, white wrought iron railed terrace. Stepping out onto it, she had an unobstructed view of the majestic Front Range. Douglas stood beside her, his forearms on the railing, absorbing the grandeur and her appreciation of it. Returning to the room, she entered a dressing area with double closets. She went through it to a white tiled lavatory which led to a stone flagged room with aqua tiled walls and an elevated tub. The master suite emanated luxurious intimacy, and she turned to find Douglas behind her, the knowledge of what she had discovered shining in his eyes. Hope for the future tingled through her.

Douglas steered her down the balcony toward the front of the house where there was a room and a half bath with small sized fixtures. In the nursery suite she leaned back against Douglas, and he covered her abdomen with his palms.

"When I am established in my career and we can afford it, we shall plan to start a family."

Before images formed in her mind, Douglas led her back along the balcony. They descended the stairs and stopped in the entry way.

"It's perfectly designed and excellently crafted. It's a dream house—a dream come true," she sighed.

Douglas bent at the knees to bring his eyes on a level with hers and laid his hands on her shoulders. "Paul said it would be a good idea for us to select our furniture together. I know you're going to be very busy this month, but could you help complete the interior?"

Surprised by Douglas' request, she waited for her mind to level off before she answered. "I would be delighted to. A bride likes to have a hand in decorating her own home." Visions of exquisite decor filled her mind, and she was eager to begin. "Do you have a tape measure?"

"What do you want to know?"

"The measurements of each room, the wall area, the size of the windows—"

Douglas recited them with such speed that she laid her fingers on his lips, laughing.

"How do you know—"?

"The dimensions?" Douglas' dark brow slanted upward. "Don't forget I designed it. And after drawing two sets—" A flush colored his cheeks and he pursed his lips.

"Why two?"

"I drew another set," Douglas said and moved past her.

Puzzled, she followed him through all the rooms again. He restated the dimensions, and she jotted them in a small leather bound notebook she had withdrawn from her purse. She added notations of color and lists of furnishings, filling several pages before she and Douglas sat on the stairs.

"What have you decided?"

"It's going to be comfortable and personal. It's going to be exquisite."

"It's going to be expensive." Douglas took the notebook and read each page then set it aside.

"I have a vision of what's possible, what's pleasing."

"What's practical," Douglas interjected.

"You don't want it done any less tastefully."

"Just less expensively. The whole house doesn't have to be finished this month. We'll have all our lives to do it. Just do the major rooms. A stove and a refrigerator, a table and chairs, a bed and a dresser. All I need in this house is you."

Flames flared in Douglas' sapphire eyes, and his mouth possessed hers. He cradled her head while his lips caressed her eyes and her hair, his lashes fluttering on her cheek. She nestled closer, linking her arms around his neck. His mouth returned to hers with a heat that threatened to melt her resistance. Her love for Douglas was too strong to let him risk what he had so diligently pursued, and she groped for strength to elude the force of his masculine magnetism. She clasped his arms and backed away.

"We must wait."

"You didn't want to wait in March," Douglas reminded, nuzzling her ear. "Now we're so close."

"But not close enough. What was true then is true now. Even though I've graduated and your house is almost completed, it's a month until we're married."

"It's going to be desperately hard. Paul was right. We're going to need all the strength we can find to withstand temptation." Douglas tipped his head back against a step and pushed his fingers through his hair. "That's another reason I want you to help finish my house. Paul suggested we do something—else—together before our wedding. But I'm not sure— Working here alone with you—" Douglas held her face in his hands and peered down at her, his gaze transmitting his impatience. "Connie, I want you as I've never wanted anything in my life."

"I want you too. You know I always have."

Douglas' smoky eyes warned her she played with explosives. She drew on her resolve and laid a restraining palm on his chest.

Douglas rose to pace the entry way then came around to face her. "I won't be able to afford what you want, but I'll have to decide— The only way I'll be able to carpet my house is if I let your parents provide it as a wedding gift."

Surprised that Douglas would even consider it, she lifted her eyes to his.

"I'll have to choose which is more important—achieving my dream or maintaining my integrity." Douglas' hands closed on her shoulders. "Promise you won't buy anything unless we've agreed."

Willingly she accepted the drastic reduction in her lifestyle. "Certainly."

Douglas' grasp on her shoulders altered to a caress. "Okay. Let's go. You're so desirable, and I—" He ran his fingers over his forehead. "It's hot in here."

Douglas hurried her out of his house with his hand on her elbow.

In the Mercedes, her ears still rang from the ferocity of Douglas' door closures. She linked her fingers together on her knees and regarded his scowl from the corner of her eyes. Self-contained as she rode beside him she let him fume, aware that being together in his house had prompted him to seize the future prematurely. Secure in the decision to deny him what he didn't truly want, she yet labored beneath his sulking.

At her home, Douglas accompanied her to the terrace where her mother and Penny reclined in the shade on chaise lounges.

"The poor wayfaring strangers hath returned," Penny quipped, raising her glass. "Tell us about your humble abode."

Douglas aimed a glare at Penny that squelched further comment.

She seated herself on a chaise, and Douglas turned to greet her father. The distance between Douglas and herself gaped wider than mere miles.

Her father seated her mother and Penny at the glass topped table set with formal beauty, and Douglas seated her. She thanked him with an upward sweep of her lashes, but his grim expression failed to soften. Piqued, she withdrew her attention from him to her mother and Penny's amiable conversation.

When dinner concluded, her father rose. "Constance. Douglas. Come with me."

Puzzled, she met Douglas' eyes; he glanced warily at her. They followed her father into the study with its waxed oak, rows of bookshelves, and brown leather furniture. Her mother arrived, and her bewilderment increased.

"This is your graduation gift, my dear," her father said from behind his desk, holding out an envelope to her. "We wanted to give it to you privately. Uncle Orville is a successful farmer, but the family is very sensitive about our wealth."

She crossed the room to accept it. "Oh, this is so exciting!" She withdrew a check, staring at the amount. Her heart skipped its beat. "Twenty five thousand dollars—?"

Douglas groaned behind her, and she turned halfway toward him.

"For the past 22 years I have been regularly putting a little something aside for your college graduation. This is what it amounts to in even numbers."

"Thank you," she said, amazement insulating her mind.

"But—"

Her father waved Douglas' protest aside. "You will recall that when you asked if you could propose to Constance, I requested she be allowed to graduate so she could receive what I wanted to give her."

"I had no idea it would be $25,000!"

Douglas' reaction pierced her with aching memories and she regarded her father.

"But before—" She groped with her hand.

"An advance. A grievous miscalculation for which I am indeed sorry. I misjudged Douglas' independent nature. I desire only that my gift add to your happiness."

Her mother, trained in the art of graciousness from the cradle, stepped forward. "Come, Douglas. We shall wait outside for Constance and her fatha."

After the door closed behind them, she asked, "This is the reason Douglas insisted I graduate?"

"Yes, my dear, but rest assured, Douglas is not interested in our money."

She continued to stare at the check aware of the irony that money had delayed her from obtaining what she desired instead of instantly providing it.

Her father came around his desk and dangled two small shiny objects before her.

"Keys!" Elated, she clasped them in her hand and brushed her father's cheek with her lips.

"Penelope received her Audi Fox as a graduation gift. You are receiving one also. Your mother and Penelope and Douglas are waiting. Shall we join them?"

In the garage, she ran her fingers along the shiny silver fender. "It's fabulous!"

Douglas opened the door and seated her in the white leather seat behind the wheel, and then he sat beside her while she scrutinized the instrument panel. She backed out of the garage and drove cautiously down the circle drive as she acquainted herself with her new car.

When she had adjusted to the feel, she asked, "Did you know?"

"No. Everything was a surprise." Douglas hesitated. "About the money ..."

She glanced at him uncertainly.

"You don't suspect that's why I waited to marry you?" Douglas' voice was uneven with disbelief.

"Yet you did wait—two years."

"It was important to your father that you graduate and receive what he wanted to give you. I had no idea it would be $25,000! I don't want it, Con. I never did. I never will. You do believe me, don't you?"

Remembering Douglas' constant refusals of any assistance and his past catastrophic response, she smiled at him, confident in his sincerity. Yet she sensed his tension and stopped her Audi at the end of Cedar Ridge Trail.

"What else is bothering you?"

Douglas turned her face to his. "I want you more than I have any right to, but I can't have you, and I get angry at myself for being so tempted. We must not give our souls, our bodies to each other outside of marriage or we'll have a nightmare of remorse instead of our dream."

"I know," she agreed.

"This could be a very difficult month," Douglas said. "It seems as if we'll never be married."

"With all the social events and activities we've planned, our wedding will be here very soon."

Douglas' lips quirked into a rueful smile. "Then again it seems too close. I'm not sure we'll have my house finished."

Vivid images of the elegantly furnished house filled her mind. "As long as I'm helping you, perhaps we could use my money."

"No way! You know how I feel about that, and nothing has changed just because you have your own money. And if you even think of using it, I'll complete my house myself—as I originally intended!"

"All right," she soothed, patting Douglas' shoulder. "We'll do it your way."

Which is better than my not doing it at all, she thought.

❧

Monday when he arrived in the office, Miss King handed him a message to call his bank. Expectancy rose within him, but he tapped his pen against his chin while he waited for an answer.

"Hello, this is Zeke Wilson."

"Hello. I'm Douglas McKenzie, returning your call."

"Yes, Mr. McKenzie. According to our records you've already borrowed the highest amount possible on your construction loan. We're unable to increase it at this time."

"Unable—? What about a personal loan?"

"Without further collateral it's impossible to approve another loan."

Impossible? his mind protested. *My dream is impossible?*

In a haze of disbelief he hung up and sank onto the bench of his drawing board. He pressed his palms to his head and impelled his brain toward a solution. He rose to pace and stared unseeing into the Denver sky.

Dear God, what am I going to do? I can't finish my house or repay Mr. Oakland.

That evening as he drove in heavy traffic and stifling heat, despite the car's air conditioning, his tension increased and the swirling intensity of Vivaldi's *Summer* played in his mind. In the foothills the air cooled, and he breathed deeply of the cedar scent until his edginess subsided.

He arrived at Oaklands', and Fenton let him into the foyer.

Penny, wearing a green blouse and a long skirt with a floral pattern, greeted him with a sultry, "Good evenen, dahling. Motha and Fatha have been detained this evenen, but fohtunately foh you, I shall be heah to entatain you at dinna."

He clenched his teeth and brushed past her.

Penny ran her hand across his back and down his arm. "Mother was able to clear tomorrow evening on her calendar, so we shall discuss further plans for the wedding and rehearsal dinner then."

Connie descended the stairs in a clingy pink dress that accented her rounded form. Her lips lifted to his and the vibrant welcome revived his spirit. Her ability to affect him so left him content and happily anticipating a lifetime of loving and caring regard.

"How are you, Darling?"

"I'm fine, Sweetheart. How are you?"

"This has been the most wonderful day! We ordered all the flowers—so you don't need to worry about any of those—and they are so beautiful! We discussed menus with the caterers and ordered the cakes. Our tier cake will be marvelous. There are decorated sheet cakes with yellow frosting rosebuds and green leaves. Now we must have our blood tests and get our marriage license."

He questioned if he should mention his rare blood type, but Connie bubbled on.

"We also need to select gifts for each other and our attendants so there will be time for them to be engraved if necessary."

Due to his depleted finances, he doubted his ability to purchase anything, engraved or not.

"With my projects in various degrees of completion, I have a variable time commitment. Perhaps we could meet downtown Friday afternoon to get our license."

"We also need to decide on the tints and patterns to complete your house."

Connie's comment caused a moment of panic, for he was incapable of completing his house. With an effort, he asked lightly, "What's your hurry?"

"Hurry? After we choose our color scheme, it's going to take time for your house to be completed and to do the painting. Then we must get the carpet laid, the draperies ordered and hung, and our furnishings selected."

A train of thought collided in his mind. *I wonder what kind of furniture Connie likes.* Certainty pervaded him. *The expensive kind. Maybe we can select a few pieces and I won't appear indigent.*

"For as far away as our wedding seems, there's an incredible amount to be done, and I think we should start right away," Connie concluded.

His own flutter of excitement surprised him, and he was unable to withstand Connie's enthusiasm. "How about Saturday?"

By then I will have received a partial paycheck, he added to himself.

"Then we would have a whole day!" Connie swung his hands wide. "Isn't it thrilling?"

Nerve wracking is more like it, he qualified mentally. He released a wavering breath.

"Are you all right, Darling?"

Using his gallantry to conceal his precarious financial state, he nodded.

"Are you certain nothing's the matter?"

I'm certain I can't tell you what it is, he knew. *You could never understand what it's like to need money.*

Connie's eyes searched his, and he wondered how well he had hidden his concern from her.

"You seem so tense, Darling. Relax now, and we'll have a nice, quiet evening together."

After a succulent dinner of what could have been shredded cardboard served with Penny's snide wit, he followed Connie to the terrace. She sat back on a chaise, glancing up at him with a charm that captivated his spirit. He removed his suit coat and tie and settled beside her.

"Would you like to swim?" Connie asked. "It would help you relax and you didn't eat enough dinner for it to cause cramps."

The idea of frolicking scantily clad in the water with Connie lightened his mind, but he tracked it in a different direction. "How would you like to have a pool at my house? It isn't fair to deprive you of all the luxury you're accustomed to."

"I've adjusted to your depriving me of everything," Connie said with perfect candor.

His soul recoiled and he offered, "If you want something I'm not able to provide, you could use your money."

"I could use it to help you furnish your house."

With a sharp and sudden irritation, he crossed his arms on his chest. "You know how I feel about that!"

"All right, so I won't help you with your house! But I won't buy you a swimming pool either!" Connie bounced off the chaise and crossed the terrace, her pink skirt twitching.

Wearily he started to follow.

"Stay there!" Connie commanded and disappeared into the house.

The unforeseen argument and Connie's departure, as well as his anxiety, combined with an unfamiliar heaviness within him. The comfort of lying quietly lulled him into waiting.

Connie soon emerged from the porch carrying a blue bowl of strawberries so plump and red his mouth watered for them. She sat in the grass beneath an elm, her knees tucked beside her, and she bit into a fat berry with open allure. He heaved himself off the chaise and strolled over to sit with her. She placed a berry between his teeth, and its sweetness poured onto his tongue.

"Hmm," he sighed and closed his eyes.

"You seem so tense, Darling," Connie murmured, rubbing his neck and shoulders.

The day had battered his spirit, and Connie's tender touch loosened his nerves. He leaned back against the elm and drew up his leg, his arm on his knee. He sampled the strawberries from the bowl at the base of the tree, and Connie drew his head into her lap. He lay gazing into the azure depths of the sky framed between leafy boughs, Connie's love a shield against the assaults of life. Her head tilted for effect, she teased him with another strawberry, a hint of amusement in her light laughter, as if she knew the effect she had on him. He reached up to caress Connie's hair, and she reclined on one elbow, her head in her palm. As she gave him another berry, her lips met his then separated. His mouth moved along the curve of her cheek to her throat and lingered there until her breath came audible and uneven, falling with her kisses against his ear. His mouth covered hers, and its rich sweetness heated his blood. Never had such pure bliss beckoned.

To have Connie now— To end the waiting—

Excitement churned in his stomach. He buried his face in Connie's shoulder and slowly inhaled to suppress it.

"Well, well, well," Penny said above him. "What <u>are</u> you doing?"

Guilt plunged through him and his heart skidded. He and Connie broke apart in haste and rose.

"What are you doing here?" he demanded.

"I live here."

His longing for Connie clashed against the crumbling wall of his restraint as he held Penny's gaze, his jaw tight.

"Well?" Penny queried, an arrogant challenge on her face as she patted her foot on the grass.

She knows, he realized. *And she's daring me—daring me to finish something I was too eager to start. But it's wrong— A physical response to being together after so long apart. Dear God, help me. I can't stop this on my own, and I must stop it—stop it now or our dream will go up in flames of passion.*

Quenching the flames with the cold water of discipline and Divine intervention, he knew he must prove Penny wrong and owe this one—who had constantly antagonized him—his gratitude, for his dream remained intact, and he had come perilously close to incinerating it.

He turned to Connie and said, "Let's go for a walk."

"I trust you will behave as a gentleman," Penny said, her brows elevated.

He thrust a shaky hand through his hair. *Only with God's help will I be able to constrain my impulses until we're married.*

His answer to Penny in his scathing glare, he twined his fingers in Connie's and strode out of the yard.

The sun had slipped below the ridge of the Front Range, and its waning strength diffused a pink opalescent glow into the cooling evening as he led Connie along Cedar Ridge Trail.

"I only wanted to help you relax, Darling."

"Someday I'm sure you will be most effective, Sweetheart, but now you achieve only the opposite effect."

Connie's glanced up at him with an expression of contrition. He laid his arm around her shoulders and removed it with a little pat.

Connie's trivial chatter was a refreshing diversion from architectural discussions or financial difficulties, and he released his mind to float along on the gentle current of her conversation.

At the end of the road, he entered the evergreen forest where lofty pines stood in jagged silhouette against the indigo sky. The spicy fragrance and dim solitude enveloped him, and he paused on the spongy, pine needle covered path. He gathered Connie into his arms, and his lips met hers with undeniable urgency. Connie's response reignited the fire in his veins, but unexpectedly a fire burned in his abdomen. His hands slid from Connie to clutch his midsection as he doubled over.

"Darling? Are you all right?"

Trying to ignore the twinges, he nodded. "It-it's just a stitch."

Sickness erupted before he could stifle it, and he averted his face, deluged with embarrassment.

"Let's go home," Connie said with a tremor in her usually controlled voice.

He remembered her aversion to illness and regretted she had seen it.

Severe cramping drove him to his knees. Connie laid her arm across his back, but he sensed her inability to assist him. Determined to walk unescorted, he staggered up. With his palms on his thighs, he lurched to

Oaklands' house, pain stabbing with every step. He stumbled at the stair, and Connie steadied him as she pushed open the front door.

"Penny! Penny, come quickly!" Connie called.

Penny pelted down the stairs and paused beside him. Bent double, he stared at the black-and-white tiled floor, humiliation burning his cheeks.

"Put him in one of the guest rooms," Penny said, her slender fingers closing on his arm.

"No," he insisted through his teeth. "I— I'll be fine."

Penny and Connie helped him up the stairs to the guest room, shards of pain severing his will power. A spasm gripped his abdomen, and he dropped onto the bed. He rolled sideways and sucked in quick, little gasps. Connie tucked a blanket around him, and her gentle distracting touch enabled him to endure.

"Darling?"

"Perhaps it was—the strawberries."

"Or excitement?"

As he recalled the sweet kisses they had shared, excitement recurred. But the pain— He hid his surprise at the sudden malady behind a smile and admitted, "You do excite me. You know you do."

Connie's violet eyes held his in acknowledgment of her effect on him and conceded his on her. Satisfaction throbbed through him, but his blood pulsed in irregular rushes.

Connie laid her palm on his cheek and then slid it to his forehead. "You feel feverish, Darling. Perhaps we should call Dr. Rhye."

Panic disrupted his breath, and the ominous strains of Liszt's *First Piano Concerto* invaded his mind.

"I can't be <u>sick</u>! I don't have <u>time</u> to be sick. I can't <u>afford</u> to be sick!"

16
Conflicts

uesday morning his alarm clock jangled its raucous summons, and he turned over to silence it. Nausea rolled through him and he lay back. While he waited for it to subside, he sorted through memories of the last evening. The shame of losing control of his impulses, when he knew he should avoid sexual immorality, mixed with a strange relief that the pain had intruded. After he felt better he had driven himself home. He explored his abdomen with his fingertips, encountering some tenderness.

I feel better than I did last night. But then, I doubt that it's possible to feel worse.

That evening seated with Connie, Penny, and Mrs. Oakland at the small, circular table in Mrs. Oakland's sitting room, he listened as she recounted innumerable details for the wedding. The extravagance of the event imbued it with a formal grandiosity, replacing the intimacy and romance he would have preferred.

"Ah trust you and your attendants have rented fohmal weah."

"I haven't been able to find six attendants. There's Terry, of course, and Mike Hall and Evan Scott, who seemed pleased to be asked, but I don't know anyone else well enough to ask him to participate in my wedding."

"What about Pastor Jefferson?" Connie inquired.

"He can't be an attendant and perform the ceremony."

A glance passed between Connie and Mrs. Oakland.

"But Pastor Jefferson isn't— Rev. Murphy is performing the ceremony."

"Since you attend church with me, I thought—"

"Your chuch isn't at all suitable for the ratha lahge affair we're plannen. Our great chuch lends itself so well to a beautiful, fohmal wedden."

As he visualized the cool, tomb-like church, disbelief trickled through him. "But still—"

"Doug-las … surely you realize we are to be married in my parents' church."

"What I didn't realize is that my best friend won't be in my wedding!"

"Ask him to be an attendant."

"As a pastor of one church, he wouldn't care to participate in another!"

"Douglas, the selection of your attendants should have been ahranged and finalized months ago," Mrs. Oakland chided.

Incapable of changing the situation, he met her gaze with a slight twitch of his eyebrows.

"I suppose we shall be able to find suitable young men to pahticipate in Constance's wedden," Mrs. Oakland said, making notations in her planning book.

"There's Blakely," Penny suggested.

"Probably not," Connie disagreed before he could. "Richard Stuyvesant would be a good groomsman."

"And Phillip Rothschild and Ashley Kennsington," Penny added.

"Do check with them and get the ties and gloves immediately or there will be no hope of havin' an identical look to the wedden pahty."

He speculated about the cost of having an identical look to the wedding party. As he analyzed the expenses for the rest of his wedding obligations, the necessity of acquiring a loan pressed heavier on his soul.

"Now we shall discuss ahrangements for the rehearsal dinna. I have spoken to your motha by phone. Since it is so difficult for her to make the ahrangements by long distance, we shall do so and infohm her of our plans."

"Perhaps an elegant dinner with orchids and damask following the rehearsal," Penny suggested. "We could have music and dancing—"

"A simple dinner before the rehearsal would be better," he said.

And less disastrous for Pop's budget, he thought.

"Yes, a formal dinner before the rehearsal," Connie added. "If we have it afterward we would stay too late, and I want to be well-rested for my wedding and honeymoon."

"You _are_ having a honeymoon?" Penny asked.

"Certainly we'll have a honeymoon," he answered with a display of confidence he little felt.

"Just remember, a honeymoon is the climax of a girl's dreams. Make every effort to fulfill them," Penny instructed.

Connie's look of love and longing quickened his pulse. He lowered his lashes over one eye in a gesture that heightened her color.

"So much for the honeymoon." Penny tapped his arm. "Douglas, pay attention. I gave up a perfectly good evening to help you kiddies plan your wedding and rehearsal dinner. Do try to be attentive. Douglas ..."

He ignored Penny and touched his forehead to Connie's, whispering his spontaneous honeymoon plans of a stern-wheeler cruise up the Mississippi River.

Penny reappeared with a blue jacquard tuxedo on a padded hanger. "Now, back to the rehearsal dinner."

Comprehension brought him to his feet. "No way."

"Now, Dougie ... this will do marvelous things for your eyes."

Not caring about the advantages to his eyes, he repeated, "No way."

"With a powder blue ruffled shirt and navy bow tie ..."

"You're pushing," he warned, his hands on his hips.

"I'm surprised you didn't balk at wearing pinstriped trousers and a cutaway coat."

"And do I have to wear a top hat too?"

"It's not going to be that formal. It's only a daytime ceremony, and Connie is marrying you, Frog Prince, not the Prince of Wales."

Indignation swept through him in a hot wave. Before it could flare into a retort, Penny patted his shoulder.

"Relax, Hero. All grooms get anxious before the wedding, but it will fall into place. You'll be all right in a few weeks."

When I'm married and living in my house with Connie.

The culmination of the dream drew his mind forward, but he compelled it to concentrate.

"You will please notify your parents of our decisions and infohm me of their reply as soon as possible?"

"Yes, ma'am," he replied vaguely.

Mrs. Oakland closed the planning book, and Connie slipped him a sheet of paper on which she had written the arrangements that had been finalized. She cupped her chin in her palm with her elbow on the table in the glow of the sunset outside the mullioned window, and he propped his elbow on the table with his chin on the back of his fingers.

"This is going to be the most incredible month of my life!" Connie exclaimed.

"If all goes well."

Connie's wide, innocent lavender gaze met his. "Everything is arranged to the finest detail. What could possibly go wrong?"

⇛

Wednesday morning she stood framed in the three way mirror, viewing the unique creation of her bridal gown. Tiers of ruffled Chantilly lace cascaded from the bodice into a chapel train, and lacy fitted sleeves tapered to points on the back of her hands. Her mother shook out the many-layered tulle veil and set the cap of seed pearls on her head. She did an impulsive little half-turn that set the sequins on her scalloped neckline glinting. Arrayed in a cloud of bridal splendor, she imagined the altar flanked by masses of blue carnations and golden gladiolus in silver vases. Douglas waited beneath blue satin sashes draped from the ceiling, wearing a pinstriped cutaway suit which accented his height and attractiveness.

"I do ... I do ... I do!" she breathed.

"Not yet you don't," Penny reminded, giving her a gentle shake. "This is just your final fitting for your photograph."

Euphoria floated thoughts from her mind, leaving her staring into free space, scarcely aware as she followed Penny and her mother on numerous errands.

⇛

He entered his apartment and dropped his keys and electric bills for his house and the apartment into the clutter on the coffee table. He lay back against the black vinyl couch with a long exhalation.

With electric rates soaring and the loan unapproved—

Tension which had coiled within him all day twined his nerves into springs, and he became aware of discomfort in his abdomen. He ran his hands down his face and loosened his tie. He recalled that Penny was going to leave Connie at his apartment, where Connie would prepare dinner for them. Then they were going to church and meet with Paul following the mid-week service. Afterward he would drive her home. He hoped for time to shower and change, but light rapping indicated she had arrived. He opened the door and she walked into his arms, her face upturned for his kiss.

Connie leaned back to look at him. "What would you like for dinner, Darling? Chicken cordon bleu, veal scaloppine? Tell me. I'll have the grocer deliver the ingredients, and I'll prepare it for you."

Opposition welled within him, and he released Connie. "You know how I feel about your using your money to buy things I would rather buy for myself."

"Only too well! You are the most stubborn person I know!"

"And after two years you're still a spoiled debutante who always wants to buy her own way!"

"But you said if there was anything I ever wanted that you weren't able to provide, I could use my money."

"I didn't mean groceries!"

"I'm sorry." Connie lowered her lashes in surrender then swept them up with tangible effect.

Drawing Connie into the circle of his arms again, he said, "I'm sorry too, Sweetheart. I'm just tired."

Connie stroked his forehead with her fingertips. "You do look tired, Darling, and you're irritable too. Try to relax before dinner."

Encroaching lethargy prohibited further discussion, and he conceded. "Do what you like about supper. I'm going to shower and shave."

After he dressed in a blue striped shirt and denim pants, he approached the kitchen with its aroma of sauteed meat and vegetables and boiling pasta. Connie had set his gray Formica-topped table as formally as possible with his Melamine dishes and stainless flatware. Her brightly colored floral jacket hung on the back of a chair; she stood at the sink in a matching skirt and yellow tank top, swishing cups and bowls through a mound of soap bubbles. Her vibrant presence brought a pang of longing for this one with whom he wanted to share his life. Wanted it with such intensity his heart rushed with it, rushed then slowed, constrained by his will.

During dinner he pushed the food around on his plate, finding he had little appetite.

"Don't you care for veal scaloppine, Darling?"

"I just wish you would have prepared something I could recognize—or afford."

Connie's habitual smile slipped and her eyes lowered in demure pique.

He was dismayed at having distressed her, but he was uncertain how to reconcile the familiar conflict. He remained silent, pressing his palms against his thighs.

"Tonight we're celebrating my culinary expertise. After we're married, we shall live on love and penury."

Connie's sunny good nature was back in force, and he lifted her hand in his, pressing his lips to her fingers. The embers glowing in her eyes warmed his blood, and he rose from the chair. He drew Connie up, and her arms curled around his waist. His mouth played softly, lightly teasing on hers as his hands glided over her back. She ran her palms up his ribs to his chest, and he nuzzled her cheek, her hair, and the softness beneath her ear. His questing kisses trailed around her neck until she murmured her delight. His lips returned to hers, each kiss richer than the last until he couldn't get enough of their honeyed sweetness. Connie clasped him to her, and his passion deepened at her response. The intemperate force within him defied propriety, and his mouth forged to hers. The intensity of their kiss seared away his last scruple. He caught her up in his arms, carrying her to his bed. He eased down beside her.

"It's been two years! Two years I've wanted you—ached through endless days and sleepless nights without you."

"But, Douglas—" Connie pressed her hand to his chest.

"I cannot resist you one more moment!"

Intense pain in his midriff made his breath quiver. He clutched Connie's hand as he waited for the spasm to subside.

"Douglas?"

"I-I'm—okay. It's just a stab of guilty conscience." He buried his face against Connie's shoulder. "Oh, Con.... I—almost went too far."

His lack of self-control chilled him and extinguished the flames which had nearly cremated his dream.

Sickness roiled within him, and he staggered to the bathroom where he hung over the bowl.

Connie appeared in the doorway, so pale he feared she would faint. "Perhaps we should call a doctor."

Alarm surpassed his discomfort. "I'm not <u>sick</u>! This always happens when I get excited."

Connie's face resembled transparent wax with two dark holes scorched in it. Her white lips set. "I've seen you when you were excited. Tonight you are obviously ill and in pain."

"I'll be all right, Sweetheart. Really," he said with the desperation of will.

He approached Connie's and cupped her face in his hands. He traced the curve of her ashen cheeks with his thumbs until the color of ripe peaches returned. Relief eased his regret at what she had witnessed, but he sagged against the doorjamb, his heart pounding.

Connie wedged her shoulder beneath his arm and helped him to the couch. She brushed his hair off his forehead, and her fingers lingered there.

"I think you have a fever, Douglas."

"You're enough to give any man a fever, Con."

"You feel awfully hot."

A chill contracted every fiber of his body and he shivered.

I feel awful, period, he admitted to himself.

"You must see a doctor. These upsets are too frequent and too severe to be ignored. We can't risk your being ill so close to the wedding. I'll come and take you to Dr. Rhye in the morning."

Automatic protest rose to his lips, but sickness threatened to precede it. He clamped his teeth together, refusing to subject Connie to another debacle. She bent to touch his forehead with her lips, and he sensed her recoil from its heat. Determined to reassure her, he arranged his face in what he hoped passed for a smile.

Connie picked up his keys from the jumble on the coffee table.

"Rest, Darling. I'll drive myself home."

With a solicitous backward wave, Connie closed the door between them.

Alone with his illness, he bolted into the bathroom for a devastating encore. Weak and perspiring, he reeled back to his bed and lay down. Sharp twinges shot through him, and he tucked his knees to his chest, rocking side to side. He clenched his hands and teeth against the torment.

No one ever died from a bellyache—not even one as severe as this, he encouraged himself.

He questioned the cause and if he should see a doctor, but fierce pangs obliterated further thought. He sought to hold his mind above the relentless throes lest they engulf him. Eventually they subsided, and he drifted into exhausted sleep.

Insistent knocking roused him to wakefulness, but lethargy held him flat. The knocking continued, and he forced himself up. He opened the door and Paul entered.

"Are you all right? You and Connie weren't at church and you weren't working on your house."

Embarrassed by missing his appointment, he demanded, "Do you always go out looking for truants?"

"Only the ones I care about."

Chagrined, he said, "I didn't feel well."

Paul's gaze searched his. "How are you now?"

"I'm fine. I can't <u>afford</u> to be sick. The money is going out amazingly fast. And without the loan—" A rising sense of urgency halted his voice. "Someone in Denver should be willing to lend me money."

"Just be sure they don't collect interest in kneecaps."

"Someone reputable. Besides, with my job and all these social obligations, I'm not sure when I'll have time to finish my house. After waiting two years to be married, everything is happening at once. The next three weeks will be unlike any in my life."

"Are you feeling well enough for all this?"

"Whenever I get excited my stomach revolts. And the last few times I've been with Connie, I've been very excited. This happened Monday night too. I'm a fairly bright guy. I think I would learn. But, Paul, she is so irresistible. Being with her, knowing that soon—but not soon enough—" With growing agitation he crossed the living room and stood by the window, twisting the drapery cord in his fingers. "We've waited 24 months. Now I'm not sure I can wait 24 days."

"But you must. Don't compromise your character for pleasure. If you do, you'll betray God's plan of taking two people and making them one. That unique oneness belongs only within the legal, spiritual, and emotional bonds of matrimony."

"I want to wait, but then I'm tempted and I yield. Why do I do what I don't even want to do?" He turned to Paul, conflict contorting his soul.

"'For what I do is not the good I want to do; no, the evil I do not want to do—this I keep on doing.'"

Paul so clearly stated his dilemma that he asked, "How did you know?"

"It isn't original with me. The apostle Paul wrote words to that effect nearly 2000 years ago." The pastor met his gaze with compassion. "We all struggle with the desire to do right and the inevitability of doing wrong. There is no way you can withstand temptation in your own strength because you don't have the power to fight it. Determination isn't enough. Jesus doesn't suggest we do what we can by ourselves then call on Him if we need help. He says that apart from Him, we can nothing. 'Now if I do what I do not want to do, it is no longer I who do it, but it is sin living in me that does it.'"

Sensing his heart's subversion of his will, he nodded.

"There is a constant battle between yielding to temptation or trusting the Holy Spirit to control you. As believers in Christ, we must appropriate the power of His Holy Spirit, who is able to give us victory. He should fill you so nothing else will make you lose control."

The concept penetrated his mind, and he turned to stare out the window into the light-pierced darkness below. To have failed distressed him. To have failed because he had neglected Paul's advice to read his Bible, pray, and avoid compromising situations angered him. He pushed his hand through his hair and flung himself onto the couch.

"You warned me this would happen, didn't you? But I had to do it my way. I was certain I could manage simply because I wanted to—planned to." He noticed Paul's sentient smile and agreed wryly, "You were right, of course. I built my house on a firm foundation. I should have built my life on the firm foundation of obedience to God's Word. In the heat of passion I ignored what was right, but I know God expects me to honor Him with my body."

In shame he bowed his head. "Dear God, what I wanted to do—what I very nearly did—with Connie tonight and Monday night was wrong, wrong toward her and more importantly wrong toward You. Only the power of Your Holy Spirit will enable me to do what is right. Give me Your strength to live a pure life and to be a clear witness to Oaklands. Perhaps they will see Jesus in me and will desire to accept Him into their lives. I ask these things in His Name."

Forgiveness removed the burden and the placid *Be Still My Soul* infused his spirit. Paul crossed the room to pat his shoulder. "That's good. Call me and we'll arrange another time to talk when it's convenient for you and Connie."

Nodding, he watched Paul let himself out.

After the door closed, memory nudged him. I forgot to tell him he wouldn't be performing the ceremony.

Paul, the most exemplary pastor he had ever known. Paul, who dispensed wisdom with tactful grace. Paul, whose exhortation had kept him from demolishing the dream before it could be obtained. Paul, whose counsel on marriage would be all he received. Paul, his best friend who, by Oakland whim, had been excluded from the wedding.

He locked the door and returned to his room where he changed into his pajamas. He slipped from his wallet the medallion which notified anyone concerned of his drug allergies and rare blood type. He hung it around his neck, an engraved albatross he avoided thinking about as much as possible. But Mom had instilled within him the necessity of carrying it with him or wearing it when he slept. Just in case....

17
Emergency

*T*he telephone beside her bed jingled its musical two-toned summons. Startled from sleep, she groped for it. "Hullo...?"

"Connie? This is Paul Jefferson. I'm afraid something is wrong with Douglas."

Coldness coursed through her and she clung to the telephone.

"I visited him earlier, and he said he hadn't been feeling well. He felt better but I've been concerned, so I tried to call him. He doesn't answer."

Steadying herself against rising panic, she said, "I'll meet you at his apartment."

She hurriedly dressed and drove through Denver lights and traffic, too dazed to think or feel. She ran up the stairs to Douglas' apartment where Pastor Jefferson waited, and she inserted a key in the lock.

"About my having Douglas' key ... I have his car too," she explained hastily.

The lock clicked, and she entered the living room, turning on the light. She ran to Douglas' room where he lay restlessly on the bed; a medallion glinted against the dark hair on his chest. A low cry escaped her and she dropped to her knees.

"Douglas?" She held his hand against her face, surprised by its heat. "I'm here, Darling."

"Con?" Douglas murmured, his eyes bright and blank.

She glanced at Pastor Jefferson in fright and confusion. He circled Douglas' wrist with his plump fingers.

"Call a doctor. Tell him Douglas has a high fever, his pulse is rapid, his breathing is labored."

She hastened to the phone in the kitchen where traces of their dinner remained. Disbelief that Douglas could be so ill when he had been so vitally, so passionately, alive mere hours ago emptied her mind.

"I'll have Margie come clean up tomorrow."

Gratefully she assented. A moment later she dialed Dr. Rhye's number, her fingers not quite steady.

Following the doctor's terse instructions, Pastor Jefferson half-carried Douglas downstairs and supported him in the backseat while she drove to the hospital her father heavily endowed.

She rocked her Audi to a stop beneath the lighted EMERGENCY sign. Pastor Jefferson sprang out to help lay Douglas on a stretcher with waiting attendants. She quickly parked and arrived in the Emergency Room after Douglas had disappeared and Pastor Jefferson had provided the necessary information to the nurse on duty. He led her to a row of chairs, but she peered at him with the familiar lightening of her head.

"Illnesses—have always had—the strangest effect on me—"

"Put your head down," the pastor instructed gently.

With her forehead on her knees, the swirling mists parted, but her thoughts continued to swirl. *How could a day that began with me trying on my bridal gown end in the Emergency Room?*

When tall, silver-haired Dr. Rhye approached in professional white, she sprang up, her head and feet disproportionately separate.

"Hello, Constance. I've examined Douglas, but I need to ask you some questions. Had he been having abdominal pain before you called?"

"After dinner."

"And before that?"

"Monday evening. We went for a walk—"

"Why wasn't he in here then?"

"He said he wasn't ill."

"Well, no doubt he was. He has acute appendicitis. He must have immediate surgery."

The shock went through her to her toes. "Surgery?"

"The operation for uncomplicated appendicitis is relatively simple. There's a place outside the surgical suite where you may wait. I'll talk to you after it's over."

She wandered into the corridor without knowing where she was going. Pastor Jefferson guided her into the alcove and sat beside her on a hard green sofa, his bulky presence in a tan corduroy suit fortifying her. He laid his hand on hers, and she clung to it, an anchor in a world which pitched and heaved beneath her as the sea. He bowed his head, and the lamplight haloed his brown curls. As she sensed his coherent communication with God, her own spirit calmed.

A week ago her prayers had dwindled to, *Dear God, please make Douglas come.* Now they were, *Dear God, please make Douglas well.*

Her mother, impeccably dressed in a beige pantsuit, appeared in the waiting area one step ahead of her father. The clouding of her mother's china blue eyes and the puckering of her brow exhibited her concern. White parenthesis were etched between her father's nose and mouth, but sympathy overshadowed his grim expression.

"Dr. Rhye called. How is Douglas, my dear?"

"Dr. Rhye will talk to us after the operation."

She performed her introductions without her voice betraying her distress, and she explained that Pastor Jefferson had alerted her to Douglas' illness.

"We are so pleased to meet you," her mother said.

Her father gripped Pastor Jefferson's hand and elbow. "Thank you for all you've done."

Her father seated her mother and himself on a green sofa adjacent to her and Pastor Jefferson.

The reality of Douglas being in surgery penetrated her mind. Suddenly cold, she stood and rubbed her arms with her hands to warm herself. She paced in spite of her mother's disapproving glance until her mother's dignity gradually infused her. She regained enough control to sit on the edge of the sofa, her fingers clenched in her lap. She needed the comforting security of Douglas' embrace, the sturdiness of his body, the strength of his character in this crisis. But he was ill, and she waited bereft of his presence. The tension frayed her nerves until they threatened to snap like violin strings while the clock ticked off endless minutes that fell into the stream of the past. She endured the uncertainty of Douglas' condition with her mind suspended.

Dr. Rhye entered the alcove in a baggy green suit, a mask hanging around his neck. Relieved to see him, she rushed forward with Pastor Jefferson and her parents following.

"How is Douglas? May I see him?"

"He's in the recovery room. He did have appendicitis." Dr. Rhye's aspect altered. "With the infection confined to the appendix usually no complications will arise, but Douglas waited too long. His had ruptured. With the extension of the process into the peritoneal cavity a host of serious results may follow. Of all the complications, general peritonitis is the most common."

Floundering in a deluge of information, she lifted her eyes to the doctor's. "He will be all right ...?"

"We've started him on antipyretics and antibiotics—the ones he's not allergic to—but they aren't too effective. He's young and strong, but he is one <u>very</u> sick boy."

She shook her head in frantic denial. "He has to be all right!"

"I know. Some patients do recover when surgery is performed at this point, but— I'll call his parents. They will want to come."

"Please, let me see him."

"Douglas is going to have to fight for his life, and you're the best reason I can think of for him to win. Go on up and wait for him."

As she rode up in the elevator, she refused to believe Dr. Rhye's dire explanation and simply rejected it. She longed solely for a reunion with Douglas after this most harrowing of all their separations.

Sucked into the mechanisms of a modern hospital with its bright lights and intimidating technology, she uncertainly entered the room she had been directed to. Expecting to find Douglas, she saw only a tautly made bed angled at 45 degrees with a row of lights and switches above it. Blank dismay held her motionless.

Dear God, this can't be happening! We're to be married—with teas and showers and lunches and brunches to attend. After two years we're so close. This—this isn't in the plan at all! she protested mentally, gesturing at the small room.

She drew her fingertips along the green wall, seeking reality in what surely must be a nightmare. She slumped into a gray upholstered chair between the window and the bed and dozed until dawn's early light filtered around the venetian blinds.

She roused when two orderlies in stiff coats wheeled Douglas into the room and positioned him in bed, IV tubing dangling around him. His head moved limply against the pillow, his tousled hair contrasting with the white linen. He uttered a low moan, and she rose to approach him, but the room dimmed and swayed. She clung to the metallic bed rail to brace herself.

"Constance, perhaps this will upset you," Dr. Rhye said as he arrived and the orderlies withdrew.

"Douglas needs me."

She regarded Douglas, his face pallid and still, the tube taped into his nose distorting his features. Involuntarily she drew back.

Dr. Rhye's troubled gaze held hers. "If you're certain ..."

She lifted her chin. "I'm certain."

A slender black nurse in a starched white uniform and cap nestled in her tight curls appeared. The model of efficiency, she checked Douglas' temperature, pulse, and blood pressure and wrote the numbers on a slip of paper. Dr. Rhye looked from it to Douglas and shook his head. Fearfulness raised mute questions, and she glanced at the doctor, finding no answers.

"I'm Kathy Parks," the nurse said. "If you need anything just push this button. I'll be in and out to check on Mr. McKenzie. Keep him as quiet as possible and don't let him pull anything loose."

Barely functional, she nodded, and Kathy followed Dr. Rhye out of the room.

Douglas' eyelids fluttered, and he plucked at the IV in his elbow. She stilled his fingers to keep him from dislodging it. They entwined hers in a feeble grip, but their hotness seared into her skin.

"Con...?"

"You're going to be fine. You've just had your appendix out."

Douglas' face stiffened, and he gripped his abdomen as if to ease the ache.

Queasiness obstructed her voice and she lowered her head, but valor raised it. "I am sorry, Darling."

She lifted Douglas' damp hair off his forehead, and he drifted into uneasy sleep. Sinking into the chair, she pushed her hair back with her fingers.

Her parents and Pastor Jefferson entered, and she managed a smile.

"We've come to see Douglas," her mother said with social grace, yet her eyes retreated from looking at him.

Her father's face sagged into heavy lines, but his tone remained firm. "How are you, my dear?"

Unable to express her inner turmoil, she spoke with perfect composure. "I'm fine, thank you."

"The docta thinks we needn't stay, so we are goen now. I must call Felicia Humbolt and cancel her luncheon for you."

"Yes, of course," she agreed blankly.

"Is there anything you need?" her father inquired.

Aware that all his wealth and corporate power couldn't recapture Douglas' health or her happiness, she shook her head. "No, Father, there's nothing."

"We'll have the jet bring the McKenzies here, and they can stay with us," her father stated.

With the arrangements made, her father and mother departed. Pastor Jefferson lingered, his solicitous gaze meeting hers.

"Call me," he said.

She sensed the wisdom of unanswerable questions not asked, of his assumption of her need and his willingness to meet it. She managed a genuine smile. He laid his hand on her head and murmured a brief benediction before he left.

During the day Douglas' fevered mumblings clutched at her soul. The strain of soothing him in his periods of pain wracked lucidity or watching as he succumbed to anesthesia and fevered sleep wore her to numbness.

Late in the afternoon, a nurse with pert features, who wore a pantsuit uniform and a teacup-shaped cap on her short coppery hair, carried in a syringe on a tray.

"Good dye to ye. I be Annie Dunbar. Yer tum be complainin' to ye, laddie? Howlin' like the very devil, is it? Ye tell me if ye be needin' somethin' for it, okay now?"

Douglas' fever-brightened eyes flickered to Annie's in mute supplication then his eyelids drooped closed. As she watched Annie inject his arm, sentience jabbed her and involuntarily she jerked.

"Ye be gettin' some rest now too, my pretty lass. Waitin' be devilishly hard on them what's close by."

Annie Dunbar left, withdrawing her Celtic vibrancy, and the room settled around her more lifeless than before. She covered Douglas' hand on the bed and drowsed on the ruffled edges of exhaustion.

She came to awareness slumped forward, her cheek on the bedspread disturbingly near Douglas' bandaged abdomen as Dr. Rhye listened to it with a stethoscope. Douglas' eyes struggled to find hers, and they glinted with silent entreaty. His suffering cramped her soul, but she stood and applied a bright, answering smile.

Dr. Rhye moved around the bed toward her. "You should go home now and get some rest. You'll become ill yourself if you aren't careful."

The doctor picked up her shoulder bag and ushered her out of the room. As the door closed, her resolution stirred and she turned, pushing it open. A bright turquoise gaze met hers, and Annie propelled her down the corridor with a surprisingly solid grip on her elbow.

"Aye, 'tis hard leavin' your beloved in the care of strangers, but we'll be doin' our best fer the lad."

In his clearer moments he knew Connie sat beside him, holding his hand or touching his hair, and her presence comforted him. Without her, specific sources of discomfort assailed him: the nasal catheter irritated his throat; the IV needle stung his arm; his muscles protested against the incision and too-tight stitches. He knew his appendix had been removed and he would miss a few days' work, but he desired solely to remain in bed and lie utterly still with Connie holding his hand.

Firm fingers moved against his abdomen and a flare of pain sparkled stars behind his eyelids. He choked and dragged his arm across his face during the agonizing examination. Annie Dunbar held his hand, imparting solace until Dr. Rhye pulled the sheet up over him.

"Ye be a bit tender, lad. You'll be wantin' somethin' to help ye."

Tenacious throes clawed at him until the sedation took effect. Then he floated in the eerie twilight space between consciousness and sleep, the peculiar swirling melody of Mendelssohn's *Fingal's Cave* accompanying him on his downward spiral.

Friday morning, dressed in a lime green pantsuit, she walked down the corridor, visualizing Douglas after a night of restful hospitalization, sitting up and eating breakfast off of a tray.

From the door, she saw Douglas leaning back quietly in bed, too quietly, his flushed cheeks advertising the fever which burned much too hotly in his body. A frown creased his forehead attesting to persistent torment. His condition downed her expectation, and she pressed her fingers to her lips to stifle a sob. She rallied and strode across the room, certain her presence would rouse him.

"Hello, Darling. How are you?" Douglas was unresponsive, and she shifted to gain his attention, smoothing his hair over his ear. "Darling...? Douglas...? Douglas?!" Frightened by his stupor, she forced herself not to clasp him convulsively to her.

Dr. Rhye appeared, and concern accentuated the lines in his face. "Constance, please come with me."

Apprehension constricted her breathing as she followed the doctor into the corridor.

"After Douglas' appendix ruptured, the infection spread very rapidly, and the antibiotics he isn't allergic to aren't very effective. His fever is up. His white count is up. The prognosis is not good. I haven't been able to reach his parents, but they must be notified."

Alarm prickled her scalp. "Notified?"

"Acute peritonitis is always serious and often fatal."

"No! You must do something!"

"We're doing everything possible."

She struggled to contain her sobs and turned away, drawing on her waning self-control.

"You may stay with him if you like."

She was certain the power of their love would protect Douglas, and she returned to stand at his side. She stroked his hair and repeatedly told him she loved him, weak, ineffective efforts to assuage his anguish.

A continuous array of MDs, MTs, RNs, and LPNs—the entire medical alphabet—well-trained to help and to heal, flowed in and out of Douglas' room, vying for his survival. His body twitching, he moaned incoherently. From the gray upholstered chair, she laid her head on the bedspread and prayed with tears for Douglas to be well.

When Dr. Rhye and Annie Dunbar reappeared, her soul searched for hope, but their inscrutable faces refuted it.

"If you'll excuse us a moment," the doctor said.

Reluctant to leave, she slid her fingers from Douglas' and allowed them to linger on his wrist in farewell.

In the restroom, she leaned back against the yellow tiled wall and closed her eyes. Away from Douglas, alone with her health and vitality, relief bloomed. Then a draft of compunction withered it. She glanced in the mirror, meeting her eyes, troubled violet pools in a pale marble face. She ran water over her hands, its flow drawing the tension from her neck and shoulders. She dried her hands and applied lotion, rubbing them together in a socially acceptable manner which helped loosen her taut nerves. She reapplied blush and lipstick and fluffed her hair with a brush—just in case Douglas should notice. Dedication urged her to leave the haven of the restroom, and she strode the length of the corridor. The weight of returning to Douglas to sit helplessly and watch him suffer caused a weariness beyond words.

Dr. Rhye's examination left spasms convulsing him, and he drifted in a solitary realm of misery. Unbidden, tears trickled from beneath his lashes until Connie patted them away with the gentle touch of a tissue.

"I am sorry, Darling. I wish I could have been here for you."

Connie's devotion sustained him, and he tried to ascend the red haze toward her. The voracious fiend devouring his vitals bit sharply, and a groan escaped.

Annie Dunbar administered medication that eventually subdued the demons. His hand on Connie's, he retreated into blissful nothingness....

He surfaced from drugged sleep, and familiar voices drifted in from a distance. With a great effort he raised heavy eyelids; with further effort he turned his head on his pillow. Connie emerged from the fog, and he focused on the one face in all the world he wanted to see.

Connie stroked his hair saying, "I love you, Douglas. I love you, Douglas."

Mom hovered above him, sponging his face and chest with a cool, moist cloth, reassuring him of her love also. Her brown eyes in her too deeply lined face were clouded, and regret that he had worried her burdened his soul.

"Mom—" With no strength for speech, his apology died unspoken.

"We came as soon as we could. I had no idea you were ill and needed surgery. Terry and I were with Pop while he evaluated a new job site near a recreation area yesterday. We just got the doctor's phone call early this morning."

"Mr. Oakland sent his jet," Terry explained from somewhere out there.

"And a chauffeured Lincoln brought us here," Pop concluded.

He viewed his family, glad that they had come. Yet further awareness brought misgivings.

His abdomen bulged hot, sore, and drum-tight. *This fire shouldn't be blazing inside me,* he thought. *This isn't normal recovery from a simple operation....Something is terribly wrong.*

Apprehensive, he sought for something to hold. Connie's hand closed over his, and her touch held his mind steady.

A pain writhed deep within him bringing a wave of sickness. With disaster imminent, he struggled against confining tubes and lines.

"Mom—!"

The turbulence erupted, doubling him over.

"Get Annie!" Connie exclaimed.

Mom and Connie knelt on the bed to support him, and he clung to them in the rending, odorous upheaval. Humiliated and shaking, he collapsed against Connie, doubting he would survive.

Dear God, no— The plea blazed in the back of his mind. *Don't let me die now! Not before I marry Connie.*

His cheek pressed against something soft, and he heard the flutter of Connie's heart. In spite of this closeness, he realized that death's sharp sickle could sever them. Unbidden, the dirge from Chopin's *Second Piano Sonata* tolled in his mind.

A deep pall descended on his spirit, and he remained conscious by a supreme effort. He knew he must hold tight or he would float irretrievably away. With the cessation of everything precious threatening him, only his hand on Connie's expressed what he felt in the final moments of companionship.

18
Critical Condition

$\mathcal{D}$ ouglas lay utterly still, and cold expanding dread filled her chest.

Dear God, he can't be dead! Please! Please, let Douglas live!

Terry reappeared with Annie Dunbar, Dr. Rhye, and a blond young man in a white tunic. He introduced himself as Dr. Tumwell and bade them leave with a curt nod. She relinquished her burden, her arms aching sweetly from Douglas' weight.

She followed the McKenzies into the corridor, and minutes later Dr. Rhye <u>emerg</u>ed from the room.

"Douglas' condition has deteriorated considerably."

Fear shook her heart. "Do anything you must to make him well. I have $25,000." She waved the checkbook she had withdrawn from her shoulder bag.

Dr. Rhye's fingers covered hers. "Money isn't the issue. In retrocecal appendicitis, a secondary abscess may form under the diaphragm. I suspect that is the case with Douglas. His condition is very critical. I called in a specialist who examined him. We'll drain the abscess, but— After developing an ileus, recovery can rarely be expected. There's not much hope."

She heard Mrs. McKenzie's stifled sob and felt herself sliding downward into a void until Mr. McKenzie's hand on her elbow steadied her.

"Constance, why don't you go home and rest?"

"I don't want to go home and have you tell me later that Douglas died!"

"Let me give you something."

Certain nothing would ease the pain of Douglas' death, she rolled her head against the wall. "Nooo," she said fretfully. "I don't want anything. I don't want to sleep. I want to stay with Douglas. I want him to be well!" She grasped Dr. Rhye's arm with both hands.

"The surgery will take some time. You may wait outside the surgical suite."

With a brief apologetic pressure she released the doctor's sleeve.

She followed the McKenzies to the waiting room and seated herself in a square green chair across from them. She clasped her fingers together, anxiety straining her self-control. Mrs. McKenzie wiped her eyes with a crumpled tissue and sniffed.

"Douglas is a very determined young man," Mr. McKenzie said. "He'll lick this thing."

Having witnessed Douglas' collapse and having held his limp body in her arms, she doubted his chances of survival. The mere idea of living day by day through the years without him was incomprehensible, and she neither wept nor spoke in her grief.

Her father and mother and Penny arrived, silvery tears trickling down her sister's wan cheeks.

"Dr. Rhye called," Penny explained.

She caught her sister's outstretched fingers in her own and clung to them.

"How are you, Constance deah?" her mother asked, laying a gentle hand on her hair.

She shrugged her shoulders in a helpless gesture. She buried her face against her father's shirt front, but his embrace failed to soothe her heart.

"We're so very sorry," her father said.

She performed her introductions, but the tremor in her tone couldn't be controlled.

Her father and Mr. McKenzie shook hands with mutual appraisal in their manner.

Her mother took Mrs. McKenzie's hand. "We are pleased to meet you."

Mrs. McKenzie clasped her mother's hand in both of hers. "Douglas has written us so much about you."

"He is such a charmen young man. We are so sorry he's ill."

Terry led Penny forward to sit beside him while she and their parents seated themselves.

"It's surprising what one thinks of at a time like this," her father mused.

Everyone looked toward him, wanting to be diverted.

"Douglas is a young man who commits himself to a goal and pursues it to an exacting end. That dedication is rare and admirable, but it has also cost him at times. He was so determined to save money toward his house that he neglected regular maintenance of his Volvo and had to buy another car. Now I can't help thinking this appendix thing—"

Her mind leaped to the conclusion it had resisted. Douglas was too stubborn to see a doctor. He waited too long—and now he's going to die.

Had she tasted the richness of love, security, and happiness, been drawn out of herself and invested in another to have it all end in hopelessness and loss?

She crossed her legs at the knees and rotated her ankle to relieve her tension. She noticed Penny and Terry as they sat together, and her heart clamored for her own dear love. Now, more than during Douglas' first surgery, she needed the sustaining force of his presence to fill the gaping empty space in her life where fear had sprung up and taken root. She sat quietly, conscious of a spreading desolation.

Pastor Jefferson and Margie entered the waiting area, and he explained that Dr. Rhye had phoned. The reason for their coming coursed fright through her in a cold wave. As she introduced them, Mrs. McKenzie's eyes reddened and Mr. McKenzie turned away.

Margie sat holding her hand in a silence more comforting than words or murmuring words that were brief and appropriate. Margie eventually excused herself with an explanation about rescuing the babysitter.

The evening crept inexorably forward as Mrs. McKenzie wept softly in the background.

Dr. Rhye reappeared in the waiting area in a baggy green suit, a mask around his neck.

Her heart labored beneath her ribs. "Douglas—?"

The doctor pressed his palm to his forehead. "He's in the recovery room. His fever is much too high. His blood pressure is much too low. He's very weak, very unstable. His chances are very poor." Dr. Rhye gestured indefinitely, turned, and disappeared behind the double doors.

Penny's gray, green shadowed eyes narrowed. "So help me, if Douglas dies and we have to cancel all the events planned in your honor and go into mourning before we've worn all our lovely new clothes, I shall never speak to him again!"

The impact of Douglas' death annihilating their dream jolted her mind. The image of him wearing his navy tuxedo in a coffin wavered before her as she retreated into blackness....

Pungent fumes penetrated her nose and blood returned to her brain, dispersing the gray wisps. From her father's arms she noticed the nurse squatting beside her. The family circled about her with a ring of unfamiliar professionals behind them. Embarrassment pervaded her inner being, but she regathered her equanimity and attempted a reassuring smile. Her father helped her to her feet, and she crossed the room unsteadily to the sofa. Pastor Jefferson sat beside her and she met his eyes. The personal sorrow in their depths stilled her heart.

With the vanishing of hope from her life, her golden future receded behind a dusky horizon. She slid the ring from her finger and stared at the diamonds, reliving the moment Douglas had placed it on the blueprints and asked her to share his dream. She recalled him slipping it on her finger when they had become reengaged and their promise that nothing would interfere with their destiny. A stinging mistiness dimmed the diamonds' luster.

"I am so scared," she admitted to Pastor Jefferson. "Douglas' love, his direction and strength of purpose are the guiding forces in my life. If he dies, I shall die."

"This needn't be the calamity of *Romeo and Juliet*," Pastor Jefferson said softly. "You are devoted to Douglas and he loves you beyond measure, but human love is frail and susceptible to tragedy. Only God's love is perfect and unfailing. He alone is able to sustain you in every circumstance."

"Perhaps in some magical way I expected Douglas to fill the emptiness in my life."

"Jesus is the only One Who can fill your life and give it meaning and purpose," Pastor Jefferson explained.

"All I want is to share our dream as Douglas planned it."

"A dream is a wonderful thing to share, but no matter how noble or desirable it is you cannot build your life on it, for it is only an illusion. You must build your life on the solid foundation of God and His Word."

"What if death intrudes?"

"Death is the hardest thing in life, but Jesus knows all about death—and dying. Because His resurrection conquered death there is life beyond the grave. The moment Douglas asked Jesus to forgive his sin he received everlasting life. We have the confident expectation of being together again."

Cold to the heart and little comforted, she objected, "I want Douglas here, now." She pressed her forefinger against the knee of her green slacks. "We have a future together— The gala pre-nuptials, completing his house, our wedding— Life with Douglas is supposed to end happily ever after, not just end."

"Connie, this is not a fairytale prince-and-princess-they-all-lived-happily-ever-after world. Despite our rejecting it and our pleas to God to spare Douglas' life, he could pass into Heaven." Pastor Jefferson's throat worked but no sound came, and he removed his glasses to cover his eyes with his hand.

With a dull horror in the back of her mind, she slid the ring onto her finger.

Each minute passed as an hour, and images from the past two years with Douglas projected across the screen of her memory.

Dr. Rhye reappeared, and she lifted her fingers to her tight throat. The family gathered around for another report.

"Douglas has been moved to the ICU. He's asking for Constance."

"Asking—?"

Douglas being alive and able to communicate lightened her spirit, and she followed the doctor briskly down the corridor.

She entered the alien environment of the Intensive Care Unit where machinery beeped and whirred with electronic and mechanical noises. A nurse directed her to Douglas, who was barely recognizable, unshaven, his hair matted. Hollows replaced the attractive curve of his cheeks, and his dark eyelashes contrasted with his deathlike pallor.

Comprehension seeped into her. *Dr. Rhye was right. He isn't going to survive this.*

Her blood iced, but she crept forward and slipped her fingers into Douglas'.

"Con?"

"I'm here, Darling."

Douglas' eyes flickered open without focusing until they found hers. "My house— It's yours. It's always—been yours ..." Douglas shuddered from pain and exertion. "Finish it— Remember me. Love you—always ..." His eyelids closed with a finality that slammed through her.

"No! NO...!" She clawed past hissing, gurgling machinery and flung her arm across his chest. "Darling! Douglas! Please, come back! I can't live without you!"

A firm grip on her shoulder pulled her away.

"You must leave at once," the nurse said. "He needs his rest."

Certain of his eternal rest, she barely managed to restrain a cry of terror.

To never see Douglas again— To be deprived of his attractive, charming presence forever— To never hear his voice— To know he exists no place on Earth— Never to experience the ecstasy of being loved by him—

Desperate to remain with Douglas, she hurled herself into the abyss of his death. "I want to stay with him! I want to die with him!" Panic transformed her usually well-modulated voice into a shriek.

Strong hands wrenched her from Douglas' side and propelled her from the ICU.

The catastrophe of ultimate separation shattered her composure. She lost her manners, her dignity, and her inbred self-control all together. She pounded her fists against the door of the ICU, screaming entreaties and uttering uncouth noises in her despair. Nurses hustled her away. Unable to prevail against them or the marauding force of death, she ran from the hospital.

Isolated from thought she drove unaware, arriving at Douglas' house in the June dawn. *"Go home," Dr. Rhye said, and this is where I came. "Finish it— Remember me," Douglas said, but it will never be a home without him.*

Inside she sank onto the bottom stair and remembered being there with Douglas only a week ago. His presence, so close yet so far away, twisted her soul. Unable to contain her anguish she wailed, the sound echoing around her. Intensively, extensively she entreated God to spare Douglas' life, panting with exertion.

"Dear God, I love him. I need him so. He has to survive. He's the center of my life. He's my reason for living."

I will be the center of your life. I will make your life worth living.

Insufficiency lodged within her, and she beat her fists against her thighs. "Without him I have nothing."

Unintentionally she recalled her disconsolation when Douglas had broken their engagement. *I thought I had lost Douglas then too, our dream destroyed. But Linda told me Jesus could make everything all right. He did then—saving me ... Linda also told me Jesus could protect me from missing Douglas so badly and help me tolerate all those separations. Jesus would comfort me. He would be there in my loneliness. But Douglas was the only thing on earth I wanted. Only his presence would suffice.*

The distinct possibility that Douglas' presence could be removed from the earth choked her so she could hardly breathe. In the overwhelming flood of grief she cried out, more desperate for God than she had ever been in her life. "Jesus, I confess. You must be the Source of my life. You must be more significant to me than Douglas. If Douglas dies and our dream dies with him, I must base my life on Something more solid than a dream. It must be based on my relationship with You."

The Lord is my Rock and my salvation, she remembered from her Bible reading.

She knelt at the foot of the stairs with her elbows on a step and dropped her forehead into her palms. "Dear Jesus, please help me."

My grace is sufficient. I AM all you will ever need.

Gradually stability settled within her, and she lay with her arms beneath her cheek as she tumbled into the vortex of exhaustion.

❧

He came awake in slow stages, certain his life would end this way, alone in the dark behind his eyelids. He wondered where his folks and the Oaklands were, but he longed for the sustaining power of Connie's presence. Her wild cries reverberated through the corridors of his mind, and he sensed their vital connection had been severed.

"Paul ..."

His friend's touch on his shoulder roused him, and he summoned his waning strength. "I don't want—another—separation. Too far—too long."

"Ssshhh." The pressure on his shoulder increased, bringing slight consolation. "'The sorrows of death compassed me ...'" Paul softly quoted.

Death hovered so close it seemed to smother him.

"'Then called I upon the name of the LORD: O LORD, I beseech thee, deliver my soul.'"

Please ...

Wavering in and out of consciousness, he only comprehended fragments of Scripture as Paul spoke.

"'Return unto thy rest, O my soul; ...'"

He heard the ethereal strains of Holst's *Venus* as the forces ravaging his body dragged him closer to Paradise. The driving force to share his dream with Connie tugged him back. Molten rivulets burned through him, and the anesthesia of death beckoned. *Let me go ... I'll go to Heaven—see the Master Planner. Tell Jesus, Thank You.* His spirit lifted, and a bright cloud seemed to draw him upward.

"Tell Connie—can't stay—" The old, cold, hard ache of separation filled his chest.

"'For thou hast delivered my soul from death ... I will walk before the LORD in the land of the living ...'" Paul continued.

He had not the energy to live nor the desire to die. Beneath the dilemma in his soul, his will functioned. *It's up to me ... if I hold on ... if I let go....* With a supreme effort he clung to his departing senses. *I will not let go. Dying isn't in the plan. I will not die.* "I will walk before the Lord in the land of the living."

Light fractured into brilliant strands, shifted, drew him to awareness, and voices drifted in from behind the billowing mist.

I've died, he thought. *Is this Heaven? There's such agony ...*

"Douglas! Douglas...?"

He was too wracked with pain to draw breath, and his mind wandered back into oblivion.

⁓

Stifling heat prickled against her face, and she awakened on the stairs. Woozy from heartache and fatigue, she dragged herself up, gritty and wrinkled. Her chin in her palms, her elbows on her knees, she sat amidst a prevailing sense of doom. Douglas could have died and no one would know where to reach her. An ache grew in her chest, but knowledge would ease the maddening uncertainty. She must know if all that mattered most to her in the world had gone out of it, but resistance halted her. She could only do that with Jesus' help. She plumbed the depths of a Source of Strength not her own and tottered to the door.

At home in her room, she discarded her pantsuit, hastily showered, and dressed.

She drove to the hospital and returned to the waiting area outside the ICU.

Penny sat beside Terry with their fingers intertwined.

"The reverend and the doc are with Douglas. They really don't expect him ta make it." Terry's face contorted and moisture glistened in his dark eyes.

"His mother had one look at him and nearly wiped out. Mother had Potts come and take them home."

"Pop and your dad are about all washed up too. They went to get some coffee. The doc will tell us when—" Terry's jaw slackened and he ran his hand over his face.

She suppressed her alarm and met Penny's eyes, gray pools that threatened to overflow.

"If Douglas dies, what are you going to do?" Penny demanded.

Sharp reality slashed through her, and her hard drawn breath ended in a soft whimper. "I've cried and I've screamed and I will again, but Jesus will be with me in the hard times. And living without Douglas will be the hardest. A year ago Easter when I faced my sin, I asked Jesus into my life. Today when I faced something I couldn't handle, I asked Him to fill my life."

Penny's tears escaped. "That's going to keep you warm on cold winter nights?"

"It will help. Only the power of Jesus' resurrection will get me out of bed and into life every morning. It will be the only way I survive."

Her father and Mr. McKenzie wandered into the alcove and greeted her with weak smiles. Alternately they paced and sat on the sofa.

Sometime later Dr. Rhye approached. "I've just phoned Douglas' mother."

She knew her heart had stopped forever this time.

19
Resolution

"*D*ouglas' blood pressure has stabilized. He's out of immediate danger. He may just surprise us all and survive."

Fright departed in a dizzying wave, and she grasped the back of the sofa to steady herself.

"Thank You, God," she murmured amidst gasps of relief from the others.

"Douglas is still one very sick boy," Dr. Rhye cautioned.

During Douglas' days in the ICU, she awoke each morning resolved to endure what the day would bring, her family, her friends, her schedule, everything outside the hospital destined to wait or be canceled. She drove the McKenzies to the hospital, observed the courtesies, kept her smile in place, her hope up, and visited Douglas for fleeting minutes at prolonged intervals. She and the McKenzies returned to her home late at night to Mrs. White's light summer dinners and her parents' solicitous questions before she sought sanctuary in her room with a weariness too profound for tears.

❦

During his days in the ICU, waves of pain, which no amount of medication could dull, undulated through him. Semiconscious, he floated in the twilight space of delirium where a kaleidoscope of lights mingled with excerpts from the tumultuous *Ride of the Valkyries*, the raucous *Bolero*, the rapid, rhythmic *Sabre Dance*, and the intense *Four Seasons*. He knew his folks' and Connie's brief presence, the touch of their hands, and their soothing voices as they repeated that they loved him.

He rode from ICU toward his room elevated in bed, conscious of needles and tubes impaling him and the fevered illness which raged through every cell. In range of his half-open eyes, a shaft of sunlight haloed Connie's platinum hair, and he seemed to be looking at her from a great distance as she receded into the mist.

❧

She sat in the gray upholstered chair while Douglas slept, his breathing rapid and shallow, his tongue flitting over his parched lips. She waited sedately holding his hand or reading Psalms quietly to him when he roused. Mr. McKenzie desultorily read magazines while Mrs. McKenzie crocheted ecru thread into mounds of lace, watchful concern in their manner.

The McKenzies excused themselves for a late lunch and offered to bring her something. Too committed to Douglas to eat, she murmured her dissent. With a dubious maternal expression, Mrs. McKenzie followed Mr. McKenzie out.

Annie Dunbar approached with her bouncy gait and exchanged an empty IV bottle with a full one.

"It's amazin' Douglas still be amongst us. But he be one ver' sick lad with a lot of gettin' well to do. It'll be a long time before he's recoverin' completely."

The concept of prolonged illness slowed her pulse. *We don't have a lot of time. We're to be married in less than three weeks.* As she looked at Douglas, so ill, so inert, a thought surfaced with startling clarity. *He can't possibly achieve the dream the way he intended.*

The dream which had buoyed her life crashed on a reef of reality. Shaken and dazed, she mourned its loss with a paralysis of mind.

Yet the dream, so relentlessly pursued, so nearly obtained, must not be abandoned.

Douglas survived—thank God!—so should our dream.

Slowly her will rose to preserve it. Only she knew nothing of the complications and technical details of completing a house. How could she proceed with such a challenge? She who had always lived in luxury and ease and to whom every whim and desire had been granted. However, she had struggled to receive her degree in home economics, and with God's strength and guidance she had succeeded. Surely the dream, so vital to her existence, was worth all the effort she could invest in it. Yet dare she?

In his dying moment Douglas had told her to finish his house, it was hers. Considering his numerous conscious avowals to do it himself, she questioned the validity of the utterance. But when he had shown it to her, he had asked for her help.

Her eyes lingered on Douglas who was so feverish, so listless, and she had no idea how soon he would be well enough to complete his house. She lapsed into regret that the dream would never be as he planned.

Confronted by the inevitable, she knew she must work on Douglas' house, and she must begin very quickly in order to finish it before their wedding. Without access to his savings, she must start with her graduation money. She knew how he felt about that—immoveableness being one of his most noticeable traits. If she assisted him now, she risked losing the dream—perhaps forever—to achieve it. The concept of life without the dream, without Douglas' love, quaked the center of her being, and her mind churned over losing them because of his illness or his ire.

In the throes of indecision, she clenched her fingers until her nails caused painful furrows, and she rose to pace.

Dear God, what shall I do? I need wisdom and discernment.

From beyond herself came a strong impression on her mind: God intended for her to share a dream with Douglas and she should participate in attaining it.

Surely he will understand, she hoped, nibbling a gold polished fingernail.

Nevertheless, even ravaged by illness, Douglas had an indomitable set to his chin. She shook her head, trying to clear it of doubt.

She continued her prayer. *If this truly is what I should do, You must provide the courage and the ability. Please help Douglas to understand, and also give him the grace—and the good sense—to accept it.*

Peace and a Source of Strength stabilized her, and she seated herself in the chair beside Douglas' bed, secure in her resolution.

She withdrew the leather notebook from her purse and opened it to what she had written only two weeks before. As she read the small pages, images of exquisite decor filled her head. She was tempted to decorate the house the way she had initially envisioned it, and the habit of a lifetime vied with her promise to not buy anything unless Douglas agreed. He was in no condition to agree on what she could buy, but she limited her selections.

Now that she was committed to her course, hope and optimism stirred within her.

The McKenzies reappeared and paused at Douglas' bedside looking down at him, their brows and lips drawn into frowns with sadness.

Eventually Mrs. McKenzie settled into a chair and resumed her crocheting.

"I'm not much of a one for just sittin' 'round," Mr. McKenzie said as he rubbed the strain from his back.

To use her time spent in waiting, she read bridal magazines, made lists, devised color schemes, and sketched furniture placement diagrams until Douglas awakened.

His fingers sought hers, and she thrust the books into her purse before she slipped her hand into his.

That evening when Dr. Rhye and Annie Dunbar arrived, Douglas roused and slid the doctor a malevolent glare.

"Now, Douglas. I know I'm not able to replace Constance in your affection, but the poor girl needs to go home and rest. She hasn't left you long enough to eat."

Douglas questioned her with a glance, but she smiled in reassurance, for his presence provided adequate sustenance.

Loyalty obliged her to stay and share Douglas' ordeal, but hospital routine obliged her to leave. She stood and trailed her fingers along the back of his hand. Mr. McKenzie rose and clasped Douglas' shoulder; Mrs. McKenzie gathered up her tote and handbag and tousled his hair as they always did before they left him for the night.

"He isn't contagious," Dr. Rhye said. "You may kiss him good night."

Pleasant wonder flowed through her. Even though Douglas appeared ghastly, love fused her soul to his. She brushed the hair off his forehead and laid her lips there, tasting the salt tang. Every particle of her being longed for his rich, reciprocal kiss, but catastrophe had eclipsed the past and shadowed the future. Stifling a low cry, she fled from the room.

❧

In the absence following his folks' departure and Connie's kiss, Annie Dunbar cut away the bandage, and the prickling of his exposed skin prompted him to peek. His abdomen bulged, bright red antiseptic painted with a drainage tube sprouting grotesquely from his neatly laced incision.

"No wonder—I hurt."

"We inserted the drain so the pus in your belly will come out into the dressing," Dr. Rhye explained. "You're sore and distended, but under the circumstances that's not too unusual. By all odds you should have died. There was a time when I thought you had."

Memories of the ethereal cloud haunted him, but gladness that he had survived infused his spirit.

A slight smile twitched the corners of Dr. Rhye's thin lips. "You're stubborn, Douglas. Too stubborn to die."

As Annie rebandaged his violated middle, he thought, *Too stubborn to die. He's probably right.*

The next morning he sensed motion and a presence and felt a hand on his. He caught Connie's fingers in a tight grip.

"Let me call Kathy Parks. She'll give you something."

"No. Want to stay—with you." He lay panting a moment. "Talk—to me. It— helps."

"Mr. Scott, Mike Hall, and people from the church have asked about visiting you. Mother and Father and Penny are very concerned, but Dr. Rhye won't allow any visitors other than your parents and myself. They will come soon. I gave your father the keys to your Mercedes, and he enjoys driving it. It gives them more freedom. Terry and Penny ride around in her car, holding hands and looking that way at each other. Pastor Jefferson calls from youth camp every day, and he will come if you need him."

Connie's light conversation distracted him, but he could scarcely breathe without undue pain. The attempt at speech had exhausted him, and he descended into an illness induced stupor.

The tumultuous *Dance of the Furies*, the frenetic *Faust,* and the pounding conclusion of *Symphonie Fantastique* pursued him through fevered sleep until much later.

In the half-light between sleeping and waking, wafts of melody from the sweetly serene *Traumeri,* the calming *Gymnopedie No. 3,* and the relaxing repetition of the *Moonlight Sonata* drifted within his brain. He rested quietly, the music transcending the pangs. The high fever no longer raged unabated in his body, and he nestled against the pillows, certain he had spent several hours in natural, healing sleep. People who had almost died then taken a turn for the better did that, he knew. Perhaps he <u>would</u> recover.

He opened his eyes to greet Connie, at once feeling the sunny, compelling contact. The awe of the love of a lifetime ran deep and ineffable.

For the moment he desired nothing more than to simply look at her, yet he longed to phrase what his spirit was saying into words.

"Hello ... Sweetheart ..."

"Hello, yourself," Connie responded, delight in her tone. "How are you?"

"I think—I'm going—to be—all right." The nasal tube seemed to impede his voice, and effort accelerated his heart, but he persisted with stoic resolution. "Your love—saved my life." He raised his finger in tribute.

Sentience glowed in Connie's amethyst eyes, and she gave him one of her purposely dazzling smiles. Affection pulsed between them while his blood sang in his veins.

⁂

Friday morning slanting rays of sunlight streamed through the three narrow, two-story windows and lay in golden swaths on the rough living room floor of Douglas' house. It seemed strangely empty and lifeless without him as she toured it. The myriad details of what all needed to be finished—from the trim and painting, bathroom and kitchen cabinets and counter tops, kitchen hardware to doorknobs, flooring choices to the lighting fixtures—overfilled her mind, and she made a note to ask Mr. McKenzie for help.

She turned to her notations of colors, furnishings, and accessories. Their home would provide an aura of graciousness and welcome to represent her and Douglas' love for each other and to honor Jesus. Unable to contain her enthusiasm, she spun in a quick, little turn before worry over Douglas' reaction squelched it. However, she couldn't risk discussing her decision with him as ill as he was.

Confident Douglas still slept, she hurried to the hospital, intending to slip into his room before he awakened. As she approached his bed, his sharp blue gaze shattered her strategy around her, and she paused. Not as calm as she appeared, she flashed him an innocent smile.

"How are you this morning, Darling?"

"My insides—are—on fire."

Empathy contracted her stomach, and she sought to distract Douglas. "Where are your parents, Darling? Surely they should be here."

"It wasn't—my folks—I waited for—all night."

Her miscalculation jolted her.

"I had no idea— That is— I thought— You should be sleeping," she chided.

Douglas aimed a withering stare at her.

"I am sorry I wasn't here for you when you awakened," she said. "I want to be with you as much as possible. Goodness knows we were apart far too much, but I—" The explanation of her absence tingled on her tongue. She swallowed it because she dared not perturb Douglas and impede his recovery. She laid her palms on his shoulders. "Rest now, Darling, and I'll stay with you."

Douglas subsided into sleep, his languid fingers in hers. She recalled his blazing eyes and remorse nudged her conscience.

Now that he's better, I must be here even more. The need to stay with Douglas complicated the formidable task of completing his house, and she closed her eyes, swaying slightly. *Dear God, how am I going to do it?*

20
Recuperation

hat afternoon the McKenzies left to get Cokes, and she sat on the bed beside Douglas. He laid the back of his hand on her cheek, and she rubbed against it, the magnetism of attraction pulsing between them.

Annie Dunbar arrived and noted Douglas' vital signs before she asked, "How aboat gettin' up and takin' a stroll?"

Annie drew the sheet back, and Douglas regarded the nurse and herself with amazement.

"You mean—I'm getting up?"

She stood aside and watched Annie swivel Douglas' legs over the edge of the bed. He winced, and she kept her smile in place with an effort. Douglas straightened, bracing his abdomen with his hands. Suddenly colorless, he staggered sideways and collapsed. The IV stand toppled down with a clatter, and the bottle of liquid smashed on the floor. She stared at Douglas' inert body through billowy hazes and clung to the foot board until she retrieved her departing senses.

Annie snatched a pillow and elevated Douglas' legs.

"He— He's—" she faltered. The terror of Douglas' dying suspended her voice.

Annie checked Douglas' pulse and raised a limp eyelid and then glanced up at her. "Yer lad be standin' up too fast. He be fainted but noon the worse fer it."

177

"This is the first time I've ever seen anyone faint. Usually I— You almost had both of us on the floor."

Douglas' eyelashes fluttered and lifted, confusion in his eyes as they met hers.

She knelt beside him. "You've fainted, Darling," she said, relief rippling into a little giggle.

❧

Connie's laughter permeated his lightheadedness, and he covered his eyes with his arm.

I thought I was getting better. But I can't even stand up! And Connie couldn't faint with me. Oh, no! She had to watch and laugh! She's seen the tears and the sickness and the pain. Why did she have to see me sprawled on the floor in a faint?

Disgrace seared his soul.

"Darling...?"

"Go away."

"Doug-las ..."

"Get out of here and leave me alone!"

His eyes stung, but he vowed, *I will not cry. And I will not faint again—ever!*

A hefty orderly in starched white deposited him uncomfortably in bed. When the shards of glass and liquid had been mopped away and Annie had inserted the IV again, he turned to absorb Connie's tender presence, but the gray upholstered chair was vacant. He had been aware of her spicy-sweet scent and fashionable appearance as she had sat beside him; her composure and fortitude had sustained his existence. Now in his pride he had ordered her away. The familiar lonesomeness recurred, and memories of Bach's pensive *Air on the G String* suited his dolor until his folks returned.

❧

Abruptly freed from visiting Douglas, she walked away from the hospital, the separation between them more impenetrable than glass and brick walls.

Why did he insist I leave? she questioned as the sting of his dismissal supplanted the shock of his fainting. *I've suffered through every second with him—my heart weeping for him, hardly eating, scarcely sleeping.*

Irritation opposed affection, and she drove rapidly in and out of Denver traffic. In front of her home she jolted her Audi to a stop. *He wants me out, I'll stay out!*

Saturday morning in the sun-filled breakfast room, she lingered over her orange juice with her parents and Mr. and Mrs. McKenzie at the oak table. "When Douglas graduated and showed me the blueprints for his house, he intended to present it to me as a gift, complete in every detail. Since he is unable to do that, I must complete it for him, but I know nothing of the complications and technical details of finishing a house." She addressed Mr. McKenzie directly. "When you're not visiting Douglas, could you possibly assist me?"

"If I take over for Douglas as the general contractor, there is quite a lot I can do to help you."

"I can refer you to the subcontractors you may need," her father offered.

"As ill as Douglas is, we must not discuss it with him and hinder his recovery," she cautioned.

The parents murmured assent.

She left her father and Mr. McKenzie to discuss the particulars and drove into Denver. She assembled her master chart of small swatches and paint samples for every room to have an overall view of the color scheme. She selected the exact tint of yellow paint, and she shopped for carpet, draperies, appliances, furniture, and accessories with a rare intensity of purpose. She recalled the plans she and Douglas had made to select their furniture last Saturday, only last Saturday Douglas had almost died. The horror of unbelievable loss froze her spine, and then relief that he was recovering thawed it. As she purchased items for their aesthetic contribution, the dream began to materialize and gratification spiraled her spirit upward.

❧

He tolerated Dr. Rhye's removing the nasal tube, but he endured the examination and Kathy Parks's changing the bandage by the sheer effort of his will.

"You're still sore and have a fever," the doctor said. "But you must exercise to maintain your circulation and regain your strength. Walking around will help."

Remembering his last debacle, he glowered at Dr. Rhye.

"Don't stand up so fast. Let Kathy help you."

The familiar nervousness crinkled in his stomach, and he balked at another failure.

The doctor's verbal prodding and Kathy's brown fingers on his arm with firm professionalism propelled him beyond his discomfort. His abdomen and legs felt too weak to support him, but he forced them to function and concentrated on setting one foot in front of the other. Stabilized by the nurse's strength, he tottered forward a few steps, his breath uneven.

"You'll get better," Kathy encouraged.

He rolled back onto his bed, and exhaustion pressed him flat against his pillows. He stared at the ceiling, loathing his painful recuperation.

Before noon a curly-haired Spanish aide set a tray on the table in front of him. She removed plastic covers to reveal clear soup, red gelatin, and tea; the mental clarion vigor of Purcell's *Trumpet Voluntary* heralded his first meal in ten days. He was so weak the spoon rattled against the dish, but the texture and flavors revived his appetite. His stomach discarded the offending fare. Disgusted, he muttered invectives through his teeth.

While he sat in the gray upholstered chair, the unperturbed aide returned his bed to spotless normalcy.

Alone he lapsed into bitter reflection. *I can't even eat! I can't walk. I can't brush my teeth. I've been too sick to spit! All I'm able to do is lie here and feel rotten. I've felt rotten forever, and I'll always feel rotten!*

⁓

Sunday afternoon she reclined on a chaise beside the pool and accepted phone calls from her friends.

Later her thoughts turned to Pastor Jefferson's sermon. "'... a man of sorrows and acquainted with grief: ... Surely he hath borne our griefs and carried our sorrows: ...' so Jesus is able to sympathize with us in our trials," the pastor had said.

She admitted her life had revolved around Douglas until he almost died. Then her perspective had been realigned. Jesus had provided comfort, help, and consolation in the life and death crisis; now she needed His forgiveness and grace for day to day life with Douglas. Still this breach wounded her, and she retreated inward until she encountered the peace of Jesus' presence. It mitigated the hurt of Douglas' rejection, and she allowed him this time alone.

The telephone rang beside her. Minimally curious, she picked it up. "Hullo?"

"Why don't you—come visit me? Now that you've seen me—sprawled out in a faint, don't you want—to see me again?"

Her pulse leaped at Douglas' voice, but his unfairness sparked her ire. "Now listen here, Douglas Alan McKenzie—"

The dial tone buzzed in her ear.

Dressed in a blue pantsuit, she rounded the corner outside Douglas' room where she found Mrs. McKenzie weeping into a tissue.

Her thoughts tumbled toward panic. "Douglas—" she managed, hurrying forward.

Mrs. McKenzie lifted her pudgy face and daubed at her red, swollen eyes. "He's so cross and impossible. Pop left, but I thought I could help."

Empathizing with Mrs. McKenzie, she laid her arm around the woman's shoulders.

The equanimity she displayed hid her vexation with Douglas as she strode into his room.

Why aren't you—ever here?"

"Ever here? I spent <u>hours</u> with you until you threw me out," she reminded, pointing toward the door. "Were you your usual intractable self to your mother until you reduced her to tears?"

Anger flamed in Douglas' eyes. "You have no idea—what this has been like! I hate being confined to bed—with this raging bellyache. I hate the incessant IVs—and injections. And I hate bed baths! I can't do one thing—for myself, and I hate—having people do things—for me!"

Douglas' vehemence shook her resolution, but compassion compelled her. She leaned against the bed, cupping his feverish cheeks in her palms.

"So much infection, so much suffering," she sympathized.

"Being sick is the worst thing in the world. And recuperation isn't much easier!"

Disregarding the unreasonableness of the ill and fretful, she laid her hands on Douglas' shoulders and soothed away his temper by degrees.

"Jesus is able to give you grace to endure. He's here with you and will be your Source of comfort."

"I know, Con. I really am glad He is. I want my folks—to know and let Him—into their lives—but how will I be able—to tell them of His love and salvation—when all I do is complain?" Dissatisfaction and fever brightened Douglas' eyes.

She sat beside Douglas on the bed. "We needed Jesus to die for us; now we need Jesus to live in us. You must appropriate His power to have victory in recuperation. I must have His guidance in all I need to do."

She contemplated telling Douglas what she had accomplished in his house, but following his outburst about people doing things for him she refrained.

"You were right, Con. When I first became ill—Monday evening, I should have let you—call the doctor. I would have had—my appendix out, but it would have been over—and done in a few days. I would be well <u>now</u>. I'm sorry for what you—and my folks—have been through—because of my stubbornness."

Douglas' remorse consoled her, and she leaned forward to lay her cheek against his chest. Hearing his heartbeat beneath her ear, she confided, "I was so afraid I would lose you."

In spite of the IV, Douglas' arms closed around her. "I was afraid—I would lose you too. But I had to live—long enough to love you. I'm so glad you're here."

She raised her eyes to Douglas, and his lips touched hers with a brief, sweet contact that recaptured the wonderful security and delight of the first kiss after so much time apart. Misty with pleasure she nestled in his embrace until all her hurt and the fear his illness had produced dissolved.

Annie Dunbar appeared beside the bed. The nurse's pause drew her attention to their position, and embarrassment suffused her despite their innocence. Douglas released her, and she stood nearby while Annie checked his vital signs.

"Aye, lad, yer heart rate be up, yer blood pressure be up too. Ye might be recuperatin' that much quicker now if yer loved ones didn't excite ye so."

Remembering Douglas' condition, she questioned him with a glance. His long, silky lashes drifted down over one eye in a gesture that cartwheeled her heart.

I wonder what that did to my blood pressure ...

⁑

Thursday morning Mom sat beside him, her eyes on the TV screen as her crochet hook glinted.

Succumbing to utter boredom, he exhaled audibly. *Two weeks ... I've been in this abominable bed for two weeks!*

Impatiently he moved then flinched and rubbed his abdomen.

"Turn that stupid thing off! Every commercial I see reminds me of my house— which isn't getting done while I lie here on my backside doing nothing!"

"Connie rented it for you because she thought it would help pass the time," Mom reminded.

"No way does it replace her."

"Now that you're getting better, she doesn't need to stay with you."

"I need her more now during these tedious days of recuperation than I did during my critical illness. What's she doing that's so important she can't visit me?"

Mom ignored his irritability, as she had when he was ill as a child, and answered mildly. "She visits you every day, but it takes a lot of time to prepare for the kind of wedding she's having." Mom laid her crocheting aside and tucked the bedding around him, giving his head a pat. "Try to get some sleep, hon."

"I don't want to sleep! I want to go home and get busy!" he said, rising from his pillows.

"You know you can't. You're only able to sit up in the overstuffed chair or walk around for a few minutes at a time."

The truth exasperated him, but he had demonstrated to himself that he still lacked strength.

"But I must do something." His brain pressed forward, thwarted by his aching, lethargic body. "Before I became ill there weren't enough hours in my days, but without anything it, a day expands endlessly!"

Impatiently he twisted the edge of the sheet. If only I could take this time I'm *wasting and save it up. If only I hadn't waited so long to see a doctor. If only it wasn't taking so long to get well.* His thoughts wavered from self-reproach to the apathy of despair.

He vaguely recalled that Mom had excused herself to go to his apartment to fix lunch for Pop and Terry, but he thought they were staying with Oaklands.

The bright stripes of sunshine slanting in through the venetian blinds slipped off his bedspread, measuring the progression of time as hours crawled past. They fell wasted into history while he waited: waited for Connie, waited to be well. In a furor of inactivity he drummed his fingers on the sheet. He telepathically entreated Connie to arrive and noticed the IV fluid dripping from the bottle. Inadvertently he began to count....

Connie entered, sweet and very appealing in a pink belted pantsuit, bringing a vitality that invigorated him. He caught her hands in his and drew her toward him. Her lips met his, and he cradled her head in his palm to prolong the kiss.

"You're the best medicine I've had all day."

Connie sat beside him on the bed and fed him his red gelatin. His interest in the unvarying, unappetizing meal revived.

"I am sorry I couldn't come earlier, Darling. Penny and I were completing our trousseau—yours and mine—and Penny loves to shop. Our mothers finalized the details for the rehearsal dinner, letting everyone know the date and place and—" Connie stopped with the spoon in midair. "What if you are still in the hospital?"

21
Jeopardy

*7*he noisy hospital routine awakened him on Sunday and he assessed his condition. Better rested and clearer headed than previously, he lay comfortably against his pillows, hearing the airy, melodic *Morning* from Grieg's *Peer Gynt Suite*. He smiled at the golden dawn pouring over him.

That afternoon Paul arrived and stood beside the bed. "Your doctor is allowing more visitors, but he is restricting us to visiting hours. You're looking better than when I last saw you. It's amazing you survived. Your father and Mr. Oakland were talking about final arrangements with me. I tried to explain that you would be in Heaven because you accepted Jesus into your life, but they were too distressed to understand. Sometimes family members are receptive to Jesus at a time like that, clinging to any hope. At other times the loss is too difficult, as yours would have been."

He had a chilly, eerie sense of viewing his demise.

"I prayed for you, my friend. Oh, how I prayed—that the Great Physician would spare your life by the power of His blood and in the authority of His Name. Since He has, we give Him all the glory, praise, honor, and worship He deserves."

Thankfulness streamed into his spirit. Nevertheless, he confided his frustration in recuperation to Paul. His friend listened in silent comfort and offered encouragement.

With the innate timing of a visit, Paul laid a palm on his shoulder in a benediction, asking God to bring healing and perseverance until his health had been restored. Then his friend withdrew.

He heard voices in the corridor and then Connie, Penny, and Terry entered.

"Well, look at you!" Penny exclaimed. "If it isn't the Tragic Hero!"

Terry grabbed his hand and worked it like a pump handle. "Boy, am I happy to see you!"

Talking simultaneously and finishing each other's sentences, Penny and Terry informed him of the obligations they had fulfilled for him. He watched them as a tennis match, amazed and amused, but hardly comprehending.

Mom and Pop and Mr. and Mrs. Oakland arrived laden with wedding presents.

He extended his hand, yellow with bruises from the IVs, and Mr. Oakland shook it with an expressive grasp. Mrs. Oakland brushed the vicinity of his ear with her lips.

Nearly bouncing in her excitement, Connie watched as he pulled decorative paper from the gifts while their families shared in the festivity. Silver, china, and crystal sparkled in his room while linens and household appliances accumulated on his bed. The tangible elements of their dream enforced his sense of isolation, and he accepted them with ambivalence.

Monday morning an aide placed his tray on the table in front of him. Unenthusiastic about more fruit gelatin for breakfast, he lifted the lids and stared at a feast of oatmeal, eggs, toast, and juice.

Later Kathy Parks arrived and sat beside him on his bed to remove the IV needle. He was free from his tether, and another bandage marked all that remained of the innumerable IVs. A tentative bubble of hope inflated within him.

"Does this mean I'm going home today?"

"You'll have to ask Dr. Rhye about that."

Kathy helped him into the blue velour robe and brown leather slippers Mom had left for him, and he tottered into the corridor. He had no degree of confidence in his knees, but Kathy's brown hand under his elbow steadied him.

"You're doing okay, but it will take time for you to regain your stamina."

Dizzy from exertion, he returned to his room and rested against the pillows.

Dr. Rhye appeared, and he bared his midriff for the doctor's examination. Dr. Rhye probed the tenderest areas, but he met the doctor's inquisitive gaze, his jaw rigid to mask the pangs. The stethoscope glided over his abdomen, up his chest, and down his back. The doctor straightened and let the stethoscope's earpieces hang on his neck, the instrument dangling.

"Can I go home?"

"It only took you a few days to nearly kill yourself, but it will be weeks before you're fully recovered."

"Weeks?"

"You're doing better than I expected, but I'm keeping you in the hospital until your temperature is normal, your abdomen is functioning properly, and I remove the surgical drain." Dr. Rhye patted his shoulder. "I'll let you know when you're going home. For now try going to the end of the corridor."

Urgency prodded him. "I have to go home and finish my house," he protested to an empty doorway.

His hope plummeted from its lofty heights. He slumped back with his immediate future as flat and blank as the ceiling above him.

That afternoon Annie Dunbar assisted him on a brief, taxing excursion down the corridor. Back in his room, he found Terry standing at the window. Surprise rivaled his weariness and he sat cross-legged on the bed.

"Hello, Little Brother. What are you doing here?"

Terry turned a straight chair around and straddled it, crossing his arms on the back. "Penny told me to come. Usually we're together but—"

"You and Penny?"

"She's a classy chick."

Recalling Penny's animosity to him, he managed a noncommittal gesture.

"You don't like Penny?"

Chivalry prevented an answer.

"Hmm," Terry puzzled. "She sure is crazy over you."

Experience defied Terry's observation. "No way. From the instant she met me, her sarcasm and snide wit have made my life miserable."

"So what's she supposed to do, for cryin' out loud? You're engaged to her sister. That girl has lots of terrific vices, but beau snitching, as she puts it, isn't one of 'em. That Saturday when we all thought you were gonna conk out, she was one shook chick. While you were in ICU, she tried to move Heaven and Earth to visit you, but the doc only let Mom and Pop and Connie in."

Groping for any elements of affection from Penny, he objected, "But she hates me."

"Not so, Big Brother. She only acts like she hates you because she loves you."

"Loves me?"

"Oh, yes. Very definitely. She let slip that it's too bad she didn't meet you first."

Horrors, he thought. *Only Connie's loyalty and tact have made life with Oaklands bearable. Penny would have devoured me.*

"As the maid of honor and the best man, she picked me up as a 'light diversion for the duration.'" Terry used his fingers for quotation marks. "But anyway. She knows all about what needs to be done. Since you're in the hospital and I'm your best man, she wants you to tell me what to do about the ring and the groom's gift to the bride."

"The ring and the bride's gift are in my top dresser drawer."

"What about the marriage license and arrangements for the honeymoon?"

Honeymoon ... His heart lurched against his ribs. Since he had become ill, he hadn't even thought of a honeymoon.

He was aware of his waning energy and the inability to establish anything in his own mind. He hastily summoned a smile and said, "I'll let you know when I need something."

"The ceremony's Sunday, and Penny—"

"Yes, I know. But I had matters nearly settled before I became ill."

I couldn't afford anything, he recalled.

Relieved of immediate responsibility, Terry grinned and rose from the chair. With a companionable clap on his shoulder, his brother ambled out.

He leaned against the pillows with his fingers linked behind his head and visualized a French provincial bridal suite. The image of Connie in white wedding night apparel floated his spirit on an euphoric crest before it shattered on a shoal of impossibility. He had never planned for a French provincial bridal suite because he couldn't afford a French provincial bridal suite. He couldn't afford the Mississippi riverboat cruise he had briefly considered. He crossed his arms on his chest.

So what will I do about a honeymoon?

The first lucid thought in weeks ran through his mind only to be halted at a dead end. He clasped his hair in his fingers while he experimented with several strategies. He agonized over each fact and question before he discarded them, the tumult leaving his brain light.

Slowly he came to the awareness that the only possibility was to take Connie to his house. Yet where better to begin to experience the art of loving than in the home they had dreamed of for two years and would share for a lifetime?

What more could I want?

The image of Connie in white wedding night apparel within the intimate haven of the master bedroom suite enticed him. Memory of the master bedroom suite jolted his fantasy; his house remained unfinished while he remained in the hospital.

It was too late to get a loan, and undeniably he could not complete his house.

How will the dream ever come to reality? The thought which had previously touched the surface of his mind now punctured it.

For two years he had taken certain things for granted, never doubting he would be successful. Now the worst had become a distinct possibility. His thoughts turned over like an hourglass and flowed in a different direction. Tenacity refused to accept the annihilation of the dream which he had lived, worked, and sacrificed for.

I must do something. There has to be a way— Someway, anyway for me to finish my house. What way? What am I going to do?

He pressed his fists to his temples and rubbed, forcing his brain toward a solution. He and Connie could stay in his apartment until he procured another loan and was recovered enough to complete his house. But that had never been the plan. Paying rent and the mortgage as well as utilities in two locations would further strain his thin finances. Now they must stretch to cover hospital expenses. He longed for enough money, speculating what life would be like without financial limitations.

Honesty nudged him. *What good is money if no amount of it will buy time or strength or health or freedom from this blasted hospital?*

He persisted in confronting the hard facts which jeopardized his dream.

The rage of the baffled possessed him and he bunched his fingers into fists, tapping them on his thighs.

The inescapable conclusion was that without time and without money, he could not obtain his goal as he had planned. With a sense of great loss, he contemplated the disintegration of his dream. That which had always given him delight and a purpose had been suddenly withdrawn and left him groping in a wide and unexpected emptiness. Now that there was nothing left—the whole edifice of hope and endeavor brought crashing down—he stared into the desolate ruins of what had been a shining future. Amidst the rubble, he spiraled into dejection, his heart beating without purpose.

Movement diverted his attention as Paul entered and straightened the chair to sit in it.

"What do you do when the most crucial thing you've dreamed of and striven to achieve has been obliterated?" he greeted.

"You trust God implicitly."

The explanation seemed too simplistic and absurdly flat. "I don't see how I can. I was so close ... now there's no hope."

"I'm sorry this is so difficult for you, my friend."

"This wasn't in the plan at all," he said, gesturing to himself in a hospital bed. "Not to be able to obtain my dream— To have lost what I've worked for all these years—" Despair constricted his chest.

"The loss must be very profound. I know how obsessed you were. However, your attempt to live life on your own terms was futile and bound to fail," Paul reminded him.

"But my life was going so well."

"When you were in control—and your resources were adequate—you didn't need God. But no plan will ever succeed if it displaces Him in your life," Paul said in his kind yet forthright fashion.

"Perhaps my passion to build my house did displace God," he conceded.

"Whatever is more vital to your life than God must be relinquished."

He considered his friend's statements with skepticism. Then as he analyzed the forces which had dismantled his dream, he said, "That seems to have occurred."

"You must build your life on the firm foundation of faith in God. Trust your life and your dream to Him, Douglas. He can do more with them than you can."

He twined his fingers behind his head and met his friend's gaze. "This is what you've been telling me all these months, isn't it? Well, now I'm in a position to understand it—flat on my back."

"God derives no joy from our suffering, but He often uses it to get our attention and to redirect our lives."

"Maybe that's what it takes. It's much easier to have a head full of nice doctrines than it is to have them as realities in life."

With a half smile Paul raised an eyebrow. "Authentic repentance shows in authentic life change."

Paul shifted position and asked, "Are you still planning to be married Sunday?"

"One way or the other. I hope we don't have The Season's Most Elaborate Wedding in the hospital." He expressed the worry which had haunted him and glanced around the room. Visualizing the scene, he shuddered. "I wanted you to perform the ceremony, but—"

"I understand."

"I don't! Connie and I set a date, and then she, Penny, and her mother took over. I didn't know a wedding could be so complicated. Why couldn't it be an event of dignity, simplicity, and tradition instead of such an extravagant affair?

"That's the way society weddings are."

"I didn't have much say at all."

"Grooms usually don't."

"But to exclude my best friend?"

"I'm sure they have their own way of doing things," Paul responded, rising.

With a gratitude beyond words, he said to Paul, "Thank you—for everything."

"I'm glad I could help. God bless you, my friend."

After Paul had gone, he drew up his knee and let his arm rest on it. The independence he possessed wasn't cocky or arrogant; he simply had been taught to be self-sufficient and to overcome life by his own will and strength. He had a naïve optimism that he could set a goal for his future and go after it, expecting a good result without including God. That inherent perception would not rout easily. If he hadn't been able to achieve his dream, the most vital aspect of his life with his own two hands, how could he relinquish it to an intangible, invisible God and trust Him to do it?

He could either continue to mourn the disintegration of all that was precious, or he could trust God with absolute faith. Engaged in an internal debate, he rolled his head on his pillows. He struggled with his thoughts, wrestled with his fears, and exhausted his human capacity to comprehend. With the basic structure of his existence shaken to the core, he recalled Paul's familiar instruction to build his dream on the foundation of God and His Word. He reached for the Bible on the bedside table and read some of the Psalms. His soul echoed their cries of despondency, but they also brought clarity.

"Put not your trust in princes, nor in the son of man, in whom there is no help.... Happy is he that hath the God of Jacob for his help, whose hope is in the LORD his God."

He recognized God's faithfulness and His desire for man to be dependent upon Him.

Humble me, O God, to the truth of Your Word.

With no amount of determination able to attain his dream, he must cease futilely grappling for it and hold on to God. Then he would be led beyond the devastation when hope was hard to find and there was no discernible solution. He had trusted God with his immortal soul for eternity; couldn't he trust Him with his dream?

Over a year ago he had accepted Jesus into his life and received forgiveness from sin. Now he accepted the Master Planner's design for his life, even though it was far different from his own. He confessed his pride, for foolishly thinking he could obtain his dream by his own means, and idolatry, for the dream had become more important than God.

A sliver of light glimmered in the dust of his demolished dream, not enough to plan his future, but enough for introspection.

It was interrupted by the ringing of the telephone beside his bed. "Hello?"

"Douglas. This is Evan Scott. There is a check here from earlier in the month and one for two weeks' sick leave in case you need them."

Surprised at this unforeseen provision, he said, "Yes, sir, thank you."

"Get feeling better and forget about work for a while," Evan Scott concluded.

After he hung up, he stared at something in the recesses of his mind, rubbing his chin with the back of his hand. One single idea emerged. Automatically he rejected it. After all his avowals to achieve the dream the way he had planned, how could he expect Connie to finish the interior alone? He had asked for her help and she had been willing, but he balked at the vast difference between her helping him and his not doing it at all. Pertinacity defied this alteration, and the chaos in his brain battered it to numbness.

Still, his hope revived.

I know she is very busy with the wedding and visiting me, but if she can fit working on my house into her schedule— If she brings in some paint chips, we can choose our colors and have Pop do some painting. He would prefer that to sitting around here or my apartment or Oaklands' house anyway. Connie and I can look over the notes she took about the type of appliances and the style of furniture she likes. After she shops for a stove and a refrigerator, a table and chairs, a bed and a dresser, we can discuss what she found. Hopefully we can agree on something I can afford. With the checks from Mr. Scott and the money

in my account, I can give her a check for her purchases. If she can arrange for
the carpet as a gift— But there isn't time to get it laid.

His alert and eager mind ran into the rock wall of reality. With little
time and little money, what did he expect Connie to do?

That evening when Connie arrived, wearing wide legged pink slacks
and a white knit top with floral appliques, her youthful exuberance brought
a current of zest to his room.

"How are you, Darling?"

"I wanted to go home today."

With an uplifting of her brows Connie acknowledged the absence of
the IV. "You must be feeling better."

"I feel fine," he said impatiently, massaging his abdomen. "Dr. Rhye just
won't discharge me until my temperature is normal, I can walk down the
corridor, and he removes the surgical drain." A belated thought surfaced.
"I can't even get out of here to buy our license."

Connie perched on the edge of the bed with her hands around her
knee. Her smile hadn't wavered and satisfaction radiated from her. "I've
taken care of it, Darling."

He observed Connie, who was too insulated by health and wealth to
know defeat. He envied her and sought to squelch her gaiety with a little
prodding. "You can do anything, can't you?"

"It wasn't easy! I had to tolerate rude remarks about getting a man
<u>before</u> I could get a license. 'It's a marriage license, Sweetie, not a hunting
license,' I was told. But with your blood test certificate from Dr. Rhye,
your adoption papers, army discharge papers, driver's license, and my
engagement ring, I convinced 'Miss Sweetie' I already had my prey."
Connie's amethyst eyes sparkled with humorous affection.

Her audacity fascinated him, and he ran his fingertip down her nose.
"You're really something. Adorable, devoted, and willful enough to conquer
City Hall."

Connie's eyes narrowed and her jaw stiffened as she leaned away. "Do
you know you have a very rare blood type, Douglas McKenzie?"

Guilty knowledge repressed speech.

"Why didn't you tell me? You who thought I was deceptive because I
didn't tell you everything."

His lips moved before the words came. "It's not that important—unless
I need a transfusion. I've come through two surgeries without one. Don't
worry about it." He tapped Connie's chin with his fingertip then rubbed
his knuckle beneath it.

Momentarily he had forgotten about his house, but a sense that something had gone badly awry hovered in his soul.

An internal void left a space for second thoughts, but Connie's quiet air of confidence began to affect him. Without alternatives, he banished his stiff Scots' pride. Humbled and dependent, he rallied his forces to make his request.

"I need you to do something else for me."

"Certainly, Darling. Anything."

Connie's calm assent alleviated his uncertainty, but it didn't alleviate his sadness.

"I'm not— Well— I can't—Will you please finish my house?"

Connie glanced up at him with a startled expression quickly controlled.

"I know you're very busy with the wedding and visiting me, but if you could fit working on my house into your schedule—"

"I— I've already started."

"Already started? When? How?"

Connie slid off the bed, stepped over to close the door, and returned to stand beside him.

"After I realized you weren't going to die, I knew you couldn't complete your house as you intended, so I must."

"Why didn't you tell me?"

"I didn't want to risk upsetting you and jeopardizing your recuperation."

"But I have been so concerned. I planned—"

"Yes, you planned. But you hadn't planned on astronomical building costs, skyrocketing interest rates, and a life-threatening illness from which it will take weeks to recover. And you had asked for my help."

"Help, yes. Not for you to take over!"

"When I began you were in no condition for me to persuade you to be reasonable."

"How could you afford—?"

"I used my graduation money."

Suspecting the answer before it came, he sat in a still cold fury. Betrayal surged through him and the blood roared in his ears.

"I told you and <u>told you</u> and TOLD YOU I didn't want you to use your money! Did you think I wasn't serious a year ago Easter? Did you think I was only being polite when I told you no way did I want you to use your graduation money?"

"At least I had it! I intended solely to start with it until you could access yours. I have learned enough from Father's business to know that more money is needed the sooner a building must be completed."

He knew that from professional experience.

"What have you done?"

"Your father worked with the crew and the painting is finished. The carpet is being installed. I purchased the appliances and furniture."

"Why did you do so much so quickly?"

"I picked up where you left off before you became ill. There wasn't much time to do everything that needed to be done before we're married."

He came to his feet. "Why didn't you discuss it with me?"

"What would you have said?"

Too angry to comment, he flashed Connie an indignant glare.

"I thought you might be furious when I used my graduation money. But I risked it. I risked your anger, risked losing your love, risked another broken engagement, risked <u>everything</u> to bring the dream to reality. I prayed that you would have the grace—and the good sense—to consent to it." Connie faced him, a challenge in her manner. "You nearly died, Douglas. You need to accept my help. Instead of being so stubborn, proud and independent, why can't you be glad and say thank you? I have invested more time and effort in that house than you could ever imagine because it's my house too. Or is it? Is it <u>your</u> house or is it <u>our</u> house? Is it a dream to share or is it your dream to hoard?"

The realization that he couldn't obtain the dream for Connie by his own means had jolted him to the core of his being. That she had salvaged it without him, without his approval, and without his finances, was irrefutable proof that his independence and determination were insufficient.

Antagonistic silence persisted between Connie and himself; their dream, their entire future, was in jeopardy mere days before their wedding. Combating his pride which could destroy what they had so very nearly attained, he tapped his fingers on his forehead in agitation.

The truth illuminated his mind with an almost tangible radiance: he had recently committed his dream to God; now God had reconstructed it.

The stiffness of rage left him, and he sank into the gray upholstered chair.

"Two years ago I never needed any help. Those days are gone. I'm not so independent and self-assured. I need your help like I never have before. It's <u>our</u> dream. Your courage and commitment to God's plan for us to share it more fully than my doing it my way have shown me a far better approach than I imagined."

He slid from the chair to his knees and laid his forehead on the edge of the bed, confessing his obstinacy and independence, his anger and ingratitude to Connie and to God.

He rose and drew Connie into his arms, savoring the nearly forgotten pleasure of her nearness. "It seems like forever since I held you like this."

Connie pressed her cheek against his chest with her hands on his back. "I want to stay like this forever."

"Not here," he disagreed softly.

Connie leaned back, a frown puckering her golden brows. "When are you going to be released from here?"

"Surely before too long. But we can't hope for much more than a honeymoon in our house."

Connie's features set in a mask. "No ... no, of course not. Not with your being so ill. I— I hoped we could take the Mississippi riverboat cruise."

"At least we'll be married and living in our house," he offered.

Awe vibrated in his veins.

22

Exercise

*T*uesday afternoon he noticed Mr. Oakland in the doorway, and the powerfully majestic opening of *Also Sprach Zarathustra* came to his mind.

That man struts when he's standing still. He smiled with a mixture of compunction and welcome.

His folks and the Oaklands had visited him last evening, but the man's demeanor indicated a business call. Mr. Oakland approached and slid blueprints from their protective tube, unrolling them on the bed. "Douglas, we have a problem. I hope you're feeling well enough to discuss these."

Interest leaped within him and he straightened, ignoring the twinge. The lines and angles he had drawn for Oakland Park communicated functional beauty, and he experienced the delight of consultation.

After he and Mr. Oakland had discussed the unresolved technical issue, the man said, "You're a very remarkable young man—ambitious, intelligent, innovative. You were doing exceptionally well until you became ill. Now here you are, days on end, without uttering one word of complaint."

"Oh, no, sir, I have complained. Mom and Pop almost quit coming because I was so irritable. I've had to learn to depend upon God to give me patience during this tedious recuperation."

"I suppose one's religion does help in a situation like this."

"It's not religion, sir. It's a personal relationship with God through His Son, Jesus."

"Whatever one chooses to believe."

/

He recognized an opening to tell Mr. Oakland about salvation. Inwardly quaking, he used the words he had heard from Paul at church. "Only the belief that Jesus' dying on the cross and God raising Him to life for all our sins is what brings forgiveness and reconciles us to God, sir."

"I haven't sinned. I'm an honest businessman, a devoted husband, and loving father."

"Compared with God's standards, we have all sinned and come short of the glory of God.'"

Mr. Oakland's hairy gray brows inched up. "Even you?"

Honesty burned within him. "Even me."

A faint smile twisted the corner of Mr. Oakland's lips. "And you admit it?"

"To myself and to God. 'If we confess our sins, He is faithful and just to forgive us our sins ...'"

"I always believed that if I was good enough ..." Mr. Oakland's pensive gray eyes searched his.

"Yes, sir, I know. This is just the opposite of that. We don't need to trust in our good works to merit God's grace. Nothing we do is good enough to come close to making us right with God. That's why He had to give us Jesus. You must agree with God that believing in Jesus' death for your sins will save you. 'For by grace are ye saved through faith; and that not of yourselves: it is the gift of God.'"

Mr. Oakland paced at the foot of the bed, his hands behind his back, his face taut with inner conflict.

He watched Mr. Oakland, every breath a prayer. "Sir, what do you want to do about Jesus?"

Mr. Oakland stopped with his head slightly down.

"'That if you confess with your mouth, "Jesus is Lord," and believe in your heart that God raised him from the dead, you will be saved.'"

Gradually comprehension lighted Mr. Oakland's expression. "The way you and Rev. Jefferson explain it makes it easier to understand. By Jove, Douglas, I do believe I've got it!"

Dr. Rhye entered and rushed across the room, seizing the blueprints. "Get these things out of here! I will not have Douglas discussing business in his condition!"

"But I enjoyed—"

"Don't you understand you are to <u>rest</u>?" Dr. Rhye glowered at him and thrust the blueprints toward Mr. Oakland.

Defiantly he met the doctor's glare. "Resting is the hardest thing in the world to do!"

"Relax, Douglas, and get well."

"No one in his right mind could relax in a hospital the week before his wedding!"

"It's the only way you'll recover."

"But I feel like working—"

"You're still weak and have a fever."

Mr. Oakland rolled up the blueprints and clasped his hand in unspoken gratitude. The man's eyes were alight with new life when he hastily departed.

Nettled by Dr. Rhye's erratic timing, he snapped, "Do you <u>live</u> here?"

"Only when someone is as sick as you, and he's Armand Oakland's son-in-law-to-be."

Abashed, he said, "Oh."

"Or if I'm waiting for another baby to be born."

After Dr. Rhye's perfunctory examination, he continued to smolder with aggravation. He jerked the sheet across himself to disperse his temper.

Dear God, please give me the patience I need to rest until I'm well. And may I please be well soon. Acknowledging his impatience, he subsided. *Help me to exercise my faith to trust Your timing.*

The memory of Mr. Oakland's decision defused his exasperation, and he lifted his clenched fingers upward in silent celebration and tribute to God.

This is what I prayed for, nearly died for.

Mom appeared in his room on her daily visit.

"Have you seen the Oaklands' house?" Mom asked rhetorically as she usually did. "Pop and I think the world of Connie, and her folks are nice people, very generous, but have you ever thought about how different their standard of living is from ours?"

"Countless times since the first day I moved to Denver."

"Your house is no doubt lovely, but it can't compare to <u>that</u> luxurious house with its staff. Now that your marriage is so close, do you have any idea how much Connie is giving up to marry you? Do you think she can reduce her lifestyle that drastically?"

He had pondered those questions more than he could explain to Mom, so he simply answered, "I've experienced theirs, Connie has adjusted to mine, and we have one uniquely our own."

"Pop and I love you both, and we just want you to be happy. It sounds like you should do okay."

Expressing what he had dreamed, planned, and worked for these past two years, he said, "When Connie and I are married and living in my house, everything will be just fine. We won't have any problems at all."

That evening voices roused him from his doze as Paul and Connie entered simultaneously. Connie greeted him with a chaste kiss and sat beside him on the bed. Paul shook his hand and seated himself in the gray upholstered chair.

"I am so glad to see you both. I could hardly wait to tell you that this afternoon Connie's father came to talk to me about Oakland Park, but I was able to talk to him about accepting Jesus, and he did!"

"Praise the Lord!" Paul responded.

Amazement recurred within his own spirit.

Connie's lavender eyes and parted lips conveyed her astonishment and excitement.

"When I tried to be an example of Christianity to my folks, I failed because I was too independent and frustrated. But after I yielded to the Master Planner's design for my life, He enabled me to exercise my freshly forged faith and worked through me to draw Mr. Oakland to Himself. Perhaps all the pain and illness were worth it. To some small extent I know what it means that Jesus suffered to bring us to God."

Wednesday morning the telephone beside his bed rang, and he answered it.

"Hello, Darling," Connie replied. "How are you?"

"Better, I think."

"So what are you going to do today?"

"There's nothing to do."

"You need Penny to plan <u>your</u> life. She has another whole day layered with appointments. Since I've been so busy the past two days and only seen you in the evenings, I hoped I could spend today with you, but it's not possible to come until this evening either." Connie's normally placid tone sounded hurried. "You do understand, don't you, Darling?"

Being deprived of Connie's presence while she prepared for their wedding and worked on their house—which they should be doing together—brought a twist of irony.

"You may not understand, but having you in the same room with me is more of a comfort than I can explain."

"I know, Darling. Me thinks the Good Fairy should wave her magic wand and speed the lovely princess, heigh ho, heigh ho, to yon pining Prince Charming."

Matching Connie's mood, he declared, "I would swim the raging seas for one glimpse of your jeweled eyes. I would cross the searing desert sands for one of your sweet kisses. I would scale the highest mountains to spend one precious moment in your presence."

"Then why don't you?" Connie responded with humorous challenge in her tone.

"Because I still have this blasted fever and the strength of a string."

"I am sorry. Goodbye, Darling."

"Heigh ho, heigh ho," he muttered dismally.

The dial tone separated her from him as surely as raging seas, desert sands, and the highest mountains....

Evan Scott, Mike Hall, and people from the church visited him, but they failed to lift his spirits; only Connie could alleviate the loneliness in his soul. She was lovelier of form and features than when he had proposed to her, and looking at her cheered him. He yearned for her vivacity and sweet gentility which would soon be his for all time.

❧

Visions of her wedding danced in her head, yet a murky specter that Douglas would not be well enough for it haunted her. From the urgency of necessity that he would be released, she continued with the planning. Stress, summer heat, and separation from Douglas chaffed her spirit, and she desired the solace of his embrace.

That evening as she changed into a sleeveless floral print dress and yellow high heeled sandals, the prospect of being with Douglas brought a glow of pleasure.

In Douglas' room, she sat beside him on the edge of the bed and leaned her cheek against his robe at the shoulder, absorbing stability and contentment.

Eventually Douglas inquired, "Have you been able to accomplish anything more in our house?"

She set her teeth in her lip to contain her enthusiasm. "It's almost finished. I developed a color scheme that is a reflection of our taste and personalities. I incorporated them into a workable, enjoyable, livable environment. Oh, Douglas, it is so fabulous!" She met his eyes with a little bounce of excitement. "I can hardly wait for you to see it!"

Inquisitiveness animated Douglas' expression. "What colors did you select? What carpet did you choose? What brand of appliances? What style of furniture? What type of doorknobs?"

She laid her fingers on Douglas' lips to halt the flow. "Now I want it to be a surprise when I show it to you complete in every detail."

She watched Douglas' mental shift. "How are the plans for the wedding?"

"Today I ran around town in the heat. A June wedding in Colorado ... All the final arrangements for the florist, the photographer, and the musicians have been made. Mother and I also took your mother shopping for her rehearsal dinner and wedding dresses. Mother arranged for Potts to meet Grandmother Oakland, Uncle Orville, Aunt Dotty, and Peggy at the airport. Tomorrow I will pick up Linda, and then she and Peggy will be fitted for their bridesmaids' gowns. Susan, Victoria, and Barbara have been fitted already. Since you are getting better, Mother thought it would be propa for me to have a luncheon with all of them on Friday. We'll need new dresses for that. Linda, Peggy, Penny, and I will set out across Denver to shop for those and for our rehearsal dinner dresses. Four girls, two dresses ..." She counted on her fingers, imagining the exhilaration of shopping as well as the chaotic dynamics.

A prevailing unwelcome thought intruded. She stood and turned with an out flung hand.

"Oh, Douglas! You and your dream didn't die, but mine did. The bridesmaids' luncheon will be lovely, but I lost all the other gala pre-nuptial celebrations I have dreamed of from childhood. You have no idea how much I regret missing the social events scheduled in our honor, having you escort me, being able to flaunt you. Not only did I miss them, but so did Mother and Penny who also planned and anticipated participating in them."

Douglas rose and circled her with his arms. "I'm sorry we missed them too, Sweetheart. I know they were important to you."

She dared ask a question even though she feared the answer. "All of us will get new dresses for the rehearsal dinner, but will you be there for it—and the wedding?"

"I'm hoping and praying Dr. Rhye will discharge me soon."

She gave the blue velour sleeve of Douglas' robe a little shake. "Please ask him when he will release you. We must give the final number for the reception to the caterer and— Douglas, you must be out of the hospital in time! I have put my heart and mind into this momentous occasion, and I would like for you to be there!" Her voice sounded high and strained.

"We must exercise our faith and trust God's timing," Douglas consoled her.

She oscillated between faith in God and craving her ideal wedding. She sought Douglas' sapphire eyes and regained her equanimity. Resolve solidified within her. "We may need to change some of our arrangements, but after waiting over two years I'll marry you here if necessary. We'll need to know as quickly as possible so we may notify our guests."

Douglas covered her hand on his arm with a tender little pressure. "We won't have to do that, Sweetheart."

Doubt shadowed her spirit, and a sigh escaped.

The next morning she stood on the balcony in her and Douglas' house, surrounded by the scent of paint, flooring, carpeting, furniture, and appliances. Good design principles and sound decorating had enabled her to plan the rooms in classically beautiful ways. After hours of innumerable decisions, matching fabrics, and careful coordination of colors, she had gained an imminently rewarding result. The total cohesive mood provided a fashionable and contemporary atmosphere. As she viewed the house, a current of achievement and relief streamed through her. During the past two weeks she had spent such a large portion of each day here, with Mr. McKenzie's professional assistance, she already felt as if it were home. Penny and Terry had helped move and arrange the wedding gifts and placed her and Douglas' personal items for use.

She descended the stairs, her fingers trailing down the black wrought iron railing. In the dining room beneath the balcony, she aligned lustrous silver service on taupe linen napkins next to floral white on white plates set on a round ecru lace covered table. Images flickered into her mind of Douglas seated across from her eating breakfast, standing beside her in the kitchen, moving around in the living room, coming down the stairs, designing in his workroom, his presence filling the house with warmth and a pulse.

This is where Douglas and I will live. Her soul clamored toward destiny.

❧

He waited for Dr. Rhye, anxiety twisting his nerves into springs. He uttered a silent, urgent prayer, but no answer immediately came forth. With his hands behind his back he prowled around the room. A persistent vision of The Season's Most Elaborate Wedding around his bed filled his mind. He shook his head to dislodge it.

In his duress he spoke aloud. "I must talk Dr. Rhye into releasing me."

"Save your breath," the doctor advised from the doorway.

Chagrined, he returned to bed.

After an extensive examination, Dr. Rhye folded up the stethoscope, stuffed it into his white coat pocket, and drew up a chair. "Your abdomen sounds clear and your temperature is nearly normal, so—" The doctor whisked out the drain.

The sharp discomfort abated and he said, "I can go home!"

Dr. Rhye raised a finger which downed his expectation.

"You said after you removed the drain, I could go home. I feel fine. I'm able to be up and walk—"

"You are indeed fortunate. You have the constitution of an ox—and you're as stubborn as one—but you don't have the strength of one. Trust me, Douglas, you don't have the stamina you think you have. If you're able to stand up during the ceremony, you'll be doing well. If you sit down during the reception, so much the better."

"I will not!"

"It will be weeks before you're fully recovered, but if you promise to rest, I'll discharge you Saturday morning."

"Saturday?"

Dr. Rhye's look threatened further hospitalization.

He acquiesced with an audible breath.

"At least you're alive to be married."

Gratitude superseded his disappointment, and he observed the doctor from beneath his eyelids.

With the surgical drain removed, he was able to shower and shampoo for the first time in three weeks. Exhilarated, he walked along the corridor to increase his endurance.

That evening he sat cross-legged on his bed, the architectural journals Dr. Rhye had allowed unable to sustain his interest. He felt neglected when Connie didn't visit him, and she had been unavailable for his phone calls. He forced his brain into the architectural concepts until he became aware of her standing next to his bed.

"Dr. Rhye said he would discharge me Saturday morning," he greeted. "We can be married in church!"

Connie engulfed him in an exuberant embrace.

"Oh, Darling, I'm so glad!" Connie's whole being seemed to relax. "For a while I was afraid— I would have done it too. I would have had the ceremony here."

Awed, he lowered his head in deference to her willingness to sacrifice her exquisitely planned wedding. "I know."

With an airy laugh, Connie said, "If we had been married in the hospital, the wedding night would have been more sterile than normal."

On Friday Pop came with Mom to visit. Pop expressed amazement at the innovative architecture and fascination with the energy efficient features of his house.

"I'm proud that I worked on the building you designed, son."

Late that evening crimson ribbons of sunset reflected from the window, but the twilight serenity failed to soothe him in his confinement. In two days all these separations would end. Connie would be there in loyalty and love, and every day of his life for as long as he lived he would have the privilege of cherishing her. Intensely bored and lonely in his solitude, he donned his robe and slippers and wandered into the corridor.

As he avoided bustling nurses, dressing trays, visitors, and other patients, he consoled himself, *I get a lot of exercise on this obstacle course.*

He recognized Connie's gait in red chunky soled wedgies as she approached from the end of the corridor, and the red sundress with a white lace trimmed heart-shaped bodice enhanced her figure. Buoyed by her arrival, he hurried forward and clasped her upper arms.

"I'm so glad you came!"

"This has been one of the busiest days of my life," Connie told him, sounding breathless. "I've been completing last minute details and attending the bridesmaids' luncheon, but you know how badly I needed to see you."

His hand rested on Connie's waist and hers on his as they strolled into his room. He cupped her face in his palms and kissed her as though he were starving for her—which he was. She gazed up at him, her eyes very wide.

"You must be feeling better!"

"I feel better holding you like this."

Connie slid her fingers into his hair, and her mouth clung to his until he moved it away to nuzzle her throat. His lips glided to her shoulder, moving slowly. She caressed his neck and chest, igniting a spark and a quiver of queasiness. He withstood further allure by the exercise of his will and reliance on Divine power and stepped back, exhaling in rough, uneven breaths.

"Perhaps I should go," Connie said, comprehension in her manner.

"No, please. You've stayed longer than this before."

"But you were ill."

"I still am," he reminded with some heat.

"You're not acting like a frail invalid, Darling."

"And you're not acting like a visitor to a frail invalid, darling," he remarked with a lift of his eyebrow.

"It would be best if I left now."

"I promise to behave if you'll stay."

Connie ran her fingertips beneath his lapels and titled a look up at him. "It's late and this visit must be brief. I have a house full of guests. You do understand, don't you?"

Envy, jealousy, and loneliness burrowed into his soul, but he assented. He escorted Connie to the elevator. She blew him a provocative kiss an instant before the doors closed.

In his room he leaned against the door until he could tame his rapid, rioting pulse. The imminence of their union burst through him, and he pressed his palms on his thighs to suppress his impatience. He had withstood the blaze of peritonitis, but he surrendered helplessly to the fire in his veins, this ageless, unmistakable need of a husband for his wife.

23
The Rehearsal

Saturday morning Connie arrived in his room wearing a blue and white horizontal striped knit shirt, white jeans, and white leather loafers. She carried a flat white box that she handed to him. He opened it to reveal a blue and white horizontal striped knit shirt, white jeans, and white leather loafers.

"This was Penny's idea," Connie explained.

Yielding to the inevitable, he accepted them. He showered, shaved, and fully dressed for the first time in over three weeks.

Connie looked up at him with delight brimming in her eyes. "It's so good to see you dressed, Darling, although you look somewhat thin and pale."

Dr. Rhye appeared and said, "I've signed your release. When you're ready to leave, ring for the nurse. She'll help you downstairs. I'll see you tomorrow. Good luck, Douglas."

"Thank you, sir," he said, shaking Dr. Rhye's hand, unable to adequately express his gratitude to the man who had saved his life.

Eager to be discharged, he pushed the call button.

Kathy Parks arrived, and Connie picked up his personal items. A swarthy orderly seated him in a wheelchair.

"I can walk," he said, but no one noticed the irony.

In the corridor the progressive strolling strains of Mussorgsky's *Promenade* from *Pictures at an Exhibition* drifted through his mind. When the heavy glass doors in the lobby opened, the splendid *Great Gate of Kiev* swelled in his head.

Outside he looked into the azure vastness arching above him, and freedom unfettered his soul. He drew in a lungful of hot, acrid, nonantiseptic air before Kathy seated him in Connie's Audi. Numb from the mindlessness of hospital routine, he glanced across at Connie seeking direction.

"Your mother is expecting us for lunch at your apartment. The rehearsal dinner is at six o'clock at the Club followed by the rehearsal at the church. Tomorrow afternoon you're to be at the church by three."

The itinerary swept through his brain without leaving an imprint on its glazed surface.

Voicing his priority, he said, "I would like to see our house."

"Everyone wanted to see it, but I'm showing it to you first."

He leaned back and closed his eyes.

Connie stopped her car, and he roused to look out the window. The house stood in the midst of verdant sod that had replaced the scarred ground and construction debris. Connie helped him out, and he accompanied her to the low front step where she unlocked the gold double doors.

He stepped into the tiled, two-story entry way, appreciating the visual impact of lighthearted yellow throughout that reflected the energy of the Rocky Mountain sun and added a feeling of conviviality. A brown and gold floral sofa and two gold chairs flanked by white wicker tables were grouped in the center of the gold shag carpeted living room with the fireplace as the focus. The symmetrical balance gave the room a formal look.

He halted in the dining room beside a round, ecru lace covered table set for two with vaguely familiar china, goblets, and silverware. A contemporary hanging lamp and ecru vertical blinds angled across the sliding glass door provided a pleasant level of illumination.

"You have arranged rooms that are attractive and comfortable."

To the left, Coppertone appliances stood on facing walls in the galley style kitchen. The sink, refrigerator, and mixing centers were on the exterior wall; the stove and serving area were opposite them. Deep green counter tops, copper tiled back splash, oak cabinets, geometric print wallpaper, and a luminous ceiling of white translucent glass panels blended convenience and safety with practical beauty.

"It's radiant and inventive," he marveled.

He glanced into the spring green utility room with a harvest gold washer and dryer and the tastefully appointed bathroom with harvest gold fixtures and luxurious matching accessories.

"The two areas are carefully color coordinated," he observed.

As if viewing a display home, he continued down the hall beside the stairway toward the front. He approached a blue low pile carpeted room painted a cool blue, which suggested spaciousness. It contained a blue velvet sofa, large contour chair, and color television. Through a doorway on the left, he saw his drawing board in the middle of a similarly decorated room. A blueprint storage chest was within reach, and his books in a bookcase on the far wall provided a familiar yet ideal workspace.

Connie proceeded through the house with him, describing her process of selection and use of accessories, artwork, prints, and plants. "I approached the decorating so it would be unique."

"Your individuality is indelibly stamped on the decor."

He wandered up to the balcony and paused in a doorway on the far right. Oak furniture, light tints of green and yellow created a freshness in the guestroom; accents in melon tones completed the serene and sophisticated scheme. In the adjoining bathroom oak flooring, white woodwork, avocado colored fixtures and two sinks sets in a white vanity added distinct character. The other bedroom, in muted yellow, served as a repository for wedding gifts.

"You have created rooms with harmony and timeless beauty."

"I designed rooms in a highly personal way that would please us both."

He entered the master bedroom where the softened putty color and walnut furniture established a feeling of tranquility and repose. A brown upholstered circular swivel rocker contrasted with the orange and brown floral draperies and comforter. The textured carpet and bright colors in the fabric combined into a warm and inviting private haven. He ran his fingers over the smooth surface of the dresser as the magnitude of Connie's accomplishment permeated his mind. The elegant touches she brought into their home appealed to his aesthetic sense, and his spirit swelled with admiration and appreciation. He waved his hand in an encompassing gesture.

"Your generosity, diligence, and skillful decorating transformed my imagination into a dynamic home. You have put together rooms of our dreams. Oh, my precious Sweetheart, it's hard to believe what you did for me."

Connie tipped her face up in acceptance of his tribute. "It was done willingly for the sake of sharing our dream."

"I hope someday I shall be able to share as generously with you."

"You've given me your love and a dream, what more is there?"

He smiled in expectation of delightful new experiences. "A lot more."

The finale of Beethoven's *Seventh Symphony* with its rhythmic, energetic sense of celebratory culmination matched the rapid beat of his heart.

After lunch in his apartment, Connie and Penny left for Mr. Maxwell's salon while Terry took Connie's family to see the house. He lingered at the kitchen table with Mom and Pop.

"It doesn't seem possible you're going to be married tomorrow," Mom said, affection burnishing her face.

A smothered feeling in his chest prevented speech.

"There for a while we were afraid—" Mom rose abruptly and cleared away the dishes.

"You had a pretty rough time of it," Pop acknowledged.

His abdomen tensed in memory. "It was difficult, but I'm sorry I was so irritable. I should have remembered that Jesus suffered too—for our sins—and that He provides grace and strength."

"It would be hard to bear what you did," Pop said.

"But if I would have behaved better, perhaps you could understand about Jesus."

"That's quite all right, hon," Mom said, laying her hands on his shoulders. "We're just happy you survived and are out of the hospital."

Mom patted his head then turned away and ran water in the sink. Pop tuned in a ball game on the radio and leaned forward to listen. Knowing the conversation had ended without the conclusion he desired, he rose from the table and went to lie down on his bed.

That evening Terry drove him and their folks to the Mountain Estates Country Club and handed the Mercedes over to the parking attendant as if well-acquainted with the procedure. Terry led them through the massive stone building to the private dining room reserved for the rehearsal dinner, and he questioned his brother's familiarity with the routine.

"I've been here with Penny—making arrangements for the dinner," Terry added.

Shaking his head, he regarded his brother in disbelief.

"Still don't like Penny?"

"She's very style conscious," he said as he gestured to his blue jacquard tuxedo with a powder blue ruffled shirt and navy accessories and Terry's beige linen one with brown accents and a yellow ruffled shirt.

"And quite *avant garde*. Her mother sees everything in black-and-white—especially evening dress. I don't think I would have come if I had to be disguised as a penguin," his brother said and ambled away.

He paused beside the white linen covered tables shaped like a U in the center of the banquet room. He viewed the arrangements of yellow carnations and blue bachelor's buttons in glass bowls on the tables formally set with crystal, china, and silver service.

He noticed Mom in a new, long yellow dress and Pop in a familiar dark suit standing beside him. "I appreciate all you've done for the rehearsal dinner."

"Oaklands did everything," Pop said.

At the risk of overstating the obvious, he remained silent.

"Clothes certainly make the man," Penny remarked, her hand resting on his back before she hurried away.

Connie appeared wearing a confection of pink chiffon with her platinum hair upswept into a mound of smooth curls. Her fingers were linked with Linda Sevenstars', who wore a straight turquoise gown with thin straps that suited her angular figure, bronze features, and long black hair. Connie met his gaze as she moved forward, each singularly aware of the other. She smiled at him with a look of adoration as tangible as an embrace.

"It's good to see you dressed so attractively, Darling. Linda, you remember Douglas, my fiance, and his parents, Mary and Terrence McKenzie."

He responded with a little bow, and his folks added their pleasantries.

Mr. Oakland approached in black-and-white dress with a group of people and reintroduced him to Grandmother Cordelia Oakland, Uncle Orville, Aunt Dotty, and Peggy, the relatives he had met at Connie's graduation—a lifetime ago.

Peggy stared up at him with unabashed admiration that prickled his skin. Terry reappeared with Penny and claimed Peggy's interest, strolling off with Penny and Peggy on each arm.

Connie laid her fingers on his sleeve and led him through a kaleidoscopic jumble of introductions accompanied by Strauss' *Radetsky March* in his head. Susan Devonshire, Victoria Ormandorff, Barbara Whitworth, the diminutive flower girl Kimberly Leighton, and three frat-type guys, Ashley Kenningston, Richard Stuyvesant, and Phillip Rothschild, were vague impressions of heights, hair colors, and facial features.

Evan Scott presented himself and his wife, who was as short and round as he was tall and lean, florid as he was pallid. "It's good to see you're feeling better."

"Yes, sir. Thank you."

Mike Hall greeted him and took Connie's hand, gazing at her with a you-are-so-lovely, where-have-you-been-all-my-life? look. He replied to Mike and extricated Connie.

He and Connie paused in front of Rev. and Mrs. Murphy, and he managed a polite smile, but the desire to have Paul perform the ceremony caught at his soul.

His energy was diminishing, but he squared his shoulders and straightened, determined to endure the formal dinner by main force.

Mrs. Oakland appeared beside him in a pastel blue floral dress. "Are you feelen well, Douglas deah?"

"Yes, ma'am, I'm fine."

"Come, we shall be seated and then dinna will be suved."

He seated Connie at the head table and sagged into the chair next to hers.

During dinner he glanced at the wedding party, and the immediacy of his marriage jostled his heart against his ribs. He laid his fork down, inadvertently rattling it on his plate.

"Relax, Hero."

He met Penny's knowing gaze, and the corners of her lips twitched in amusement.

"Don't you care for pheasant?" Connie inquired quietly.

"I don't feel much like eating."

Following dinner tuxedoed waiters circulated to pour champagne, and then Terry rose and lifted a goblet. "To my brother Douglas and his beautiful bride-to-be, Constance. May they be very happy as they begin their new life together."

Connie's violet gaze clung to his, glowing eloquently as he touched his goblet to hers with a clink.

After the other toasts had been drunk and the dessert plates removed, Terry appeared with a package laden tray. Connie stood and presented small yellow wrapped gifts to her bridesmaids with gracious ease. Nodding discreetly, she indicated his obligation to his groomsmen. Speculating on the source of the gifts, he rose and distributed them.

One small square blue and one flat yellow gift remained. He recognized Terry and Penny's magic that had produced the groom's gift to the bride. He gave the yellow box to Connie with a flutter of anticipation. Curiosity in her expression, she ripped aside the paper and opened the black velvet case. She gazed at the glistening pearls, her lips parted over her round, even little teeth in astonishment, and then she flung her arms around him in a mound of chiffon. She handed him the remaining box and he opened it, staring at the gold tie clasp and cuff links, each with a diamond set in a sunburst.

I give her pearls. She gives me diamonds. Will it never end? Certainty pervaded him, and he shook his head.

"Don't you like them?" Connie asked, puzzlement in her tone.

"They're very nice." He snapped the box closed, pondering when and with what he would ever wear them.

Penny and Terry stood, and Mrs. Oakland directed the wedding party to the limousines. The import of the rehearsal set his blood pulsing.

"If we're rehearsing the wedding, shouldn't we rehearse the wedding night also?"

Connie clasped her arms around him with a yearning in her eyes that reflected his.

He inclined his head and his mouth sought Connie's, her lips moving beneath it until he said with assumed calm, "They're waiting for us."

Inside the church, he stood on the blue-carpeted platform between Connie and Terry. He listened to Rev. Murphy explain the ceremony procedure while fog drifted behind his eyes. With something akin to panic he realized Dr. Rhye was right; he didn't have enough stamina for this. He concentrated on Rev. Murphy's instructions, but the words dinned in his ears. When Connie passed a bouquet of white ribbons to Penny and practiced making the turn, the floor tipped beneath him. Teetering on the edge of a void, he groped to steady himself. Terry's hand closed on his forearm.

"You all right?" Terry whispered in his ear.

He lowered his head and bent forward with his palms on his knees as he waited for Earth to correct its orbit. A touch on his sleeve drew his attention to Connie, and her eyes met his with anxious tenderness.

"Darling...?"

"I'm fine," he assured her, his pride enforcing his will.

"You look as if you're going to faint. Do you need to sit down or have a glass of water?"

He waved away Connie's offers and lowered his lashes over one eye in a gesture calculated to achieve its effect. It failed to distract Connie's gaze from probing his to discern the truth. He turned toward Rev. Murphy to proceed with the rehearsal.

Penny appeared and thrust a glass of water toward him. "Drink it," she said, her lips barely moving from her fixed smile. "If you faint, I'll pour it on you."

Annoyance beat through him, but Penny's unrelenting stare and the close observance by the others compelled him; he drank the water. It collided with the nervousness and he swallowed against a wave of sickness. Resolutely he held himself together.

Rev. Murphy continued, and he stood with his feet wider apart, certain his firm intentions and Terry's shoulder against his would enable him to function during the remainder of the rehearsal—and one of the most elaborate weddings of the season.

24
The Reception

*O*n her wedding day, she entered her mother's conservatory where the June sun glinted from the glass panels in myriad rainbows, and the floral tranquility slightly assuaged her restlessness. She seated herself on a marble bench and leaned back, her fingers linked around one knee. The awe of being united with the person she loved more than life itself expanded within her, yet even as she contemplated a lifetime of contentment and security, the solemnity of marriage stilled her soul.

Dear God, thank You for the privilege of loving Douglas, of having him in my life, she prayed, gazing into the turquoise sky. *I'm going to need Your love and wisdom to succeed in this. May I always accept Douglas the way he is, not expecting perfection that belongs to You. May I be swift to praise his strengths and always look at him kindly, seeing him through Your eyes of love. May I respect him, honor him, and give him the devotion and obedience he deserves. May I have an abiding faith and the inner beauty of a gentle and quiet spirit which will always attract him.*

She beheld a future shining with promise and radiant with opportunity. Lost in wonder and appeal, she didn't notice when Penny sat beside her.

"The wedding should go all right. So long as Terry holds Douglas up as he did during the rehearsal. You know he nearly fainted," her sister said smugly.

She recalled Douglas, wan and gaunt, his eyes fogged with fatigue, but defensiveness rose within her. "He'll be fine."

"He's something very special," Penny mused, pensiveness shadowing her features. "You actually found Prince Charming. I envy you, Con. I truly do."

"You mean you <u>like</u> him?"

"<u>Like</u> him? I could have gone for Douglas McKenzie myself."

"But you—"

Penny's brittle gaze silenced her. "Love at first sight, the best kind. But you had sighted him first. What was I supposed to do? We never did snitch beau."

"One look and I was hopelessly in love," she said to Penny. "Douglas had captured my heart. I found an acceptance that didn't depend upon my being Armand Oakland's daughter or a propa society girl. I had never known such adoration and tenderness of manner as I had with him. From the second I saw him, he was the sun in my universe around which my life revolved."

"But the sun nearly blinked out—that night." Penny's fingers closed over hers, sharing memories of mutual despair. "I'll never understand how you, who faints at the least little thing, could withstand that harrowing ordeal."

"I found someone I loved more than myself." Honesty flowed from the depths of her soul. "But it was Jesus Who gave me grace and strength. He knows all about suffering and pain. He died to forgive our sin so we could be born into God's family and have eternal life."

"Come along," Penny said, starting up the path. "We must assemble our clothes and be ready to leave for the church in half an hour."

Regretting that Penny failed to understand about Jesus, she sighed and followed her sister to the house.

In a green room at the church, she stood amidst layers of tulle and Chantilly lace, her pulse visible beneath her scalloped bodice. Penny in a cornflower blue tulle-over-satin gown and the bridesmaids in their gold tulle and satin gowns clustered around her giggling excitedly. Her mother positioned the shy, blonde flower girl in her blue satin dress with a sash tied in a bow. The reality of the details were as she had envisioned them, and she stored the images in her mind.

Her father arrived, distinguished in formal attire.

"You look very lovely, my dear. When did you grow to be such a beauty? Douglas is a very fortunate young man, and you are fortunate to be marrying one such as he. You will make each other very happy. If there is ever anything I am able to do ..."

She reached up to brush her father's broad cheek with her lips in affectionate gratitude.

The photographer reappeared, and she smiled with practiced ease until he concluded the numerous poses.

Her mother kissed the vicinity of her ear and was escorted out by one of the ushers as the signal for the ceremony to begin.

The traditional, stately strains of Wagner's *Bridal Chorus* from the great organ penetrated the room. She knew Douglas was entering the front of the church with the groomsmen. She was impatient to join him, and she turned to receive her bouquet of white roses and stephanotis from Penny. Her father laid her hand on his arm and covered it with his. He stepped out to escort her down the long aisle behind her bridesmaids and the flower girl. With fluid grace she matched his measured gait. In a hushed rustling, the guests rose around her and all heads turned in admiration.

Douglas, who was very handsome in his black and gray pinstriped trousers, gray cutaway coat, wing collar shirt, and gray ascot, turned to watch her approach. His face paid her tribute higher than mere words, and he took a step forward.

As she proceeded down the aisle, images of the pavilion and the blueprints with the engagement ring on them wavered against the candlelit, floral background, and she heard Douglas ask, *"Will you marry me and share my dream?"*

Yes! After all the separations, sacrifices, and suffering, yes, yes, YES! Her spirit went dancing to meet him.

Within the circle of candlelight at the front of the church, she glanced up at Douglas, noticing his resolutely calm exterior.

He's stubborn, but that annoying trait will get him through this.

She passed her bouquet to Penny and laid her hand in Douglas' for the ritual of uniting their lives.

"Dearly beloved, we are gathered here today in the sight of God, and in the face of this company, to join this man and this woman in holy matrimony ..." Rev. Murphy proceeded with the solemn formality of the ceremony and eventually paused to ask, "Douglas, wilt thou have this woman to be thy wedded wife, to live together after God's ordinance in the holy estate of matrimony? Wilt thou love her, comfort her, honor, and keep her, in sickness and in health; and, forsaking all others, keep thee only unto her so long as ye both shall live?"

"I will," Douglas vowed, fervor vibrating in his voice.

"Constance, wilt thou have this man to be thy wedded husband, to live together after God's ordinance in the holy estate of matrimony? Wilt thou obey him and serve him, love, honor, and keep him, in sickness and in health; and, forsaking all others, keep thee only unto him, so long as ye both shall live?"

The pledge of a lifetime became audible. "I will."

Douglas took her right hand in his, and his sapphire eyes met hers as he repeated, "I, Douglas, take thee, Constance, to be my wedded wife, to have and to hold, from this day forward, for better for worse, for richer for poorer, in sickness and in health, to love and to cherish, till death us do part, according to God's holy ordinance; and thereto I plight thee my troth."

She held Douglas' hand in hers and recited, "I, Constance, take thee Douglas to be my wedded husband, to have and to hold, from this day forward, ..."

❧

Following Rev. Murphy's instructions and Terry's assistance, he slipped the ring on Connie's finger while he recited, "With this ring I thee wed, and with all my worldly goods I thee endow." When he recalled that Connie had finished his house, the words faltered on his tongue.

Connie slid a gold wedding band with a diagonal row of diamonds onto his finger. "With this ring I thee wed, and with all my worldly goods I thee endow."

Connie's eyes behind her veil held his in private renunciation of her wealth.

"Inasmuch as Douglas and Constance have consented together in holy wedlock ... I now pronounce them husband and wife. You may kiss the bride."

He raised Connie's veil and clasped her to him, triumphant joy in that kiss.

Mendlessohn's jubilant *Wedding March* filled the church, and he swept Connie up the aisle.

After innumerable photographs and all the documents had been signed and witnessed, Connie directed him toward a white limousine. Devoid of endurance, he slumped against the soft white leather seat and closed his eyes. He twined his fingers in Connie's and rested them on his thigh, the ride to the reception site allowing him to regain some energy.

In the reception hall, silver bowls of cornflowers and yellow carnations adorned numerous round, white linen covered tables. On the bridal table, sheet cakes with yellow rosebuds and green leaves flanked a six-tiered wedding cake. A brimming silver punch bowl, silver coffee and tea service, and a lavish buffet on silver platters occupied their own white skirted tables. The reception was even more extravagant then he had envisioned, and he glanced down at Connie, finding satisfaction in her manner.

Mrs. Oakland positioned the wedding party in the receiving line beneath an arbor of greenery. From an alcove, the string ensemble began playing softly as the line of friends, business associates, and family members inched forward. Surrounded by her veil, Connie's porcelain features were enhanced by a bridal radiance. With her usual decorum she conveyed cordiality in a few brief words. He managed a strained smile and handshake while he stood rigidly, exertion trembling in his legs.

You have to make it through this, he told himself. *All of Denver is here.*

Inconspicuously he braced his shoulder against Terry's and felt it stiffen, sharing his weight.

Mom and Pop paused in front of Connie and himself, Mom's face resembling sunshine after the rain as she hugged each of them.

"We always wanted a daughter, but we couldn't possibly have had one as sweet as you," Pop said.

His folks moved on, and Paul and Margie Jefferson approached.

"You are so beautiful!" Margie exclaimed quietly to Connie. "I am so happy for you."

He clasped Paul's hand with both of his, absorbing strength and stability from his friend. Exhaustion ached in his back, but he clung to his dignity.

"Here come the ushers. We're nearly through," Connie told him softly.

He escorted Connie to the bridal table where she and her bridesmaids laid their bouquets in a floral row. He seated Connie, but his knees threatened to liquify, and he sank into a chair with the groomsmen sitting to his left.

The guests served themselves from the buffet while uniformed waiters served the bridal party. He was vaguely aware of the merry chatter around him, but he was too tired to eat and simply looked at the food before him.

"Are you going to feel like dancing?" Connie inquired.

"I don't feel like <u>walking</u>."

Weakness tempted him to lay his head on Connie's shoulder, and he desired solely to go home with her.

Go home with Connie. The goal fulfilled ...

After the toasts, the expectation in Connie's gaze, his devotion to her, and his social obligation lifted him to his feet for the ritual cutting of the cake. He covered her right hand on the blue beribboned knife with his left to slice a morsel off the bottom layer. Connie placed the sugary bite in his mouth with an airy little laugh. He swallowed the symbol of sharing, aware that they would participate equally in their future. He gave Connie the next piece, her palm delicately beneath her chin. Exhilaration sparkled in her amethyst eyes, and his love for her, a deep, sweet pain, halted his breath.

The ensemble continued in the background, and uniformed caterers cut and served the cake while Connie guided him across the reception hall to mingle with their guests. She paused to chat, accepting the homage to which she was accustomed with casual effortless charm. Exhaustion extinguished the embers of his excitement. His heart beat erratically and a strange mistiness floated through his head. He glanced around to locate Paul or Pop or Terry and discovered them to be occupied. He willed himself to behavior befitting an elaborate wedding reception. He swayed above the floor and mentally tightened his grip until he stood very still, trying not to sway, not to faint.

I can't faint. I will not disgrace myself in front of Connie and her parents and their guests.

Connie peered up at him. "Come sit down, Darling. I'll throw my bouquet and then we may leave."

"I'm okay."

The floor receded from beneath his feet, and he slid into blackness....

He floated to the surface and waited for his mind to level off. He kept his eyes closed, but he was uncomfortably aware of the curious stares of the wedding party and the guests crowded above him.

Dr. Rhye loosened his ascot and collar and felt for his pulse. "He fainted, but he'll be fine."

Connie's wedding dress rustled next to his ear. "Are you all right, Darling?"

He wanted to reassure her, but he was embarrassed beyond speech.

"It's not propa for the groom to faint duren the wedden reception!"

He wished he had died from peritonitis rather than mortification here on the floor of the reception hall. Paul and Terry grasped his arms, and he came up by degrees. As everything settled into place, he saw Connie's look of horrified disbelief.

"You didn't injure yourself, did you?" Connie murmured, tucking her hand under his arm to steady him.

"Douglas?"

He waved Paul's query away.

Doug—?" Mom said softly beside him.

He felt Pop's hand on his back. "Mr. Oakland has arranged to fly us to St. Louis, but will you be all right?"

"I'm fine," he said, his tone as measured as his smile.

The ensemble increased its volume and tempo, and Penny began to dance with Terry. The wedding party and some of the guests followed.

Connie quickly said goodbye to her family and friends and left the reception site with him by a side door. He knew adjustments had been made very rapidly, eliminating the joyous dash beneath a shower of rice and rose petals.

He seated Connie and himself in the limousine that waited to drive them to their destination. Connie's voluminous skirt crinkled against his leg, and he gazed at her across the barrier of unspoken words and feelings, recognizing an acknowledgment of his weakness in her expression.

"I'm sorry ..." Misery lodged in his throat.

"Let's go home so you may rest."

This can't be happening. His disbelief that the reception had such an invidious climax revolved into awful certainty. *Oh, it happened all right.*

25
Sharing the Dream

*S*imply walking from the limousine to the front door of the house depleted his energy. Inside he sank onto the sofa, his feet out in front of him, his chin sagging onto his loosened ascot.

"Douglas—? Are you going to be all right?"

He was aware of Connie's meaning in the gently stated question. Certainty settled within him, and he observed her from beneath heavy eyelids. He longed for the culmination of the dream with such intensity it clutched at his heart, but the hurt of inflicting disappointment on Connie grated in the depths of his spirit. He caught her fingers in his and drew her down beside him.

"I love you. I've loved you from the instant I saw you, and I've existed to live in this house with you—loving you. I know this is our wedding night, but I hadn't planned on being so sick or it taking so long to recover. I am sorry, Sweetheart."

Speech had exhausted him, and he seemed not to have an atom of stamina left.

Connie's eyes glistened, but she said, "Rest and get well."

He laid his lips on hers in a chaste, quiet kiss which said as it always had, good night. Connie rose and ascended the stairs with a rustle of lace. He slumped over on the sofa and closed his eyes, Chopin's brooding *Raindrop Prelude* echoing the tears which fell in his soul.

The humiliation of fainting during the reception and his inability to experience the ultimate moment with Connie withered his pride.

If my will and dogged determination weren't sufficient to finish my house, keep me on my feet during the reception, or make my body respond, how will I ever succeed in marriage?

He recalled that day in the hospital when he had entrusted the most crucial element of his life to God. Now he needed to trust God in all the circumstances, not only in the crises.

O Lord Jesus, there are things in my life beyond my strength and ability to accomplish. I need You. Forgive me for foolishly thinking I could obtain them by my own means and not asking for Your strength.

Trust began to fill the space left by his departing persistence, and his spirit fluttered free of its despondency. Yet his body felt wooden and pressed flat to the sofa as he drifted into slumber.

⁂

She closed the door in the master bedroom and backed against it, pressing her palms to her chest to ease the ache there. For two years she had dreamed of nuptial bliss with Douglas. When she had finished this room a few days before, anticipation had bubbled in her veins. Even though they had to postpone their honeymoon trip, she had savored fulfilling their love in their home. But as she recalled Douglas' haggard face and the exhaustion which had rendered him incapable of exertion, she knew no matter how long, how keenly she craved him, she couldn't have him on her wedding night. Unaccustomed to being deprived of what she desired, she considered her usual resources: wealth, influence, temper, tears, and tempting, none of which had alleviated the effects of Douglas' illness. In the overwhelming excitement of marrying him, she had nearly forgotten how critically ill he had been, and she had assumed that their marriage would proceed with the flawlessness of the ceremony. Then her dream of having a wedding reception—one of the most important social events of her life, something beautiful to remember always—had been unexpectedly dashed. Buffeted by dissatisfaction and regret, her soul recoiled from the loss, and she sank to the floor.

Since Douglas had been feeling better, she had reverted to seeking her emotional stability from him, only to discover that he had failed to meet her expectations, not intentionally, of course, but because of his humanity. She hadn't come far in this shiny new marriage before she realized her contentment could not be centered in Douglas: it must be centered in Christ. When Douglas had walked through The Valley of the Shadow of

Death, Jesus had been with her, and she had grasped the importance of building her life on something—Someone—more solid than Douglas and their dream. The Holy Spirit had granted her courage and fortitude, grace and peace to endure life without Douglas; now she must rely on Him to endure daily life with Douglas. The assurance that the Holy Spirit would be faithful through life, through marriage, and even through this empty night steadied her.

Kneeling by the bed, she prayed, "When I asked for Your help this afternoon, everything seemed so happily ever after. Almost immediately I need patience in my disappointment and the ability to love Douglas with a pure, unselfish love that flows from You as its Unending Source." The magnitude of it engulfed her. "I won't be able to do this on my own. You must empower me."

She sensed a fresh infusion of forgiveness and a refined concern for Douglas.

From the balcony she could see him lying on the couch. She hastened to where the wedding presents were stored and carried a pillow and blanket downstairs.

She paused beside Douglas, noticing his features were strained even in slumber. The temptation to awaken him for her own purposes prodded her, but he needed sleep more than she needed him. Drawing upon her new reserve of undemanding love, she removed his shoes and covered him. She sensed the irony of herself in her bridal gown and he sleeping in wedding attire when they should be enwrapped in reverie, wearing only tranquil smiles. Aching to touch him, to kiss him, to utter his name, she backed up the stairs and paused to blow him a kiss and a silent, *Sleep well, my darling.*

❦

The mountain dusk was filtering through the three tall, narrow living room windows when he roused to wakefulness. He eased the blanket and formal clothing from around him, and the incongruity of the bridegroom in the living room still vexed him. He had been mindful of Connie's ministrations, but he had lain quietly, too lethargic to acknowledge them.

He half-raised with his arm on the back of the sofa and observed the room. He marveled at the conversion of lines and angles, which he had drawn the night of the Sweetheart Dance, into this vibrant dwelling. The miracle of inhabiting this house where he and Connie would live and love and share a future awed him. He longed to approach her and give substance to the dream.

He felt mussed and wrinkled, and he sat up, pushing his hands through his hair. He found a nominal reserve of energy, which he knew wouldn't last, but he began with a shower in the downstairs bathroom.

Invigorated by his damp cleanliness, he ascended the stairs in a yellow terry cloth towel. In the master bedroom, Connie sat on the bed supported with pillows, wearing a filmy white gown and a robe with feathery trim on the sleeves and hem. Using a breakfast tray as a desk, she wrote out thank you notes with a white plumed pen, her face serene in repose. The two boudoir lamps on the headboard haloed her platinum hair.

Eagerness perfused him along with the familiar queasiness.

This internal upheaval is ridiculous. He pulled his shoulders back and inhaled to quell it by an effort of will. *I will not let myself get so excited it interferes with my marriage.* His agitation increased, and he conceded he could not expect a good result without including God. He abandoned the futile, lifelong struggle with fear of failure, and his spirit unfurled the white flag of surrender. *Dear God, please help me not to be so nervous. Help me to relax and to remember I'll only find success for every situation in You.*

His nerves uncoiled and he crossed the room. "Good evening, Sweetheart."

❧

Startled, she glanced up.

"Did you sleep well, Darling?"

"Very comfortably, thanks to you."

"I thought you would sleep the night through."

"I'm sure I shall, but not on the couch." Douglas' tone accelerated her pulse.

Douglas transferred the tray to the floor. She rose to pull back the sheet and comforter, and slid into bed. Douglas drew her close to his side and his lips sought hers. She curled her arms around his neck and tangled her fingers in his hair, her love and need of him surging into that kiss. Douglas' mouth tarried upon hers, then their lips met and met again, each kiss, each touch longer, richer than the one before. Alive and virile in every way, Douglas was as dedicated to starting his marriage as he had been to starting his career. His sapphire eyes touched her with the warmth of promise as their love fused in the strong, pure bond of matrimony.

Douglas gazed at her with the look of a man who had received everything he ever wanted. "Being married to you, sharing my life and all my dreams, is going to be glorious." His lips quirked into the infinitely charming smile she loved. "With hard work and dedication all our dreams can become a reality as we entrust them to the Master Planner."

"Dreams to share," she whispered with love's sweet promise.